GOTHIC

GHOSTS

Forge Books by Charles Grant

Jackals
Symphony
In the Mood
Chariot

Tor Books by Charles Grant

For Fear of the Night
In a Dark Dream
The Black Carousel
The Pet
Raven
Something Stirs
Stunts
Tales from the Nightside

THE OXRUN STATION NOVELS

The Hour of the Oxrun Dead
The Sound of Midnight
The Last Call of Mourning
The Grave
Nightmare Seasons
The Bloodwind
The Orchard
Dialing the Wind

Tor Books Edited by Charles Grant

Midnight
After Midnight

THE CHRONICLES OF GREYSTONE BAY

Greystone Bay
Doom City
The SeaHarp Hotel
In the Fog

Other Works by Wendy Webb

Co-editor of *Phobias* and *More Phobias* anthology
Author of several short stories and articles on various subjects

GOTHIC

GHOSTS

EDITED BY

WENDY WEBB

AND

CHARLES GRANT

TOR®

A TOM DOHERTY ASSOCIATES BOOK
NEW YORK

This is a work of fiction. All the characters and events portrayed in this book are either fictitious or are used fictitiously.

GOTHIC GHOSTS

This book is printed on acid-free paper.

A Tor Book
Published by Tom Doherty Associates, Inc.
175 Fifth Avenue
New York, NY 10010

Tor Books on the World Wide Web:
http://www.tor.com

Tor® is a registered trademark of Tom Doherty Associates, Inc.

Library of Congress Cataloging-in-Publication Data

Gothic ghosts / [edited by] Wendy Webb and Charles Grant. — 1st ed.
        p.   cm.
    "A Tom Doherty Associates book."
    ISBN 0-312-86684-4
    1. Ghost stories, American.   2. Ghost stories, English.   I. Webb, Wendy.   II. Grant, Charles L.
    PS648.G48G67   1997
    813'.0873808054—dc21   97-13696
                                                         CIP

First Hardcover Edition: November 1997
First Trade Paperback Edition: September 1998

Printed in the United States of America

0   9   8   7   6   5   4   3   2   1

Copyright Acknowledgments

Contents

Introduction

So what did we look for when we began this project?

Mood.

Atmosphere.

A return to traditional, character-driven stories.

Real people in normal situations that, with a simple twist, become not normal at all.

It was out of the nineteenth century that the short story as it is known today emerged. The focus of those works was primarily the "what" of the story—the circumstances or event in which the characters were immersed. Now we are more interested in exploring characters through motivation and conflict. We want to know them, sympathize with them, and connect in some way their situation to experiences of our own.

So what did we look for?

Some have said that the principal elements of Gothic are the presence of the supernatural and a quality inherent in the work that arouses such feelings as fear or terror. To some degree, that's still true, but instead of castles and stark terror, today's Gothic atmosphere, and what we sought, can be found in narrow alleyways, a moonless waterfront, or the corner of a familiar room where light always falls short.

And it can be found deep within each of us.

Not the late eighteenth- and early nineteenth-century literary trappings of a ruined Gothic castle or abbey to set the scene. Then the work was filled with ghost-haunted rooms, secret passageways, and the door that should always remain closed. And while this volume shares those ghosts with our English literary ancestors, perhaps now the door that should remain closed is the one in our mind.

A good ghost story isn't always scary or unsettling at first. Sometimes, in fact, it seems perfectly innocent. Melancholy, perhaps, or even sentimental. Playful, or even humorous.

But it always has an unexpected bonus—like the souls of the dead, it returns . . . and lingers. With a touch to the back of the neck, or a gentle caress down the spine when you least expect it. A chilly draft when there is no wind. A sound you know doesn't belong.

So within these pages are stories of repressed memories, desire and despair, lost connections, questionable gifts, and second chances. Different styles and different voices.

But innocent?

Not likely.

Be careful what you wish for, for you may find it here.

It is the human condition.

With a Gothic twist.

Wendy Webb and Charles Grant

Nuestra Señora

Carrie Richerson

𝔄 drench of white moonlight slides through tall, narrow openings in two-foot-thick walls that once held the blistering border sun at bay. Waves and neglect have eroded the plaster that once protected the soft sandstone blocks and brightened the interior; now tiny ripples in the water reflect the light in writhing, silver skeins over the crumbling umber walls and the polished pine beams of the roof a short distance above. With only the tiniest movement of the oars I guide us around squared columns that rise into the perfect arches for which Guerrero's stone-masons were famous. Time and weather and the rising and falling lake levels gnaw away at these ancient stones, but it will be the arches, locked into symmetry by obdurate keystones, that are the last to go.

It is a mild night, the day's heat finally spent, and a cool stirring of air occasionally wanders into the old church and puffs against my cheek. To ward off a faint chill that is not from the breeze, I lounge back in the skiff and pull the flask from my hip pocket. My knee taps the oarlock, and the clunk echoes over water and stone. I hold back an irreverent word and offer the flask to my passenger in expiation.

He waves it away with gnarled fingers and returns to twisting his straw hat in his hands. "Why does she not come?" he whispers anxiously. "Why, *señor?*"

For José Domingo Ruiz Menchaca de Atlan I have always been "*señor*," or "*Señor* Francisco," never "Frank," never once in all the thirty years I have been bringing him here on Midsummer Eves, sharing his vigil, respectfully observing his hope and pain. "Shhh, José—she will come. She will be here at midnight, as always."

He twists around in the boat to stare at the windows. "What is the time? Oh, I cannot see *la luna,* it is too late already—"

"No, José." I stroke the oars lightly and move us beneath the part of the roof that has collapsed, where the nave lies open to the wide sky. "See—there is the moon. She's still rising. It's"—I angle my wrist to the strong light—"it's only eleven. Be patient, old *amigo.*"

José's shoulders slump. The battered straw Stetson hangs limply from hands scarred by a lifetime of ranching. "Why does she not come?" he repeats dully to the floorboards.

I am used to this; I ignore José's mutterings and look around the half-lit Nuestra Señora del Refugio again. Its eerie nighttime beauty never fails to move me with admiration for its builders and sadness for its present state. On sunny days the light comes through the old windows in golden bars that shine right down to the sandstone slabs of the floor, six feet below waterline. One can still see the patterns worn in the stone from the impact of thousands of feet over the church's 194-year history—the feet of petitioners and penitents, celebrants and mourners, hot-blooded boys with their first mustachios, shy girls resplendent in their *quinceañera* dresses. Shuffling or striding, or crawling in on bloody knees as an act of contrition or supplication. For all the weight of that history, these stones should be pocked from the acid tears of faith and grief and joy, but time has worn the tracks smooth and serene.

The penitents and petitioners still come, as tonight José and I have. Nuestra Señora del Refugio didn't stop being a church to the *peóns* and *indios* of the valley just because one has to visit it by boat now. On a shelf halfway between waterline and roof, someone long ago fashioned a shrine to the Virgin Mary. The strong moonlight almost washes out the flicker of votive candles that are always burning before the laminated picture in its cheap, silvered frame, but seems to enhance the fragrances of vanilla and sandlewood on the moist air.

I sigh. Too late now to regret the decision made by the Mexican and American governments forty-two years ago to sacrifice this little town of Guerrero and its beautiful church to the making of Falcon Lake on the Rio Grande. Water for the agricultural empires of the big downstream landowners, but a watery grave for Guerrero and its beautiful cathedral: the neoclassical, columned cloister; the mission-style facade; the distinctive three bell towers.

I don't feel like spending the next hour cloaked in such sadness, so I guide the boat carefully through one of the windows into the open lake. "*Señor!* We mustn't leave now, she will come soon, I know!"

"We've plenty of time, José. I want to do a little fishing."

We have the whole Mexican side of the lake to ourselves tonight; an unusual occurrence, since the few families that still live in the area depend on fish from the lake to supplement their tortillas and beans. But then, everyone who lives around here knows that José and his Anglo friend are out here tonight, and why. I don't expect any intrusions.

I steer for the arches that mark the old town's *mercado*. Many of the town's houses and shops have melted away into half-submerged piles of rubble, but the keystone arch is so stable a structure, and was engineered with such skill throughout Guerrero, that it endures where simple walls have collapsed. Drowned Guerreo Viejo is now a town of portals that open into nothing, gateways into an invisible past.

The fish may not bite in such strong light, but a fisherman is an inveterate optimist. I try a few topwater spinners, to no avail, then a plastic worm. Something strikes at it, but veers off before I can set the hook. On a normal night I would have set out a short trotline with a few blood baits for catfish before I rowed out from shore, but this isn't a normal night and catfish seem too ignoble for the evening. Bass or crappie would be better.

I edge closer to the columns and cast a buzz bait with small double hooks into the shadows there. Something hits it immediately. Be damned if you can't spend your whole life fishing and still be surprised by what those crafty water-breathers will like. I set the hook and a flash of silver rises into the moonlight, dances on its tail for a handful of seconds, then falls back in jeweled spray.

The fish fights like a little tiger for five minutes before I get it landed. A nice black bass, almost two pounds I reckon. I thread a stringer through its gill and out its mouth and drop it back into the water. The other end of the stringer goes around the oarlock; I can hear the captive bumping against the boat as I row to a new spot.

José fidgets and asks for the time again, and I tell him it's eleven-thirty. The moon is close to zenith and there aren't many shadows left, but I find a small patch west of an old store wall and cast in the same buzz bait. Another immediate hit, and soon I have a second bass on the stringer.

That's enough. I don't need to fish as much for food now that I live alone, since Anna passed. I fish more for pleasure now, for quiet and time to think. I find that the less I have to do, the more I have to think about, now, at the end of my life.

I check my watch, then lean on the oars and let us drift. Over toward the American side of the lake, where the water is deeper and colder, mist is starting to rise. Behind me, way off in the brush on the Mexican side, something coughs, and the sound carries clearly over the still water. For a moment my heart leaps—*El tigre!* No, not likely. Maybe forty-two years ago, before the government evacuated the residents of Guerrero to the raw, cinder-block ugliness of New Guerrero, maybe then a solitary jaguar might stalk a goat or sheep from the village, and maybe that bold cat might be stalked in turn by a stout-hearted *vaquero* like José. And if he was lucky and skilled, if his horse was steady and his aim true, he might present a properly cured jaguar hide to his new bride on her wedding day. Or, if the wedding was called off for some reason, he might just sell the hide to some wealthy *gringo* and drink up the profit in his rage and shame.

José is fretting. It really is time. I clean and pack away my lures, then head us back toward the church. Around us the mist thickens, turning the clear moonlight blue and soft. I row us to within a few feet of the church's great doorway, then keep us there with tiny movements of the oars.

When the floodgates of Falcon Dam were closed in 1953, hydrologists calculated it would take almost three years for the lake to fill enough to inundate the city that was already being called Guerrero Viejo. The area lay in the iron grip of a multiyear drought. Plenty of time to organize an orderly evacuation of the still-resisting Guerrerans.

Nature doesn't read weather reports. A tropical storm slipped across the Mexican interior and settled over Texas's Big Bend, where it proceeded to rain, and rain, and rain. The Rio Grande turned into an angry torrent, and Falcon Lake filled in three weeks. Guerrerans barely had time to grab their most precious possessions and get out. Artisans and priests removed Nuestra Señora's holy treasures, its bells, and its magnificently carved oak doors even as the muddy waters swirled at their feet. The precious items were taken by wagon and burro to their new home in Nuevo Guerrero, thirty-six miles away. But the new church looked more like a blockhouse than a house of God, and the huge doors never fit in the tiny structure. Nuestra Señora's lovingly crafted architectural wonders disappeared over time, and now she lies calmly open to sky and water and wind.

And on some midsummer nights like this one, to the mist that thickens and moves with strange purpose to surround the old church and plaza. The light seems to come from every direction now, and the flakes of silica in the old sandstone walls glitter like stardust. José rises to his feet, his hat crushed in heedless hands, his eyes fixed to the east. There the figure of a young woman carrying an infant separates itself from the swirling fogs and skims over the water toward the church.

She offers José her hand. He bows and kisses it, then turns to me. "*Señor* Francisco," he says for the thirtieth time, "I present to you Maria Escobar Portillo, who will be my wife."

Careful not to overbalance the skiff, I stand and bow in turn. "*Señorita,* I am honored to meet you. I am at your service."

She nods graciously to me but does not speak. Still holding her hand, José steps out of the boat and to her side. I hand him the jaguar pelt I have pulled from beneath my seat, and he drapes it reverently around Maria's shoulders. Then he takes the infant from her arms, kisses the top of its sleeping head, and settles it on his hip. I row the skiff a polite distance away and watch the couple promenade through the ruined town. I can hear the murmur of voices but not the subjects of which they speak.

It is an old story, forever new. José has told me much of it, and other details are common knowledge among older Guerrerans. Maria was a beautiful young woman, though it was whispered that, generations past, there were those in her family who had been touched by God or the Devil and were not right in their wits. José laughed at the soft voices. What did he care about the past? It was the bright future he had planned with Maria that concerned him. The arrangements were made between the families, the *padre* cried the banns, the date of the wedding was set for Midsummer Day, some months off.

And then it became apparent that Maria was with child. She swore no man had touched her, not even José; the child must be a gift of God. Certainly she had had a dream of an angel speaking to her in a haze of glory, naming her *blessed,* but she had thought it only a dream. The *padre* shook his head and urged her to confess her sin; the village murmured against her, the murmurs growing ever louder and uglier; and José hardened his heart.

The baby was born, without benefit of midwife, two hours before the scheduled wedding. Maria herself defiantly baptized it, since the *padre* would not attend. At the time appointed for the nuptials, Maria rose from the birthing bed, took up her son, and walked to the church. José waited at the door. Three times she invoked the Father of All to witness her innocence and asked José to accept her. Three times he refused her in front of all, called her a whore, and spat at her feet. He said he would not take soiled goods, nor raise another man's child as his own. That night Maria drowned herself and her infant son in the waters of the Rio Grande.

A suicide may not be buried in hallowed ground. Maria's parents gathered up the bodies when they were found the following day, and buried their beloved daughter and her child a short distance out of town to the east, on a slight rise overlooking the church and plaza. Until they grew old and died in turn, they tended the site regularly, whitewashing the stones that marked the grave, trimming the mesquite and retama that threatened to overrun the hill, planting coreopsis and poppies to brighten the little clearing. Every *Dia de los Muertos*, they took *pan dulce* and *galetas* and sugar skulls to the grave, ate a picnic lunch under the trees, and sang songs to Maria and her unnamed, unparented son. On one of those All Hallows' Eves, José—older, wiser, more compassionate and less self-righteous— joined them. After their deaths, he tended the gravesite weekly until it slipped under the rising waters of Falcon Lake.

Years later I met José walking on the road from Nuevo Guerrero one Midsummer Eve and offered him a lift to the lake. I've been part of this ritual ever since.

José and Maria pause in front of the remains of the elegant Hotel Flores, built in 1871 as a stop on the road from Matamoros to Nuevo Laredo. José points upward through the ruined stairwell: Is he re-calling the vanished splendors of its ballroom? Did he and Maria share tender summer dances there, before their beautiful dreams were shattered? There is so much here that has been lost to time, and I feel so old, thinking of those I have lost. Anna . . .

And then it is one o'clock. José and Maria turn their steps back to the church, and I row to meet them. The baby is awake; he looks at me with eyes as grave and piercing as his mother's. Who can know the truth of another's life? The old Guerrerans I ask, who know *why* I ask, cross themselves and answer frankly and fearfully— but none of them know who the father of Maria's child might have been unless it was José himself, and José has said he was not. I be-lieve him. So was Maria innocent, or merely ingenuous? Is this ever-nameless infant angel or devil, or merely a human bastard? I will never know the truth; and at the thought, the child nods at me as though in confirmation.

José hands the son he never had back to Maria and brushes the blue air of her cheek with his lips, then hands me the jaguar pelt and steps back into the skiff. *"Gracias, señor,"* she inclines her head to me. "I thank you for this time with my husband."

"Until next year, *señorita.*"

We watch until Maria's form merges into the blue mist and the vapors themselves begin to disperse. José is silent all the way back to shore. My bass occasionally bump the boat on the end of their stringer, but they are as much prisoners of history as José and I, and there will be no pardon. My truck's headlights pick out thirty-six miles of potholes as we jolt our way to Nuevo Guerrero.

I pull over beside the new church and lean across to open the door for José. The predawn air is thick with scent—the sweetness of datura and moonflower, the bitter tang of creosote bush, a lingering trace of incense from the church—and the stark little building of whitewashed brick glows in the light like a bitter mockery of the graceful curves of its antecedent. The same moonlight picks out the track of every regret in José's long life on the map of his face.

"She will come again, *señor? Por favor,* tell me she will come?"

"Next year, José. She will come."

"And you, *señor?*"

I hesitate. It is a lot to promise, perhaps not even within my power.

"I'll be here, *amigo.* For a few more years yet." I feel its truth as I say it, and close my eyes in pain. *Anna . . .*

José steps out of the truck and jams the straw Stetson onto his head. *"Gracias, señor.* My regards to *Señora* Anna." I have told him for three years running that Anna is gone, but José's world does not admit change. He strides into the graveyard beside the little church; his boots are silent on the gravel underfoot. I watch until I can no longer distinguish his form from all the other shadows that move and murmur there.

Maria was just seventeen when she died; José, a year older. He lived another fifty years, and never married. He died in the hard winter of '65, of pneumonia. I met him the following Midsummer Eve. On my way home to the American side of the lake, I think about what my life would have been like without fifty years of Anna.

The light in the window of my cabin makes it look a little less lonely. I'd brought two old lovers together for a short time, and I had fresh fish to fry up for breakfast. Not a bad night's work for a seventy-year-old coot.

Anna will be proud of me.

A Mirror for Eyes of Winter

Jessica Amanda Salmonson

Is there anything so sad in this world as an old, old man whose deeds, undone, cannot be dreamed again? I think there is. That sadder thing is an old, old dog not smart enough to guess what the thing is that makes the rabbits so much faster than once they were, and the light of day so dim. I saw my husband die without a single dream come true, without one scheme out of many ever bearing fruit of success or happiness. "Wasn't our love something?" I said, smiling at him as I sat by his deathbed, holding his palsied hand. He said to me, "I've left you nothing. I gave you nothing." These were his last words. He died with tears in his eyes. And Enoch, the old sheepdog that my husband loved, came into the room and placed his enormous paws upon the foot of the bed and looked on, uncertain why I cried, but knowing it was sorrow, and so began to whine as well.

Enoch, like his master, had slowed with age. Even so, the clumsy old fellow managed to hop upon the bed, onto Carl who lay unmoving. He licked my hand that clung to Carl's, and he licked Carl's face as though to say "Wake up, old boy! Your wife is crying!" And when the wet tongue couldn't win response, the big foolish animal leapt onto the floor and stood looking at the wall, then paced oddly around the room searching for the flown ghost. And maybe dogs do understand something of death, for he gave a howl of regret such as I had never before heard from his long throat.

Carl was laid to rest in Deephaven Cemetery, a rolling field of snow punctuated with leaning monuments like upraised fingers twisted with rheumatism. Those acres of buried bones were hemmed about on three sides by trees whose naked branches scratched the early winter sky. The fourth side was a steep slope that overlooked the rocky cove, wherein lay even more bones of Deephaven's generations of fishermen, taken by the unforgiving Atlantic.

After the funeral, I could remember little of what transpired. So numb was my mind, I had not heard Parson Williams's prayer of comfort, and could not recall who of the village had been in attendance, what words they may have spoken me, or I to them. There lingered in my recollection nothing of Carl having gone into the ground, as though memory rebelled at the possibility. Yet I could still feel the slap of a stinging wind, and retained a vision of overhanging clouds heaped up like slate tiles, and amid those clouds a face, gray and awful, glowering upon the cemetery, upon all of Deephaven, like a pitiless god.

In days and weeks that followed, I fell into idleness and deepening depression. It seemed to me that death was an icy terror that displaced the soul; it was a dark, dark cloud, iron hard even though insubstantial. I understood only that all things vanish away. There is left of us no remnant of the evil or the good that is in us, and we might just as well never have lived at all. I read my Bible and tried to think lofty, beautiful thoughts. But each thought turned like a worm in my brain, becoming poisonous. God had taken my Carl. God had left me with nothing but my lonesome misery and spiritual doubt. I had no future but to await unpitying Death, to wait alone, powerless in Death's hovering presence, forlorn in my heart, cold to the marrow, with the Maine winter howling at the eaves in grim sympathy with my mood.

It felt as though the only reason I perceived the world was because things just carried on by force of habit, even though the world ceased to exist a thousand years before. Everything and everyone I had ever known were mere shadows in a book; nothing had a firm sure existence; nothing was certainly real, save woe.

It was strange how Enoch attended me. I had never liked the old dog much. Not that I'd ever disliked him, but he wasn't mine. It had never been my task to feed him. He always had stayed close to Carl, and whatever affection the animal showed me along the years was restrained in comparison to his doting love for Carl. But now, of a sudden, we found each other. And having to care for him forced me to care for myself, for otherwise it might not have occurred to me to eat or bathe or comb my hair. In the weeks that followed, Enoch stayed by me near the fire, stretched out beside the footstool on which I rested a vein-sore leg.

It can be very surprising how a life must change when a loved one leaves us. We can think we're prepared, but there is not much we can really apprehend beforehand. As well to prepare oneself for the vanishing of the earth, as though there would be anything else to cling to.

The winter grew colder and the wind blew ever more mournful with each passing week. Certain routines that had been Carl's became mine, and other routines that had been my own, and had been so important to me, centered so much around Carl that there was no longer any use for once-habitual actions. It was not only that I had lost a part of myself in losing Carl, but most strangely, he had taken over a part of me, *possessed* me in a commonplace sort of way, as I performed his duties and lost all mine.

Enoch seemed to me symbolic of this possession. I had daily to brush his long coat, clean his rheumy eyes, mash and warm the dog-food that his old black gums and nubby teeth could hardly eat otherwise, and walk him though the snow on my way to the Deephaven post office in the afternoons.

The post had been Carl's task too, and doubtless I could have convinced Mr. Harris to send a boy around to my lane-end home, given my age. But I owed it to Enoch, if not to myself, to maintain a stolid front.

After years of daily strolls with Carl, Enoch had come to expect the walk to Mr. Harris's general store and post office. If in my disheartened preoccupations I forgot the time, Enoch would be at the door snuffling and woofing and reminding me of our scheduled walk. And the post was an odd sort of consolation to me at first, since no week went by that some letter didn't reach me from somewhere, some friend of mine or Carl's or both, having only then heard of Carl's passing, writing me condolences. I began to correspond with several people as a result, who kindly and eagerly replied even if their hand was more crabbed and illegible than mine. Thus our walks were mutually gratifying, for Enoch and myself.

Parson Williams dropped by one day, stomped snow off his boots, and took off coat and hat. Then, holding my hands in his, he asked, "How are you doing, Claire?" He had wanted me to move into the home next to the church with some other old widows, to sell the big old house and, as he said, "Live well on the profits until the end of your days, surrounded by your good friends." I gave it some thought. I might have done it but for Enoch; the Widows' Society did not permit dogs. I owed it to Carl to look after Enoch. Besides, Enoch, more than the house that Carl built with his own hands, seemed my last connection with warmth, love, and the man I had lost.

"I'm doing well, Parson," I told him, and led him to the chair that had been Carl's. The old sheepdog looked up with sudden curiosity, his foggy eyes scarcely able to see, with or without the heavy bangs that brushed his face. Was this his master? he seemed to wonder, and exercised his nostrils, though even that sense had deteriorated. But in a moment he settled down before the fire, discounting the possibility of his master's late return.

I made the parson tea and he spent an hour or more with me. I did not let on that I was just frightfully sad and lonesome. I never said the things I felt, of my feeling that lingering in life was useless and unwarranted, that I was ready to die. "Yes, everything is going as well as can be expected, Parson. I've lots of friends, you know; more than I considered." And I indicated to him a pile of recent correspondence, again not letting on that in the two long, cold months since Carl's death, and with my renewed interest in letter-writing, already two old friends had passed away, leaving me only a scratchy letter or two by which to conjure up some sense of who they once had been.

Before he left, his kindly voice and sentiments broke through a layer or two of my defenses. I confessed, "Old age is a terrible thing, Parson. I don't know which is worse, to die, or to remain." I held back tears, but wallowed in the parson's comfort for a few minutes more. Then I gave him the chance he needed to be on his way, since I was not his only parishioner sitting lonely on a winter's eve.

The next day Enoch and I took our slow walk through the snow toward the post office. The leafless trees of the lane were all thick with freshly added snow, fallen in the night. The world was muffled and beautiful, yet cold and distant too. It was not an easy walk, not for Enoch or myself. With my aching legs, and his arthritic haunches, we were certainly suitable partners as far as speed was measured, plodding through heaps of white powder.

We turned at the end of the long lane and struck the edge of town, which didn't extend particularly far along a stretch of coastal road. To call our country setting a town was to give it the benefit of the doubt. It had once aspired to become a city, but that was in days of the tallships, and no one living was old enough to remember those long-lost days of Deephaven's grandeur and glory. Once-grand houses built for captains' families, with widow-walks where anxious wives would stand watching the deadly sea, were neglected relics with broken porches and decaying foundations. There were a few of these "painted ladies" restored and transformed into Victorian bed-and-breakfasts, owned and run by escapees from the big city— strangers to Deephaven, really, who would always remain so to those of us who've always been here. Yet if it were not for these holiday getaways as well as the cove's resort marina that was likewise never busy save in summer, I suppose Deephaven couldn't even support its one combination general store post office.

I dallied to speak with Mr. Harris.

"Why, hello, Mrs. Ledderer. You must be a regular snowplow, coming on a day like this."

"Old Enoch's the plow," I said, almost laughing, which Mr. Harris alone could make me do with his pie-faced smile. "I merely walk along in his paw prints and do just fine."

All I had was a letter and a catalog, which I took from Mr. Harris's warm hand. I bought a slab of salted pork and some dogfood, and that added up to as much as I could carry. Enoch stood the whole time on the store's stoop looking in the dusty window at me, or at the shadow that was all of me his feeble eyes could see.

Can a dog be depressed? It seemed to me that Enoch became more and more downcast as winter nights rolled on. Or it may have been that he reflected my own feelings, a mirror of my own depression, and if only I could cheer up, so would he. Despite everything one may attempt to suppress, hide, or avoid, it's funny what a beast can understand.

One day, as we started toward the post, he got as far as the front yard gate, then looked back toward the house to woof quietly, calling to Carl to hurry along with us. When Carl wouldn't come, Enoch refused to budge, as though his life had at that moment acquired one brick more than he could carry. He stood with his legs half buried in snow, whined a moment, then became a motionless heap. I felt that he was trying to remember something, or figure something out that was just beyond a dog's ken.

"Mail, Enoch," I said. "Time for the mail."

But he wouldn't come; and I, feeling halfway betrayed, trudged through the snow to the post by myself. It was a sad trip without him. Really, I was tempted to follow his example and stay home and pout; just cave in and do nothing ever again. But I had become addicted to meaningless little talks with Mr. Harris and needed especially those dribs and drabs of mail that came to me now and then.

The letters had become a blessing and a curse. There were five trips to the post a week, but many a day there was no mail for me, not even the consolation of a few subscription ads. That would spoil the rest of my day. I always had letters of my own to send off, for it was obvious that if I didn't send them, there could be no replies. When there was a letter, or occasionally three, how brief they were, compared to the long ones I had written. A typical missive, so badly scrawled that I had to study and study every word to figure it out, was often nothing more than "I am doing fine," followed by "write to me again." The worst ones said such things as, "Arthur died and I am so unhappy, Claire, I wish that I was with him," which was anything but healing for my own frame of mind.

Yet, what beyond these letters did I have in my simple existence? Those letters, and Enoch, were the sum total of my reason to go on. All too well I knew those letters underscored the purposelessness of my life and of the lives of those who wrote me; but I clung to the expectation of further correspondence as firmly as a lame man clings to crutches.

After that first day when Enoch chose not to take the short walk into town, he seemed to be losing what vitality he had left, and never again walked farther than the edge of our yard. Sometimes he would walk me to the door, taking each step like a rusty automaton. He'd sit inside the door and stare up at me as I put on my boots and heavy coat, his moist apologetic eyes dull behind his bangs.

Other times he sat outside at the edge of a snowdrift, waiting for my return. When I got back from the walk, he'd be in the exact same place, almost invisible with snowflakes settled on him.

It got so I could scarcely look at Enoch without an unbearable pity engulfing me, for myself as much as him. We had become so much two of a kind, neither of us quite able to find a new rhythm for our lives, or grasp the reason for the increasing difficulty of managing daily needs.

His days were otherwise spent before the fireplace. He hardly ate, but expended so little energy that he was able to keep up his weight even without much nourishment. It was mightily disheartening to see his last bit of energy fading day by day. Yet there was a good feeling in my heart when I returned from my near-daily constitutional and heard his tail thumping on the throw rug and his growly old voice giving me welcome. It seemed always a relief to him to have me back, and my talks with Mr. Harris became shorter in consequence. It worried Enoch each time I left, and I think he fretted that I, like Carl before me, might one day leave him forever.

At the height of winter a terrible storm came on, nothing un-expected along the Maine coast. I peered out the window for hours, hoping it would let up so I could head for the post. It was a Monday, and I hadn't been for the mail since Thursday. I hoped this meant an extra amount of mail awaited me. I also had a batch of my own letters ready to send.

It was blindingly white outside. As my vision strove to pierce thick white flurries, I thought I saw someone moving past the kitchen window, heading for the front of the house. I went to the front window and saw an indefinite form, obscured by white swirls, near the gate. The shape had sagging shoulders and a familiar pos-ture. I thought it might be a neighbor's hulking teenager, who had been helping me with firewood and odd jobs once or twice a week. Eager for unexpected company, I opened the door, calling out, "Are you the Lambert boy? Come on in out of the weather."

The shadowy figure swelled to enormous size, then fell to pieces. I realized I had been watching nothing more than a whirl of snow. Enoch raised his head and was whining from his place on the throw rug. I shut the door and went over to him, told him not to fret, and put a couple of extra logs on the fire. Enoch wouldn't settle down, although nowadays he showed his agitation by little more than his upraised, blindly attentive face.

"I won't be long, Enoch," I said, pulling on my boots. "I'm going for the mail."

He started to get up. I told him to stay still, as I knew it hurt his hind legs ever so much to stand after a long period of immobility. He got his front legs straightened out and was loosening up his haunches as I fastened my heavy coat and put on my gloves. He woofed feebly that he wished to come along, or wished that I would stay. I knew he wouldn't go any farther than the gate, and the weather was so intolerable, I didn't want him sitting out there. I shut the door on him just as he reached it, then I heard him howl a sad lament that like to broke my heart.

It was impossible to see through the wind-driven snow. But I knew the route by heart, down to the exact number of steps it took to reach the end of the lane. When I struck the main road, I moved out into the part where studded truck tires, or car tires with chains, had flattened a track. I stayed alert for the sound of a vehicle, pulled my muffler tight around my throat. With my head down I pushed on to Mr. Harris's.

I was surprised to find him closed. As he lived in back of the general store, I banged the door, and soon enough he came to let me in. It was too cold to trek back without warming up first; that, at least, was to be my excuse. The truth was that I had to know if there'd been any mail.

"Why, Mrs. Ledderer, what are you doing out!" he said with alarm. "Come in here. Come in and warm up."

His potbelly stove was putting up a roaring fight with the wind that strove to poke its way down the flue. I stood by the stove and said, "If I'd thought, I would've known you might not have opened on a day like this. But even in a storm, people need supplies! I need a couple of things, and thought I'd get my mail."

"Why, there weren't but a little pile of things brought in this morning. The mail's clogged all along the routes. The storm should pass over us in a day or two, but in the meantime deliveries are bound to be erratic."

"But there was *something* for me, wasn't there?" I asked, rather pathetically I'm afraid. "It's been since Thursday."

"Oh, a few things. I haven't sorted them, but it isn't much. Here, wait a minute."

He grabbed a handful of unsorted mail from his postal cage and thumbed through the stack, removing but one item. "Oh, my," he said. "I'm afraid this is all there is."

He handed me one of my own letters, marked "Deceased. Return to sender."

I must have appeared absurd to him, as tears were brimming, and I barely suppressed a long sigh of sadness and disappointment. "Another friend gone before," I said softly. "And I was only just getting to know her again." Mr. Harris put an arm across my shoulder and patted me gently. It was bold of him, but a great comfort.

"Can I walk you home?" he asked. "It's simply not possible to see out there."

"Oh, I'd know the way even if I went plum blind," I said, making myself sound cheerier. "I better get back to Enoch. He's feeling mighty poorly lately."

The storm drew tight about me, furious as a thousand needles pricking my cheeks. I tried to hide my face in my muffler and collar as my breath was sucked right out of me. I'd only gone a little way down the road when Mr. Harris's general store vanished behind me, and I felt as though I were drifting in a white void. I counted my steps, but the deepening snow changed the length of my stride. When I turned onto what I thought was my street, I soon came to a dropoff, so hurried back to the main road. I went again and again to edge of the road, but could detect no side road or driveways. It occurred to me that I may have passed by my street, and went back searching; the weariness in my legs and lungs was awful. No, it wasn't possible I'd passed my street, and I didn't want to go back to Mr. Harris's. I turned again, and found myself somehow in the midst of a stand of young maples, their thin black branches like cracks in the whitened sky.

By now my lungs were gasping. I coughed feebly. I was in a sudden panic realizing I had somehow lost my way. The road was undoubtedly a few feet left or right. But how could I choose my steps? What direction should I turn?

Then to my relief, I saw a shambling figure ahead of me in the snow. It had to be the Lambert boy. I tried to call out to him, but my throat was constricted from the cold. He was lumbering away, his dark coat a blur amid the flurries. If I could only catch up with him! If I could at least keep him in sight, I'd find my way to the Lambert house, or wherever that ox of a boy was headed.

I don't know how long I followed him. It seemed forever. He was just beyond reach. Then he seemed to have stopped up the way a bit, and raised his arms in the air, threw his head back as though to capture snowflakes in his mouth. "Michael. Michael Lambert," I croaked. Icy winds whistled amid the trees, and he couldn't hear me.

When I reached him, my heart sank, for there was only a black stump of a tree with two limbs reaching upward. The cold had slowed my thinking. I was panting wildly, my mind whirling with a giddy fright. How could I have been following a stump?

In the midst of my alarm, I half laughed, for I recognized the stump. It was something of a landmark, visible up the lane from my own front yard. I knew where I was now! I oriented myself, strode forward a scant ten or so difficult paces through a drift, then collapsed alongside the road. I felt such an extraordinary relief, despite the fact that I could not get up. In my giddily irrational frame of mind, I thought I had made it, I was safe, and now I could rest.

I could hear Enoch howling in the house. It seemed so near. Yes, I thought, I'm home now. I needn't struggle any longer.

I know now that only a miracle could have saved me. No one would be out on the roads on such a day, and I was not apt to be found. If a snowplow came through, the driver could not have seen me covered with new snowfall, but would have plowed me right into a snowbank where I'd not be discovered until spring thaw.

But Enoch somehow knew that things were amiss. I must have latched the door insufficiently, for his efforts to get out succeeded. My eyes were half closed as I saw that shaggy animal materialize out of ghostly swirls. He prodded me with his front feet; he licked my face; then he lay upon me to keep me warm. I could no longer hear a thing, not the storm, not Enoch's howling; but I could see his throat stretched upward above my face, and I knew he was calling for help. When still no one came, Enoch got up from atop me, took a step or two, then looked back at where I lay. Then he set out, as near as I could judge, in the direction of the parsonage.

It's funny, but as I lay there, the depression of the last months lifted from me. I wasn't afraid of dying. I was relieved that it would soon be over. The dog, foolish friend, might've saved me had he stayed until the storm lifted. As it was, the heat was rapidly leaving my body. "Carl," I said, if only in my mind, "Carl, if you're out there, I'm coming." For a moment, I was certain Carl indeed heard me, for I saw him nearby in his long black autumn dress coat.

I was about to scold him for wearing his autumn coat instead of something warmer. But it was the parson, fussing about me in a terrible dither. He was not a big man, but strong enough to carry an old stick of a woman. He lifted me in his arms, and I was thinking he was an angel taking me to Carl. He half wrapped me in his own long cloak.

By the time we reached the front door of my house, the parson's warmth had restored some of my senses. He put me down by the door and fumbled to get it opened, as I whispered hoarsely, "Where's Enoch? Where's that fool dog who saved me?"

The parson looked me straight in the face, and I realized he was abnormally pale, and there was a wonder in his expression. He answered, "I don't rightly know. When he came to the house all agitated, I thought there was trouble. He led me to you, but then . . ."

"My lord!" I said, horrified. "You lost him out there?"

By then the door was opened. The parson got me inside. The fire in the hearth had died down; nevertheless, the room provided a warm blast in comparison to where we'd been. I saw that Enoch was still lying before the fireplace, in his usual spot. It was a great relief, though for the life of me I couldn't guess how he got out and back in. The parson put me down in a stuffed chair—Carl's chair, which I never sat in, it seemed a sacrilege—then, finding three blankets, he tucked me all up warm, and threw logs on the fire to build it up.

My consciousness faded into sleep. Whether minutes passed or an hour I don't know. But when I opened my eyes, the room was toasty, and the parson was sitting in my chair across from me.

"Claire," he said. "You'd better brace yourself, for Enoch's dead. It must have been some other dog found you out there in the snow, and fetched me from the parsonage."

I looked toward Enoch's still form, so natural looking I'd thought him alive, although I now realized his tail for the first time had failed to thump the floor when his name was spoken.

"I'll carry him to the church's tool shed, where he'll keep until it's possible to dig him a grave. If you like, I can take you over to the widow's house to stay a few days, so you won't be alone. I know what that dog meant to you."

"Do you really think it was another dog, Parson?" I asked, my head sticking out the heap of blankets.

He licked his lips. He knew as well as I there wasn't another sheepdog within thirty miles. "I guess it couldn't have been," he admitted.

"That's right, Parson, it couldn't't've been any other dog. And I have to tell you, if you'll forgive my saying it, that when Carl left me, I kind of stopped believing things. If there was a life beyond, how could I have been left to suffer so, and Carl not feel sorry and come back, just for a moment, to reassure me? Now I know he did come back, Parson; I saw him out in the snow, but he wasn't old, and I mistook him for the Lambert boy. Carl came for Enoch's soul, Parson, and they both of them saved me from the storm before going on their way, to a place I'll go too, in time, and be with them again."

"We do need faith, Claire, without expecting to possess all the answers. But a dog's soul? I don't know, Claire, I don't know."

"Now don't you go telling me an old dog can't have a soul, or any business in heaven, because that's the thing I'm holding onto right now."

The parson was a good man, of course. But his theology was narrow. Carl had never liked to go to church because of it. I looked at him, and remembered how pale and confused he'd looked on my front porch when I first asked after Enoch. It seemed to me he was ruminating on our shared experience, like a cow chews its cud, and I suppose he'd been ruminating on it even when I was asleep in the chair. He looked at the inert, peaceful animal between the chair and the fireplace, then he looked back at me. I think he felt his own mortality just then, for he shivered in the heat of that room.

It was then the storm lifted. Where a moment before the wind cried aloud like an anguished beast, now there was the silence of fallen snow, broken only by the sound of a crackling fire. I lay my head on the back of Carl's chair, closed my eyes, and fell dreaming into a place where grief is healed and life again has meaning.

In the Clearing

Brad Strickland

The hilltop clearing was easy for the two women to reach. It took Sarah and Lynda twenty minutes of rough driving over a rutted dirt road, and then another thirty of chest-burning climbing in muggy September air up trails that may have been broken by hikers or bears.

The hilltop clearing was difficult for the woman to reach. It took Sarah Hallford twenty-one years, the mystic three times the mystic seven, to feel desperate enough to dare the darkness.

Sarah's last memory of Alan alive: On a bright April morning he saunters toward his beloved Volvo, and she calls, "Take care, love." Without turning, he waves a careless hand in a loose-elbowed, over-the-head farewell. His dark curly hair gleams in the sun. Ahead of him is a winding road up into the mountains, a little patch of land where one day they will have a summer house, a small hilltop clearing in the woods.

Homebody Sarah does not need to visit the site so often, does not need to reassure herself that stone and branch remain as she left them, that the clearing has not fled to other climes. Let Alan see the hilltop with the eyes of a dreamer, listen with the ear of fantasy to future children laughing in the sun. She, kneeling, returns to the salvia she is transplanting. The scent of turned earth is rich with promise. With the red of the flowers in her eyes, how could she see the blackness to come?

"There are ways," Lynda told Sarah kindly one tumultuous July night of thunder and wind-whipped hail.

In Sarah's house, the only one Alan had ever called his own, they sat cross-legged on the chestnut-colored carpet before the enormous stone fireplace. Blazing oak logs crackled and gleamed yellow, throwing shifting patterns of light and dark over the two barefoot women, over the cards laid out in cruciform pattern on the floor: Sarah's Queen of Wands, covered by the King, reversed, crossed by the Tower, with the Nine of Swords beneath and Death as the crown.

Sarah, already tipsy, sipped from her brandy snifter. "There are ways and there are days," she intoned. With a smile edged in deep creases, she murmured, "You needn't try to seduce me, dear. My tastes never ran in that direction, and my juices have long since dried."

With a reproving smile, Lynda shook her head. She was raven-haired, her forehead bead-banded, a woman ten years younger than Sarah. "Not that. Not that. I knew that was not part of you. But"—her long, carmine-tipped finger reached to touch the card of hopes, the Lovers—"you still have needs. Your farewells are all unsaid."

"On the contrary. I have said my good-byes too many times."

What did the Fool, reversed, mean? Why did it lie before her? "I think," Lynda said slowly, "you are asking for something without understanding what it may bring with it."

Wind whistling in the eaves. Lightning photographing a thrashing landscape of storm-tossed trees outside the front window. Before the wild white light faded, the slam and shatter of thunder. The house vibrated. Concentric circles appeared in the red dregs of brandy. The Lovers blurred.

For a long time after the April afternoon when two State Troopers, both so red that they looked boiled, broke the news of the automobile accident, Sarah talked to Alan's pictures. One particularly, the one of him standing behind her on the steps of their new house, his arms around her, his hands possessively grasping her shoulders, the wind lifting a long strand of her golden-brown hair (it was long then, and unsilvered) to waft in a tendril under his chin. She is smiling, wide mouth, white teeth. His chin is lifted slightly, avoiding the tickling hair, and the gesture has pursed his lips. His eyes are merry and loving. He is always twenty-eight in the photograph.

Sarah told the twenty-eight-year-old of the horrors of mortuaries, the ghastly consideration and condescension of those whose business is with the dead. She told the picture of a word she had learned from the Director of Arrangements: "cremains."

Ashes to ashes, and dust to dust, and Alan to cremains.

In later years, she confessed the awfulness of the struggle to keep the house, to hold together their nest, to come to terms with a nursery doomed always to be empty. Her life became a maze of stratagems to cope, a bad job giving her time to study, a degree giving her a marginally better job, the burning need to find meaning in the leftover life she lived driving her to an advanced degree, a teaching position, the chair of the department, then the division.

Sometimes you run too hard to stay in place.

Sometimes you are so lonely that you lose yourself among people.

A year came when she covered her face in the photo with the base of her thumb. Picture and mirror no longer agreed. She found a different photo, a snapshot, of Alan as he had looked a few months before the closed-coffin service and had an artist specializing in portraits render it as a likeness in oils. The artist, who taught adult-education art courses for Sarah's college, began as one of her good friends and grew to loathe her. Sarah looked over the woman's shoulder every day, critical, pointing out small mistakes, fallacies of color or line. The portrait finally matched Sarah's memories, and the day she hung it on the wall of her lonely bedroom was also the day she took all the other photos, the ones of herself and Alan, off her walls and put them in an attic box.

One night she stared into the mirror at her long hair, entirely, prematurely silver. Another woman might have reached for a package of color, or for the telephone to make a hairdresser's appointment. Sarah reached for the shears.

She wept as the hanks fell into the bathroom wastebasket. The shag she left herself startled the other teachers. Some complimented her on the new look. She smiled and ached.

At the top of the trail, rounded shoulders of granite hunched through the red-brown drift of pine needles and the pale-green barbed-wire tangles of blackberry briars. "There," Sarah said, pointing. From here the hillside rolled upward to a gentle rounded crest, clothed in armpit-high grasses, yellow after a drought-dry August and an early, warm fall. Sarah breasted the grass: no paths now.

Lynda followed in her wake, saying nothing. She wore buckskins and silver-hoop earrings. A patterned red cotton scarf covered her hair.

They reached the summit, and Sarah, wearing a thick red-plaid flannel shirt, jeans, and boots, hugged herself, not for warmth. Despite the clouds, the day was almost oppressive for fall, laden with an unseasonable, drowsy heat. The hill fell away on all sides to a wooded plain, and beyond the plain on all sides rose blue-green hills, and beyond them pale-blue mountains. To the north, a speck of hawk rode a high thermal against a lowering sky. That and three distant brown spots that were cows eating their way across a cleared pasture were the only moving things in sight. Sarah glanced at Lynda, who stood with her head back-tilted, like a Gypsy in Indian garb. After a long moment, Sarah told her, "Every window would have a view."

"It's a beautiful spot."

"He loved it." Sarah hacked the grass with the heel of her boot. Moving in an expanding spiral, she pressed the dry growth flat. The thought crossed her mind that some low-flying pilot would see her work and report a flying saucer nest, a crop circle on a remote hilltop. Her boot hit something hard, and she cried out in satisfaction. "Here," she said, kneeling, caressing the grass away. "Here, see here."

A steel stake, its surface oxidized to chocolate. Etched in the rounded top were three small figures, hardly visible in the diffused light: A&S. Alan and Sarah.

Their initials stabbed into the flesh of the hillside, marking the place where Alan dreamed a house.

Sarah touched it with a tentative forefinger. Beneath the whorled pad of her flesh the steel was cool and rough.

A moment on the very edge, seven years after Alan's death.

Sarah, huddled in thick quilted robe and pajamas, in front of the fireplace, hunched over a lap desk, marking papers from a senior class in nineteenth-century fiction. Some hapless student, a twenty-year-old boy who looked pubescent, all big nose and black-rimmed glasses and erupting face, had turned in a neatly printed term paper: "Visitations from the Dead in 'The Turn of the Screw.' "

The paper asked: What if Henry James's ghosts were real?

The house was cold and silent with the chill of late February. Sarah clenched her grading pen with fingers that felt numb. Without once making a mark or comment, she read all the way to the last part of the final paragraph: "If, then, the apparitions were truly the spirits of the debauched couple, then the reader must conclude that our neurasthenic governess, far from being the dupe and the villain, is the true heroine of the piece. For if the dead return to trouble the living, their victims become the protectors of a society complacently swathed in the comfortable pseudorationality of a science-worshiping age, a society ruled by dictatorial patriarchs of the material world who must not and cannot admit the deeper mysteries beyond the grave."

Sarah, remotely astonished, saw her hand slash out letters half an inch high, the color of blood, on the blank space at the bottom of the final page: THE DEAD DO NOT TROUBLE THE LIVING THE DEAD DO NOT CARE OH YOU—

Five seconds later she carefully ripped the paper, leaving only the typed lines. The three-quarter page with her scrawled obscenities she dropped into the fire. It curled, the deeply scribed lines of her words standing out at first like cuts in cinnamon-colored skin, and then everything was bright flame and black ash.

Sarah dropped the term paper on the floor and walked barefoot through every room of the silent, cold house, turning on lights, calling Alan.

She ran a steaming bath and popped a single-edge blade from Alan's old razor. Staring at her reflection, Sarah undressed, letting the thick robe drop, then the nightgown, then the white panties. Gooseflesh crinkled the slopes of her breasts. She felt something hot touch her there and knew she was crying only because her reflection wept.

She left the tub to cool. She opened a closet door and pulled armloads of shirts and trousers, his things, from their hangers. She fell asleep naked, with his clothing locked in the embrace of her arms and thighs.

The next morning she drained the tub, threw away the blade, took a shower, and telephoned Goodwill, asking if they could use some clothes in good condition, trousers size 34–32, shirts size 16–32. They asked her to drop them off, which she did on the way to the office.

In the faculty workroom Sarah carefully photocopied the mutilated last page, worked with fingernails to straighten the left-corner staple holding the term paper together, replaced the torn page with the copy. She gave the paper a B-minus and recommended some articles to the student's attention.

For the dead do trouble the living.

"Are you sure?" Lynda asked. The drowsy afternoon had waned to early dusk.

Sarah gave her a bitter smile. "I'm sure of nothing. But, yes, we might as well."

"Give me your hands."

Lynda's eyes were brown and direct. "You must understand. You must want this. You must want it more than anything."

Sarah's smile twisted. The hilltop felt airless, hushed. "If you only knew."

The brown eyes did not blink. "Many people fool themselves, Sarah. They hold on to a memory, and the memory becomes the person they miss. But you must remember, a memory is *not* a person. If we call him and he answers, he will see you as you are. You must see him as he is, not as you remember him." For a moment she paused, looking troubled, then added: "The living grow and change, Sarah. The dead never change."

The unspoken question: What would Alan make of what Sarah had made herself? Flickers of memory, faint as distant moths, whirled around Sarah, Alan's exasperated comment about women in the workplace, his eye-rolling impatience with a woman executive at work, his sarcastic remarks to television anchorwomen. But those women were not Sarah, and her love for Alan was large enough to contain such moments without hesitation or doubt.

Implacable, Lynda asked, "How much do you want this, Sarah? Be sure of yourself. For God's sake, be sure."

Sarah tried to pull her hands from the other woman's grasp. Lynda did not allow her. "For twenty-one years and five months," she said, "I have wanted Alan every second of every minute I was conscious. If I could see him again, if I could only tell him what I feel—"

Lynda sighed. "Very well." She let Sarah's hands fall. "But there are rules. First, we have to wait until full dark."

"The witching hour."

"Don't be insulting. We don't have to wait for midnight, just for full nightfall. It's just that the world is different in darkness, that's all. There is a full moon tonight, if the clouds let it show. That would be good. Moonlight can be a bridge. Next, we have to prepare for your safety."

On an outcrop of smooth weathered granite, they cleared away leaf-drift and branch-fall, two tidy housekeepers making nature a little neater. Using a flat piece of pale-blue chalk, Lynda expertly drew two concentric circles, the smaller six feet across, and within them a five-pointed star. In the curving space between the circles she drew marks that looked like Hebrew letters.

"I can't believe I'm doing this," Sarah said, watching her.

Lynda gave her a quick tomboy grin.

From a pouch at her belt, Lynda took a small vial of oil. Carefully, at intervals, she poured drops of oil on the periphery of the outer circle, muttering some incantation. Then she raised both of her hands to shoulder level and murmured what sounded like a prayer many times repeated. At last she stepped back from the circle, nodded, and came to sit beside Sarah on the fallen trunk of a storm-toppled pine.

"That's it?" Sarah asked her.

"That's it. Now we just wait. You didn't eat anything, did you?" Sarah shook her head.

"That's good. One thing: When we begin, I'll ask you to step into the center of the circle, the heart of the pentagram. You are to stay there. Do you understand? You must not leave the center."

"Or the demons will get me."

With an exaggerated sigh, Lynda turned her back on Sarah. "No, the demons will not get you. But you'll break the connection, sever the tie, collapse the bridge. One try is all you will ever have."

"I won't leave the circle."

"That hawk," said Lynda, staring up into the clouded sky above the mountains. "She must feel so free."

The day that Sarah received word of her promotion to full professor she felt more strongly than ever Alan's absence.

After the congratulations, the perfunctory handshake from the portly Dean of Instruction, the jokes about Ph.D. meaning "piled higher and deeper," she returned home and stood before the portrait of Alan.

"You wouldn't know me now," she told him. "I'm not as silly as I used to be. I'm not as much fun to talk to."

But oh, her heart said within her, at one touch of your finger I would burst into blossom like a rose in bloom. One kiss from your mouth would make me immortal and eternally young. One caress would cause me to become anything that pleased you. I would give up all that I have become for one last night together with you.

Oh, if you spoke one word, you would have me again, know me again, possess me body and soul.

She got as drunk that night as she had ever been. She skipped school the next day, though everyone forgave her and made small lame good-humored wisecracks about the perils of celebrating the gifts of Dame Fortune.

At times alone in her office at school, Sarah closed her eyes and tried to call back Alan, his shapes and textures, scents and flavors.

She was losing him. She was losing him.

Time is the most terrible thief.

For a time during the settling of dusk they switched on Lynda's small flashlight. Then, deciding they might need to conserve the batteries, they turned it off and sat side by side. The clouds had thinned in the east, and the blurry orb of a bloody moon showed through them not long after sunset. "A little longer," Lynda murmured. "Not too much, though."

"You believe this," Sarah said.

She felt Lynda shrug. "I have no choice."

Sarah's mind drifted to their chance meeting, at an organization dedicated to preserving the environment. Her first sight of Lynda had tripped the phrase "aging hippie" in Sarah's mind, but Lynda's conversation had been by turns amusing and sensible. They saw each other at the meetings, had a dinner one night together. Lynda mentioned her sexual preferences only once, and Sarah said that she didn't share them but didn't mind. And while Sarah dismissed Lynda's dabbling with the Tarot, with scrying balls and I Ching,

Lynda took her skepticism with good humor and with no offense. Opposites in so many ways, the two became friends.

Only after they had known each other for more than a year did Sarah realize how much she had revealed to her friend. She had shown Lynda all the empty landscape of her life, the half-spoken regrets and unacknowledged longings. No one else knew half as much about her as her black-haired mystical friend.

Sarah tolerated the casting of cards, the reading of omens, never for a moment believing them. But as day succeeded day and the pain inside her wound tighter and tighter, like a rubber band twisted in coil upon coil, she listened to Lynda with something more than amusement, something far less than belief.

And when Lynda had mentioned that the spirits of the departed often remembered places of power they had left behind on the earth, a vision of the hilltop came unbidden to Sarah's mind.

"It's as good a time as any," Lynda said, snapping the thread of Sarah's reverie. With unerring aim, she shone the light on the center of the pentacle. "Just stand there, quietly. And remember—"

"I know," Sarah said, taking her station.

"All right then." Lynda snapped off the flashlight. In the gloom she began to undress.

It had been a drizzly day in April when Sarah brought the small package here. Then her hair clung to her cheeks and neck. The misting rain had soaked her well before she reached the summit and the clearing.

Back then the grass was short, cropped by deer, perhaps. Low clouds hid the crests of the mountains, drifted like smoke in the valley.

Sarah spoke no word as she opened her package and scattered the ash. There were no words to say.

The ashes drifted to the earth without a sound, the wet ground welcoming them. Rain soon tinted them the same color as the granite. They flowed from the box, and the box was an hourglass measuring the years of a man's life.

Sarah had climbed the hill in the rain, and she walked back in the rain. She never looked back.

And then, on that remote day, she could see only darkness ahead of her.

Standing in the center of her circle, Sarah heard a rustle in the dry September grass, whisper-quiet. The drumbeat of her pulse resounded in her ears, filled her chest with an aching pressure. She hugged herself, feeling the warmth of her flannel shirt, his flannel shirt, the only one she had spared from the Goodwill bin. Around her the night grew deeper, impenetrable. Lynda had begun to chant as soon as she had dropped her clothes to the earth, and for what seemed like an hour her chant continued, counterpointing pulse-beat, stirring something in the night.

A wind, not cool, touched Sarah's cheek. She felt it lift a long tendril of hair, realized that her hair was too short for that feeling, had been too short for ten years now. She closed her eyes, seeing red spots behind the lids, blooming and fading with her heartbeats, systole and diastole. Her throat clamped on his name, transmuted it to a subvocal sob.

When she opened her eyes, the moon shone through a break in the clouds. It had climbed into the sky, had become a high cold orb the color of silver. Lynda was a metal statue, sitting naked, cross-legged, on her discarded buckskins, her head thrown back, black hair falling below her shoulder blades. In the blue-white light she sat in three-quarter profile to Sarah, her smooth belly pocked with the black cup of her navel, grounded with the dark triangle of her sex. Her moon-silvered breasts and outspread arms made her look like a life-size pewter sculpture of a shaman-woman.

And—Sarah was almost sure—something stirred in the tall grasses, a darker shade than night.

The chalk circle seemed to glow with a light of its own, an unearthly pale blue, almost fluorescent. The five-pointed star seemed to spin, with Sarah as its axis. The disk of the world whirled about her. She wanted, oh, she wanted—

"Please," she moaned through tears. "Oh, please."

The wind hissed, warm, scented of spring and turned earth.

"Oh, are you there?"

In the bending grass did the moving darkness have shape? The moon did not touch its inky secret core. Was it moving toward her, or away?

The drone of Lynda's voice, patient, endless, a cicada mourning the lost life of summer.

Coldness of moonlight on the bare granite, a snowfall of no depth, a winter chill.

Rustle of autumn leaves.

Scent of spring.

"Oh. Oh, please."

Her heart drumbeating.

And then—

"Sarah."

At the whispered name she jerked as though she had touched a live electric wire, felt her chest squeeze on the breath within it, felt the prickle of fine hairs on arms and back of neck. Close, close, behind her—

She willed herself to believe, to accept. The surface of her mind saw the hilltop as it was, the granite barren and empty, touched only by moonlight and wind.

But something deeper, some stronger tide, rose in her now. She gasped, pronounced his name, a question, a prayer. She closed her eyes. Oh, she would give anything if the whisper had been real, not the voice of her wishes.

"Where is Sarah?"

His voice. Undeniably his.

"Oh, here," she breathed.

Uncomprehending silence answered her.

The living change. The dead do not change.

A touch, a caress, hands on her shoulders. An imagined weight? Was there something rough in that contact?

The living love. The dead have forgotten how.

"I want us to be together."

Who said that? She or he? Do the dead have desires?

"I want you to be mine."

Do the living trouble the dead?

She opened her eyes, tear-blurred, and saw Lynda standing, just outside the circle, mouth open, eyes shocked, arms reaching.

Sarah reached forward to touch Lynda's outstretched hands, to ask for reassurance, for human warmth, for life. Without knowing she was about to do it, without intention, she screamed, a harsh, throat-ripping shriek, a cry for help, for life.

And then the hands—the other hands—found her throat.

Cinder Child

Stuart Palmer

You may call this your room for the night," said Miss Ballam. "Though, naturally, once you are employed on the estate, the master will never more show you favor."

I stared nervously with pale blue eyes, unsure what she meant.

"You will then be housed in the workers' cottages," she said sternly, "on the edge of the estate, where you belong."

In the flicker of the candle, I looked round the small room. It was oppressively furnished, with a sturdy wooden bed and dresser. The air was cold and dusted with the smell of damp linen, as though the door had been locked for a hundred years. Across the fireplace, on heavy black hinges and strong bolts, were sturdy wooden shutters. It was an uncommon sight.

I looked quizzically at Miss Ballam, but her expression forbade enquiry. Her thin lips pulled tight as though on a drawstring and her hand brushed at the sleeve of her starchy black dress. I was pained by the coldness in her soul.

"That you are the master's nephew affords you nothing beneath this roof," she said, ignoring the silent question and lighting a second candle to guide her back downstairs. "Consider yourself favored that the master agreed to employ you at all."

"I do," I said, endeavoring to mask my bitterness. "Truly I do."

"And ask no questions within these walls," she added severely. "The master will see you after noon. Trouble yourself to bathe and change your filthy attire."

I noticed trousers and a rough cotton shirt arranged on the bed. My body was grimy from carriage and road, my blond curls crushed and dirty.

"You may be the poor and disreputable end of the master's family, but the master does not take scullions in his chamber."

The door closed and I was alone with a hundred questions and a hundred fears. On my journey from home I'd not seen a friendly face. I'd huddled my small frame against the dying afternoon, trying hard to remember my mother's face. Such a mixture of hard and soft, bitter and loving. She'd not waved, just watched the carriage pull away, like a mourner at a funeral.

"It's for the good," she'd said. "It's for the good, Thomas. Gershom knows you're coming and he's agreed to you working the land, and there'll be wages and a roof and . . . It's for the good. I know it is, Thomas. You're fifteen now and it's all for the good."

I touched the shutters over the fireplace and wondered at their purpose. I felt small in the strange environs, crowded by strange faces and miles of road, only half alive. Why had she sent me away to this cold prison?

Careful to be silent, I opened the door and peered out into the hallway. The house spoke to itself. It spoke of age and decay, and this artery of bare boards and wood-paneled walls groaned with the tales of generations. Dusty faces stared down from cracked portraits on the wall. Their eyes were forbidding, and I hastily closed the door and turned to the bed.

Unhappy, I undressed, snuffed the candle, slipped beneath the starchy sheets.

Tomorrow I would meet Uncle Gershom Taberford. It was a daunting prospect.

Sleep was elusive. I lay as stiff as Miss Ballam's corset. My eyes studied the ceiling and the square of anemic moonlight that filtered through the window.

A noise. What was it?

At first, I thought it mice scratching in the wainscoting. But the sound was too loud for tiny paws. Rats? No; the sound was too regular. I sat up in the bed and looked about the darkened chamber. Could it be birds in the chimney breast?

Yes, birds, I told myself. Nothing but birds. It's nesting season. The fires in this wing can't be in use, that's why they're shuttered.

The noise again; scratching, now tapping out a gentle tattoo. Birds were musical, not rhythmic. My heart trembled in my scrawny body. Fearful, I pulled the covers about my head and listened for footsteps on the boards.

"So, you're the nephew, are you?"

Uncle Gershom stood by the immense marble fireplace, his crimson face framed with excessive gingery sideburns, jeweled with a purple nose.

"I am pleased to meet you, sir," I said, vaguely inclining my head as I'd seen servants do to men of class.

"Thomas," said Uncle, critically. He mulled the name on his lips, turned to look at a portrait of a young girl in a gilded frame above the mantel, as though asking her opinion. The girl had Uncle Gershom's dark hair and rosy complexion.

I felt uncomfortable, but tried hard to fight the awkwardness in my bones and stand tall. I was dwarfed by cabinets of polished oak and chairs with backs that jutted like turrets. There was a must in the air that tightened my jaw. It came from the tattered velvet drapes that framed the mighty windows.

"A scrawny young chick," said Uncle. "Hardly fit for roasting, and not an ounce of work to wring out of those bones."

I wanted to defend myself, but did not dare. My eyes kept low, away from his, studying the threadbare rugs, for fear that my soul would be consumed.

"Have we worked the fields before, boy?"

My head lowered further.

"No, of course not. What's that sister of mine taught you, then?" He dug his hands into his waistcoat pockets and strutted the room like a corpulent rooster. "Been teaching you the evils of the Taberfords, has she? The injustice that befell her and how we're heartless?"

"My mother seldom spoke of family, sir." I felt bullied, tricked and trapped. "When she did, it was to mention your kindness in accepting me here."

"Sight unseen, I hastily add."

"She said no more than that, sir." It was true. I had known nothing of the family until Mother returned from a trip; to my knowledge, the only trip she had ever made. She had news of Uncle Gershom and had secured for me a minor position on his estate. That my family was moneyed came as a great surprise. We had never seen a penny of it.

"Taberford's a noble name," said Uncle, "but a damnation to your mother."

I kept my head low, but I was interested. Mother lived in poverty, bitterness her only friend. Why she had fallen from grace was something I had wondered, something I had never dared ask.

"That the name's yours tells the world all it need know." Uncle laughed and continued his strutting.

I felt him circle, like a bird of prey. He had hungry brown eyes, large eyes shot with veins of crimson.

"An unholy child," said Miss Ballam from the door. "Hardly a fitting subject for mirth."

I felt Uncle's eyes lift. When I dared look, those eyes were glaring at the willowy housekeeper. They burned with such intensity that the woman looked away, straightened her apron, and brushed a string of iron gray hair from her brow. Her icy composure was clearly fractured.

"Think there's some of his father in him, do you?"

The woman seemed concentrated on her primness.

"Afraid he'll turn you into something evil, twisted and hateful?"

"It was merely an observation," she said, adding with evident discomfort. "Forgive the intrusion, sir."

"The boy'd be far too late to turn you into a hateful crone," said Uncle Gershom. "Should I require judgment, Miss Ballam, I'll ask for it."

The interview passed without further incident, but I felt tension stretched like cat gut. I was relieved when leave was granted. I stepped out into the hallway but kept my head lowered so as not to catch the eyes of the fearsome portraits that so severely watch over this house.

I hurried to the hallway's end where pale light filtered through a window. Outside I saw the estate: a cluster of barns that sat black as cankers against the furrowed fields. My hands were fists, knuckles white.

And every desperate measure of loathing that came from my body seemed to be returned by the walls and floors of this labyrinthine manor. I did not wish to remain, and yet I knew I could not leave.

Work started the following week; today was Wednesday. I thought perhaps my protracted stay in the house was the housekeeper's punishment for whatever ill she'd spoken. She took it with brittle courtesy, but it left me uneasy. I felt like a pawn, and now had more questions, for my mother had never spoken of my father.

Late afternoon, I found myself in the kitchens. The sun was low across the fields, making the dust on the windows glow like sheets of gold. Wood pigeons cooed in the trees about the grand house. Cook fussed over the burnished black stove, calling for onions and carrots, a pinch of wild herbs.

I sat on a rough wooden chair and tried to be invisible. Uncle had made no intimation that he wanted again to see me. Miss Ballam gave me only judging glares. I watched Cook and the few servants bustling across the stone flags, between the cathedrallike columns. I watched Paget, the ancient butler, buffing shoes at the table. How small and resentful I felt beneath the kitchen's vaulted ceiling.

"Must seem strange after a small village," said Paget, "what with the comings and goings of farm hands and a house the size of this."

"I find the house the strangest, sir."

Paget laughed, his face cracking open like a walnut. "There are no sirs in this part of the house, lad."

I apologized, lowered my head. This was a new world to me.

"I'll take it as a compliment," said Paget.

His head raised on a neck of tendons and leather skin, and dim eyes stared kindly at me from beneath heavy lids. "So what you reckon's strange about the house then?"

Cook turned and I was aware of silent communication passing between her and the butler.

"The shutters on the fireplaces are strange."

Paget nodded and turned the shoe beneath his cloth.

"And I heard noises in the night."

"Expect that'll be the hens out in the roost."

"It was here, in the house."

Cook glanced at me then returned to her pot. Her plump cheeks were pink. Paget never broke from his chores. His gnarled hand swept back and forth across the shoe, working up a sheen.

"Why are the chimneys boarded?"

"Keeps out a draft, lad, when they're not used. Why else would it be done?"

"I heard tapping, steady as this." I drummed out a beat on the table, added a little roll. "Last night in my room, right at the top of the house."

"Oh, nonsense, dear," said Cook.

"Rats have talent in this house," said Paget, and he would say no more.

My questions went on, but no servant answered, and when food was served, I was handed a bowl and sent to my room. Politely, of course. I was still the master's nephew, and no servant would cross me for fear of reprisal.

Still the unanswered questions made me wonder.

When I reached my room, the shutters were drawn back and there was a meager fire in the grate. It surprised me and gave the room a new air. The paneled walls seemed to shudder as shadows danced. The aroma of dry woodsmoke masked the dampness that the walls breathed into the gloom.

The flames burned low as I ate, and I watched them and warmed myself and tried to think of Mother, many miles away. It was difficult, as though she had died, and I felt grief at the land that lay between us. Grief, and something that I thought was anger. How could I now be stranded so far from her side?

Staring into the smoking embers, I heard a pop of igniting wood and watched a spark circle up into the chimney. Its light was star-bright and brief as surprised. Less than a second and it was gone. Still I stared, enchanted by the glowing wood, then just staring and not thinking of the fire at all. I thought of Mother. I thought of the priest who had educated me. I thought of the village where I was born. There was little work there. Mother survived on bread and late-night calls from drunkards. They did business behind the pantry door and made noises that I had slowly come to despise.

The thought of those noises sickened me. I blinked, frowned, realized I was watching something move in the hearth. At the back where the blackness was almost total, I saw moving gray sticks. They were vertical. They passed across the opening; crossing, straightening, limping. Above them were rags, more sticks, eyes as shiny as silver.

I shrieked, fell back from the grate. The eyes were white, whiter still for the ashen face that housed them.

The door slammed open. Miss Ballam marched in, skirts hoisted and a broom in her hand. She wore an expression that would have won the Battle of Inkerman without a fight, and she hooked the shutters with the broom handle and smacked them home across the fireplace. The broom dropped. The bolts were hammered into place. She stared down at me like a school ma'am before an impudent pupil.

"I saw . . . I saw a child," I said, terrified by the thought.

"You saw nothing, foolish boy," she said. "By God, never leave a grate without a fire, foolish, stupid boy. Never beneath this roof."

"I . . . I don't understand."

"You need understand nothing. Obey me, you wicked child."

Fear gave me a little courage. I stood, tried to pull myself up as tall as the housekeeper. "What was it?"

"Impertinence! I should take a cane to your hide and beat the devil from you."

"What was it? Was it a sweep, or—"

"Silence yourself. I will not be—"

"Tell me!"

Her eyes sparked like flints, but there was fear there too. She touched the skin about her left wrist, and I saw a livid purple burn.

"I did see a child," I said. "I know I did. I saw it clearly."

"Always shutter a dead fire beneath this roof," she said, and retreated from the room.

"Paget, you must tell me."

"Nothing to tell, lad." The butler hobbled down the sun-dappled path, headed for the village. I ran behind, hoisting up the trouser bottoms that hung into the dust over my oversized boots.

"If you've sense in that head of yours, you saw nothing and heard less."

"I know what I saw." I was shouting, aware of field workers straightening their backs and staring between the tall hedges. "I saw a child, Paget. It was younger than me, maybe seven or eight. I saw it, Paget, I know I did. Miss Ballam, she saw it too."

Paget stopped by a sapling birch and shook his head. "You're a lucky one to be in the house still. I know old Ballam tried to get you moved to the workers' cottages that same night, and would have an' all, had there been space. Now there's no good you asking me about the children, so—"

"Children? There's more than one?" I felt a shiver of horror, imagined the house like a cheese infested with maggots.

"I said nothing of the sort."

"You said children."

"If the master heard I'd been talking, my job'd be worth a groat and a marching order, not more than that."

"But you did say—"

"This one's an old man, and he gets confused." Paget snapped his wrinkled lips together. The journey to the village continued in silence.

The moon was a pale-blue sheen that stained the foot of the bed. I lay still, hardly dared move. My breath was held for seconds at a time, and I started at every noise. All I heard was the house speaking its age in the night's hush.

My feet were chafed and blistered from the boots Uncle Gershom had given me. I was small for my age, but thought I would never be of a size to fit those beaten leather boots. I rubbed at my toes and my heels and thought of a village far away.

Then there came a knock, loud and clear against the shutters. I saw the bolts jiggle in the bolt cups. Something dragged tiny fingernails against the wood, now tapping, now drumming hard.

"Wh-who are you?"

The drumming went on.

"Who are you in there?"

Bolts rattled in their holders.

I wanted to close my eyes, cover my head, but I knew the noise would remain. I was hypnotized by its urgency, terrified by the thought of little hands.

"Release us," whispered a tiny voice.

"Please," said another. "Please, help."

"You must," said the first.

I stepped down from the bed and lit a candle. It guttered, threw shadows up the walls and the dresser. Still I could not bring myself to approach the shutters. I hung back by the bedposts, trembling in my nightgown.

"Who are you?" I called again. "Please, tell me."

"Lost . . . without home," said a tiny voice. "Please . . ."

"No." I thought of children squirming behind the walls, and the thought was repulsive, raising horror in my chest. "Why are you there? Who put you there?"

The pleading started anew; three voices building in a whispered chorus, gentle and sad as any words I had ever heard.

"Pernicious lies."

I shrieked at the booming voice. It was loud, at my shoulder. I turned, saw Uncle Gershom loom over me, sideburns like flames about his cheeks. Afraid, I shrank against the bed. The man was deep purple, eyes like black gems. His boot lashed out, smacked hard against the shutters. They made a sharp cracking noise. There were tiny whimpers, scuttling and clawing, Uncle's swearing, then a moment of purest silence that held me in awe.

I stood paralyzed. Then the silence passed, and in its place I heard gentle sobbing. I stared at the shutters, and realized to my shock that Uncle Gershom was crying.

"Evil . . . evil monsters," he said. "Never listen to their malice, boy. They're evil."

"But . . . but what are they? Please tell me, sir."

Uncle shook his head, face creased with pain. "Our family never forgave your mother . . . my sister . . . never will."

I felt sad, knew she wanted this above all else.

"But I did," he said. "I forgave her. A certain understanding, you see. I slept—" Plump hands cupped his face in shame. He sat on the bed, staring at the shutters. "I was seduced by a whore from the valley. I was innocent and she . . . How could I know? I was young, eager, ignorant of all things, as . . . as you are ignorant."

I did not dare turn my face from him.

"She was rich with sorcery, and she was as hungry for land and wealth as I for . . ." He sighed and looked away. "I paid what I owed, no more than that, and I left her to her idle dreams."

I had heard of sorcery, seen its effects on the farms around the village. In that moment, I felt pity for Uncle and knew he would hate me for that emotion.

"This is not the end," Uncle added. "Oh, no. Years passed. I took a wife, conceived a daughter . . . beautiful child she was." His voice cracked with pain. "And then the produce of my unholy deed returned to torture my soul. Three child-monsters, young harpies and demons. They demanded my fortune, my life, all I had, and . . . and when I refused, they killed my beloved Mary." Tears glistened in his eyes. "And they killed Hannah."

I wanted to console him, but fear kept me back. Instead I watched like the worst voyeur, and tried to show my sympathy.

"I would have sustained them, as was my duty, but they craved all I had. For months they hounded me, drove away my servants, friends, family." Uncle wiped his face and his eyes became hard.

"Did you . . . did you tell the police, sir?" I asked.

"And reveal my sin to the world? My un-Christian act of lust? No. My mind . . . my temper . . . it snapped. I tricked them, imprisoned them in an outhouse . . . and I razed it to the ground, killing them all."

My sympathy withdrew, shocked by the revelation. Contemplative silence hung heavy in the room, and I tried to speak, but there was nothing to say.

Uncle's lips pulled tight, and the story went on.

"Their mother's sorcery . . . Fire could never kill them. I saw their faces in the ashes of every fire in this house. I heard them walk from the grates, and I made it their prison, boy; shuttered and bolted when there's no fire to hold them at bay. That's the way it stays."

I nodded, but now doubt wormed beneath my pale skin. The huge man was resolute again. He stood and cursed the shuttered fireplace.

"Never open it. Whatever they say, they lie." Uncle leveled a finger at me. "They're evil bastards and I'll cheat them of satisfaction."

To pass the day I took to helping Paget. I was enthusiastic, remembered Mother telling me to impress Uncle with my zeal. I could go far now. I could do better than a job on the land.

But I had another motive for helping Paget. Constantly I thought of the children scurrying in the soot behind the walls. Constantly I thought of Uncle's confession and tears. Sleep came in small portions. Every tiny sound made me think of children's fingers. What was the truth of Uncle's tale?

Saturday afternoon, my chance came. Paget cleared a tray of drinks in the study. Uncle had gone hunting with acquaintances. The light was bright, bathing the leather chairs in warm sunshine.

I stared up at the portrait above the fire. "Paget? Who is this?"

"Miss Hannah. Dead now, poor thing, but . . ."

"Dead?" I feigned surprise. "How did she die?"

"Fell to the fever's what I heard, lad." The old man shrugged with shoulders like brittle sticks. "Why? You fancy the look of her, do you?"

I gave him a mock reproach.

"Before my time, you see," he said. "I used to work a few miles north on the Polkinghorne estate. They were a fine pair, they were. I only came here a dozen or more years ago, and blessed happy I was to get away from Jemima Polkinghorne and her harmonium."

"Would Cook know?"

Paget shook his head. "Been here no longer than me that one, lad. Seems the master took to sacking all his old servants, told them to . . . well, go away, shall we say?"

I looked a little longer at the portrait, then followed Paget from the study.

That night the farm workers had a party. From my room I heard them singing in the barn. From my window I saw their lanterns and their dancing shadows. I had no light for myself, not yet. The room was almost lost in shadow and I kept an unlit candle by my side, but tonight the darkness was something to relish. I did not know why. It felt safer than it had ever done on the estate. It felt right.

Hour after hour I watched the party. Until the darkness was complete. Then the noises began. First came the patter of fingers, gentle but persistent. I listened with numb fear, moving close to the shutters and listening intently. They knew I was there. I felt it in my trembling heart.

The voices began, frail and small. "Help us, please. Please help. Let us out."

I lit the candle and sat by the hearth. "What are you?"

The voices stopped.

"Tell me what you are." I felt a promise implicit in my words. "Tell me what you are, maybe I'll help." I rested my shoulder against the shutters and listened for noises.

"We're lost," said a child. "Lost."

"Fatherless," said another. "And we came to find him and . . ."

The smallest voice of all began to cry in tender sobs.

"Mother told us he was here." It was the first child. "She said he lived here. She said he'd help, but . . . He hated us, and in shame he sent the servants away and tried to beat us."

"He did that," said the second child. "He beat us."

"He hated us." The first child was close to tears. Its voice grew smaller. "He got cruel when his daughter died of fever. She died, and his wife too, and he got cruel. He locked us up, burnt us."

The other children repeated the final words.

"But your mother was a sorceress," I said. I felt suddenly calm. "Her powers kept you alive in the ashes of this house. And here you are."

"Alone," said the children, "lost."

"And we can't sleep," said the first child. "While he's alive, we never can sleep."

The calm faltered. I stared at the wooden shutters, heart fast and high in my chest. "You want to—"

"We have to. To sleep. To finally sleep."

The children made an echo of the words, repeated them over and over in tiny, aching voices.

"But . . . but killing him?"

"It's the only way."

I considered, tried hard to imagine the children's pain. Concentrate on that. Do not think of murder. Think of flames closing around you, skin and hair burning, senses screaming as your flesh crisps and cracks in the heat. Imagine a scald that gets hotter and hotter, that goes on and on, deeper and deeper into your body. Imagine smelling your own meat roasting around you.

Imagine being lost from your mother's side . . .

"I'll release you."

I heard expectant movements from the fireplace. My tremulous fingers reached for the bolts and tugged them loose.

"No!" Uncle was in the doorway, face pale, eyes wide with terror. In his hands was an ax.

My fear leapt high.

"Foolish child." Miss Ballam was close behind, spitting as she spoke. "Foolish, damnable child."

I drew back the final bolt. Terrified, I pulled at the shutters, rolled aside and lay frozen against the wall as something stepped into the hearth,

Miss Ballam crossed herself then clutched at her skirts.

I saw a foot. It was a bundle of blackened twigs. Every footfall produced wisps of smoke that curled about stick-thin legs. Burnt meat hung in strips. The legs bulged at the knees, then on the thighs became thin as fingers. They joined with the bones and charred rags of a body, a body so thin it barely supported the crumbling head.

White eyes stared out. They were beacons of hate. Teeth were like little pearls inside lips of burnt leather.

Three children stalked forward. Uncle screamed at them, telling them how it gladdened him to see them burn. Miss Ballam shrieked like a bird and fell back against the door, calling on the saints to save her.

A hand of spent matches reached toward the pair of them.

The ax fell. The hand severed at the wrist, but there was no blood in the veins. The hand fell and lay flexing on the boards. The stump of arm stuck out, caught Miss Ballam across the face.

She ignited at once.

I sat up. What was Miss Ballam's part in the children's fate? They'd spoken only of Uncle. A child now closed on him, forcing him closer to Miss Ballam's collapsing form. Her flames were bright and high, filling the room with acrid smoke and a stench of hot lard. They took to her dress, melted the fat beneath and soaked into the cloth. She was a spasming candle.

A finger extended and tapped Uncle on the hand. He combusted without sound. Within seconds the flames had eaten at his jacket. A few seconds more and they had taken his hair and blistered his face.

I was on my feet, pressed against the wall. Terror held me frozen as the smallest child edged slowly forward across the floor. Its hands raised as though to embrace me. It stumbled like a baby. It grinned with perfect teeth.

"No," I screamed. "You said . . . you said you wanted Uncle. You said—"

"We want life," said the tallest child. "We want freedom."

"Freedom," said the smallest, stepping closer.

My head shook, nerves ice cold with fear.

"No, please." I saw the finger come for my chest. I felt it touch like a hot needle against my skin. The pinpoint scorched, spread out across my shirt. I screamed and dropped to my knees. Burning hair was all I smelled.

Now I live in the warren of chimneys. I scramble through sooted passages. Occasionally I see the sky through a pot.

There is no time here. All is dark and encased in soot. There is no smell but the stench of fire damage, no food but brittle cinders.

And sometimes, when I see a slit of light, I press my eye to it and gaze out into moonlit rooms.

I see strangers in their beds.

I see plump children in their new home.

The Place of Memories

Thomas S. Roche

There had been no rain this year, or last.

The wind and the sun had abused the bright-yellow police tape across the door until it was only a battered string like dry parchment, a representation of an authority that held no power here.

The door was nailed shut. I returned to the beat-up Chevy to get the ax and the .357 while I was at it. I slipped the gun into one of the big pockets of my fatigue jacket, hefted the ax, and started on the door. After about twenty minutes, the door finally gave, creaking on its hinges, allowing the bowels of the underworld to open up and issue forth their evil seed.

Coughing, my eyes watering, I tried to enter the house, found myself unable to take the step. My belly froze.

Gradually I lowered myself to my knees, setting the ax and the lantern on the porch. I lowered my head, tears welling in my eyes.

Two Our Fathers and six Ave Marias later, I had composed myself. I stepped inside the house.

Flights of dust angels rose to greet me.

* * *

The ancient tapestries remained on the walls. Spiders and rats infested the carpets and couches. Except for the chittering of rodents, the silence was absolute. My footsteps did not make a sound on the sodden carpet as I stepped over the faded outline.

The plush red velvet of the antique divan had long ago turned rotten. I had a memory of Andrea, stretched on the divan, nude, all silken jet and flawless alabaster at the height of her beauty. The memory became a vision, and I regarded her slender white body, graced by the wave of black hair that scattered about her shoulders, reclined upon the rotting rat-piss red velvet with her arm cast above her head, her full lips curved in a seductive smile and her bright green eyes laughing and innocent. Her hand spread across her throat and down her body, inviting me gradually to the promises of erotic splendor. Oh, God, how I remembered her.

I shook my head, banishing the vision of Andrea.

The small altar stood in its proper place by the stairs, defiled by filth and damnation. I knelt there and whispered a heartfelt Nicene Creed, crossing myself when it was finished. I picked up the lantern again and crunched my way over rat bodies to the foot of the spiral staircase.

As I mounted the stairs, I caught another vision/memory/hallucination of Andrea, this time sprawled at the door.

I set the ax at the foot of the stairs, knowing it would be of no use to me on the upper level.

Gradually, reluctantly, as if ascending the infinite staircase toward judgment, I climbed.

The bedroom remained intact, though mold and dust stained everything. The flowers had not died; the impression on the silk-covered feather pillow was undisturbed. The bedclothes were tangled and ancient and rotting, but living flowers scattered their way in damned salvation across the room. Many dozens of roses still lay strewn on the bed, floor, and vanity, looking freshly cut as they had so many years ago, thorns and buds alike undamaged. All the living things were preserved as in that frozen moment when our bliss peaked brought the jealousy of all creation, and thus its wrath, down in lightning sheets upon our bed.

The wedding dress still lay in a crumpled heap by the bed.

I stood by the shattered window, regarding the overgrowth of trees that had grown in to protect the house. Slowly I felt the sheets from the bed creeping up and spiraling around my ankles.

The sheets fastened themselves securely and pulled me back onto the bed. I lifted my arms and squirmed and fought as the cords from the velvet curtains began to work my buttons, but moments later the energy went out of my muscles and I lay limp, a ragdoll plaything: harmless, inert.

I didn't have the strength to resist any longer.

We drank late at the reception, the party continuing to all hours. The champagne flowed freely and Andrea and I danced on the dance floor, danced to the strains of the harpsichord and string quartet with bass guitar and drum machine. We received many kisses that day, and presents of silver and gold and silk.

We returned to the house on my motorcycle, Andrea's veil flapping in the wind and her shrieking in delight as the white fabric tore around through the two-hour ride in delicious soft summer breezes scented with flowers.

Once we were in the house, I carried her up the spiral stairs and we tumbled together into the bedroom. Mommy and Daddy had provided the room full of roses, red and white. We tumbled amid the thorned flowers on the bed, the white wedding dress staining with droplets of blood. Rose petals scattered about us in doomed abandon.

I had lived alone in the house, ever since the unfortunate accident that had befallen Grandpa. I know for sure that the house had always resented his presence, and was glad to have me to itself. While he was around, Grandpa had taken my attention away from it.

My early days were spent wandering the ancient stairways and corridors, feeling the velvet beneath my bare feet, investigating the multiple basements and subbasements and sub-subbasements, gazing out the attic window at the melancholy droop of apple trees outside and the majestic peaks beyond. Sprawling on the rich carpets, constantly aware of the presence, the benign, nurturing presence of the house, stroking my furrowed brow, whispering soothing words in my ear, bringing me pleasant dreams of treehouses and amusement parks, kissing my head, ruffling my messy hair. The house indeed resented the presence of the old man, whose attentions to me ranged from letting me sit at his feet while he read crumbling books in the library or the bedroom, to yelling at me and taking his aggressions out on me with the back of his hand. He also did other things, much darker things that I couldn't even remember, really. Just sort of, when I thought about it or when I was very sad or upset. Other than that, the things he did were lost in a cloud of memory and obscured by the gentle caresses of the house.

Grandpa had taken care of me for as long as I could remember—I had been very young when Mommy and Daddy had disappeared. I had heard many stories about the accident, most of them conflicting, and I didn't remember any of it so I couldn't ever know what really happened. I do, however, remember Grandpa's accident. It was unfortunate and, I suppose, unlikely. Finally ruled a suicide, I think, though that's also pretty hard for me to recall. I was too busy playing make-believe up in the attic. But I knew, deep in my heart, that the house had finally been pushed too far, and had been forced to protect me. Grandpa had been the target of its rage.

Since then I had been alone except for occasional court-appointed custodians whom I largely ignored. The house itself had cared for me. Early mornings, the alarm clock having set itself or the house waking me with a gentle whisper and shake; lunch packed in a brown paper bag and placed (with a note) on the dining room table as I left for school; dinner prepared at sundown by pots and pans and butcher knives that moved of their own accord in the kitchen.

Occasionally, as I have said, the court would appoint custodians, but they tended to vanish periodically, until finally the state left me alone. I was well cared for, and always would be.

Years passed in solitude. I went away to live in the city, enjoying the many pleasures of my inheritance, becoming involved, then somewhat obsessed, with the club scenes there and meeting many friends. I visited the house periodically, still sensing its benign and loving presence, but I never brought my friends home to visit there. I was saving that pleasure for my wedding night, when finally I could share the nurturing affection of the house with my one true love, whom I had met at the Orphanage and gradually fallen in love with: Andrea. Our friends had blessed us and our wedding had been planned for the Orphanage, largest and most extreme of the Goth clubs in town. Ancient rites would be enacted and I would give Andrea sweet kisses as we joined together to live forever in the house in the country. The house would dream its dreams, gently kiss Andrea's forehead, and forevermore be loving mother to us both. It had begun to rain.

Andrea's black hair tangled in the lace veil. Organ music played on the stereo as we made love.

The house trembled in the wind. The rain increased outside until it was a pounding torrent, though it had been sunny at the reception in the park. Lightning flashed like nightmares and apocalypse. Candles lit our wedding chamber, dribbled wax onto the carpet amid the rose petals.

I thought it was an earthquake, but Andrea obviously did not feel the shaking. She continued to kiss me. I moved to sit up suddenly, but Andrea's weight held me down. The floor pitched and the walls shuddered. The house gave off a deafening moan. I heard glass crashing downstairs. The mirror in the bathroom shattered.

Andrea heard nothing. She was oblivious to the destruction. I reached down, trying to get hold of her to push her away from me, but I suddenly realized that the velvet bedspread had tangled about me with some force—and would not allow my arms to come free.

"Andrea!" I screamed desperately, but the sound was hoarse and weak in my throat and she was unable to hear me, being occupied as she was. It was then that the pillows came down on my face and began to smother me.

The shaking continued. I was sure it was an earthquake. But part of me knew that it was much more than that. I heard the thunder, felt the lightning hitting the attic with a deafening explosion. The bedclothes had tangled about my body, and Andrea's. I could neither see nor breathe, but I felt Andrea being pulled off of the bed and hurled to the ground by the velvet bedspread.

I squirmed, tearing sheets and pillows off of my body. I finally ripped the pillow away, gasping for air, stars shooting across my darkened vision, but as I fought to get off the bed I found myself held down as the sheets knotted about my wrists and ankles. It was then that I saw Andrea.

The velvet bedspread had wrapped itself around her body and was strangling her. Her cries mingled with the explosive sounds of thunder and the rain and shuddering of the house. Lightning hit again and the windows blew in, scattering glass all about, sending shards and fragments against my flesh and Andrea's.

I fought to get off the bed. Andrea struggled to her feet. The door slammed shut. She pulled the door open and regarded a wall of butcher knives and cleavers floating in the air, regarding her curiously, having risen from the kitchen.

The knives paused momentarily as horror overtook Andrea; then they set upon her.

Andrea pushed through the wall of blades, screaming. She leapt for the stairs, trying to reach the front door. Lightning struck for the last time and all the lights went out as Andrea went over the edge of the spiral staircase.

I screamed as the sheets knotted themselves more securely. I was trapped, and the presence of the house was all around me.

Don't do this . . . I said, but only to myself. The house was not listening, and Andrea's pleas drizzled off into the sound of the rain and became as whispers in the dark.

It finally released me, hours later, after she was finally gone and I could not save her. I stumbled off of the bed, my swollen, bruised face hot and my tears salty, my body ravaged and torn, my bare feet bleeding as I made my way across a floor strewn with broken glass. I finally fell to my knees, smearing blood on the carpet as I crawled down the spiral staircase.

I made it to her body and felt for a pulse, a heartbeat, a breath. Nothing. Her lips had gone blue and her eyes were still wide open in terror. Sobbing, I kissed her brow and then her cold lips. There were many holes in her body, and her blood still darkened the entryway. One of the butcher knives was imbedded deep in Andrea's abdomen. I tried to summon her ghost, to feel the presence of my dead lover. I could not. Andrea was dead.

It was then that the numb fear struck me, the realization, the knowledge that I would be blamed for this. I stumbled upstairs, searching for my clothes.

Oh, God. I had to get away.

I had some cash in the safe downstairs—not much, but enough. Once I was dressed and had stuffed the money into my pockets, I returned to where Andrea had fallen. My tears came again, mingling with her blood on the carpet.

Furniture began moving toward the door, barricading it, and I kicked and pushed it away. The door locked itself three times, and finally I broke the window with a chair and leapt, running for the motorcycle.

I heard the keening of the house, felt its shuddering, its trembling of desperate need, as I mounted the bike and got it going. I slammed into first and hit the gas, my rear wheel skidding as lightning crashed around me. The house gave a final moan of betrayed horror as I skidded onto the street and opened up the throttle.

That had been so many years ago. And now the house had me again.

The moldy, rotten sheets finally released me, crumbling to nothing as I tore free. The house was finished with me, for now, but I did not seek to run away. Not just yet.

Instead, I groped in my discarded fatigue jacket for my pack of cigarettes. I lit one and lay there on the bed, considering the feel of the dank and rotten bed beneath my body. Faces seemed to swirl in the smoke.

"You thought you owned me," I said to no one. "You thought you had possession of my soul. Until I brought her in here . . . and then your rage was absolute. . . ."

I was really only reciting bad Goth poetry to myself. But there was a response, somewhere: a hand on my thigh, a gentle stroking of a rotten sheet on my stomach. I swatted it away and tossed my cig-arette onto the bed as I got up.

Feebly the decayed sheets tried to grab my clothes away from me. I fought with them, ripping at the damp moldy strips of cloth until there was nothing left. I finally got the pants on, the boots, then the shirt. Holding the jacket, I tried to pull away from the curtain cords that had made their way across the room to grasp me.

I yanked out the revolver and pumped a few rounds into the bed, sending clouds of mold and dust into the air. My ears rang. I cursed at nothing as I groped my way downstairs. A curtain cord got around my ankle and I went flying, the gun skittering over the edge of the stairs. I kicked at the cord, then fought my way, crawling, kicking, screaming, down the stairs inch by inch.

Finally the cord gave, and I lost my balance and began to fall.

I tumbled down the stairs, hitting hard on the bottom level. I tried to focus my eyes and felt them rolling back in my head. Blood ran out of my nose.

Finally I managed to get to my knees, backing away from the divan and the velvet chair as they inched across the room to-ward me.

I kicked out at the divan, and its pillows leapt off and assaulted me, bearing me down onto the carpet amid the ancient bloodstains. I kicked and fought my way to the door, which had slammed itself despite the fact that it was barely hanging on its hinges. Big gaps of the door were missing where I had chopped them out, but it held tight as I threw my weight against it. I would have to use the win-dow. But all the windows were boarded.

I managed to get the ax off the floor before the big velvet chair slammed into me. I had to wrestle it onto its side to get back on my feet. My leg felt like it might be broken at first, but held my weight just the same. I launched myself at the window, hacking violently at the boards.

The carpets pried themselves off the floor, reaching for me. My limbs felt leaden. I gritted my teeth and began to tumble through the broken window.

The boards gave, and I was out. Blood scattered about my face, from a nasty cut in my arm. I bunched my jacket around the cut as I crawled through what had been the flower bed, going for the car.

The influence of the house diminished now that I was outside. I made it to my feet, though my leg was badly hurt and I could barely walk. I stood looking at the house as the sun slanted against it. Never again would it do this to me.

I popped the trunk and got out the canisters. Ten cans at two gallons each. I unscrewed the tops and threw two of them one at a time through the open window by the front door, knowing they would land on their sides and pour the contents over the entryway. Perhaps the carpets and furniture would be able to right them, but in the end it wouldn't matter—for there had been no rain this year, or last. Then around the house to the back side, pouring another two gallons of gasoline over the dry grass and weeds around the base of the apple tree.

I had chosen September because I knew, intimately, the dry summers in the region. Nothing could save the house.

I set off the flare and gave a good toss onto one side of the timber-dry roof. The flare rolled off and landed harmlessly on the asphalt driveway. I picked it up again and tossed it in through the front window. Then I tossed another flare, which caught in the rain gutter at the edge of the roof. The gutter creaked and broke, of its own accord, and the flare fell back into the driveway. But I smelled the smoke and knew I'd gotten the shingles this time.

That's when the gasoline caught, and I felt I must be going.

The house gave off a horrid moaning and shuddering as I slammed the car into gear and floored it. Vines leapt to tangle around the car. A giant fruitless mulberry cracked and started falling across my path; I swerved and missed it by inches, the branches tearing off one of my wipers and laying a spider crack into the windshield. The leaves clung to the bumper, slowing me—but only for a moment. I heard the tires spinning and downshifted. The gears slipped but then the clutch caught and I felt the car moving again. I smelled burning asbestos. The ground shook and the moan rose to heaven as I hit the road and the tires screamed. Then I was gone.

When I looked back, the sky was apocalypse black. I heard the shatter of glass as the upper-level windows blew. Sirens screamed in the distance.

The smoke drifted above the highway. Traffic was nothing, and soon enough I had left the house far behind me. It was over.

I thought of all my dead, and the tragedies that had befallen them. Tears drizzled down my face as I turned on the radio to listen to news of the conflagration. Firefighters had been unable to catch it in time, and the flames had spread to the surrounding woods. I mumbled last rites around the butt of my cigarette, interspersed with a few creative obscenities.

The house had loved me, in its way, and had done horrible things to preserve the sanctity of that love. Andrea had been its unfortunate victim, as had Grandpa, for different reasons. Possibly even my parents. Grandpa's death doubtless saved me, but Andrea's death caused the complete destruction of my life. No matter. It was finally over.

The wind picked up and the smoke from the house seemed to move in my direction. Conflicting winds came up and the smoke scattered angrily on the sunset. I leaned on the accelerator.

With a choking sob and a left-handed sign of the cross, I bade farewell to my beloved Andrea, wishing I could have saved her. As I drove, I thought of our days together, of Andrea's erotic splendor, of the many good times we had, of my love for her. I thought, too, of the beach house, thousands of miles away across the ocean, where Caroline had lain, where the nightmares had come to feast upon her, in a darker and more horrible fashion, where the Hawaiian-print sheets had nearly strangled me while they had their way with my body and with hers, and where I had wept over Caroline's shattered and ravaged body in the darkened bungalow with the wind flapping the pink and orange lei about my tear-stained face.

I popped the glove compartment and checked my plane tickets. Window seat. Business class.

The sky streaked blood-red in my rearview mirror.

Traffic was clear all the way to the airport.

The Heart Is a Determined Hunter

Thomas Smith

The moment Lloyd McPherson dialed the telephone the world went dark. At least that was the illusion created by the first dark clouds of the coming storm as they pushed the October sun out of the way. As it was, Lloyd barely noticed. His connection had already failed twice, and the one that was coaxing the second ring from the phone on the other end was tenuous at best.

He had debated the idea of calling the Steadman Resort for almost two days, and, right or wrong, he had finally placed the call. The line popped and crackled; the ghosts of past conversations unaware they were long finished. Lloyd's finger hovered over the tiny plunger that held the power to terminate the connection. Twice he had pulled back at the last second. Scant seconds from the comforting buzz of a new dial tone. He was still not too sure.

"Thank you for calling the Steadman Resort. How may I be of service this afternoon?"

"What?" The world swam back into focus in one large wave. "Oh . . . yes, I'm sorry. I was a little preoccupied."

"Of course, sir. How may I be of service?" The voice was steady. That sort of well-bred, professionally aloof hotel voice. A voice that implied the sort of patience gained after a lifetime of serving the public's whims and fancies.

Lloyd stopped drumming his fingers long enough to pick up a pen and start tapping the capped end on a weekly organizer pad: Stupid Stuff I Gotta Do This Week. He tapped number three. Call the Steadman. "Yes, I was calling on the off chance you might have a room available for the next two or three days. I know this is rather short notice, but this was a spur-of-the-moment idea." The lie tasted funny.

"If you'll allow me just one moment, I'll be happy to check for you, sir. I believe we may have a room available tonight. Could you hold, please?"

"Yes."

The line went silent. At that moment the idea of severing the connection before the reservations clerk returned was almost overwhelming. Though he needed to go back, this might not be the time. Maybe in a couple of months. That's it, he thought. I'll wait a little longer.

With that in mind he reached for the plunger. Just as the voice returned. "Sir, we have an ocean-view room available, and I will be more than happy to hold it for you if you'd like."

Lloyd hesitated. He was still not 100 percent sure about this decision.

"Sir . . ."

"Oh . . . right. That will be fine." He fished for his American Express card. "I'm sorry if I sound a little out of it. To tell you the truth, I wasn't sure you would even be open. I thought I remembered someone telling me you were in the process of remodeling."

"No sir, that's all finished. We are right here and ready for your visit."

"Okay, that sounds fine. My name is Lloyd McPherson, and my American Express number is . . ."

"Mr. McPherson, you of all people don't need to secure a room. You're a valued guest here, and it will be our pleasure to have you stay with us again. As a matter of fact, I look forward to serving you personally."

Lloyd sat back in his chair. "Thank you, that's very kind. I'm looking forward to staying"—*another lie?*—"for a few days. I'll probably arrive sometime after nine tonight."

The voice, smooth as polished wood. "We'll be waiting. Have a pleasant trip."

The world went dark again. "Thank you."

"Good-bye then, Mr. McPherson."

"Good-bye."

Lloyd replaced the receiver and stared at the telephone. Stared like a man waiting for the next word from God Himself.

The open road and the subliminal hint of salt in the air cleared his head a little. Lloyd had been driving for almost an hour and a half before he so much as sighed. He hadn't sung with the radio, hadn't even yelled at the Volkswagen full of college kids that pulled out in front of him earlier. His silent grief had been gray and deep, just like the weather. But even with the thickening clouds overhead, the sea air began to work its magic. Slowly. So slowly.

He and Carrington had always loved the beach. Before they could afford a place on the ocean, they dreamed of having their own place. Then, when money was no problem, they found they enjoyed going to various hotels or renting a condo for a week or two. That way they could enjoy one another and somebody else could worry about maintenance, grass cutting, and all the other little headaches that go with owning their own place.

And now the ocean was starting to soothe him somewhat. But not before he had replayed the events of their last day together.

They had read about the Steadman Resort in a regional travel magazine and immediately fell in love with it. The tennis courts, racquetball courts, ocean view, bicycle trails, and attentive staff was just the tip of the iceberg. The location—the Outer Banks of North Carolina—was secluded enough to afford them privacy when they wanted it, but they were close enough to the quaint shops and historic sights of the surrounding area to immerse themselves to their heart's delight. And immerse themselves they had.

Their days had been filled with walks on secluded beaches, picnics on the shore, treks to such exotic places as Duck and Nags Head, and wonderful evenings of dinner, dancing, and romance. The resort had a grand ballroom and an orchestra that played big band and swing music until the wee hours of the morning. They had enjoyed their first trip so much they had spent the past five Thanksgivings there.

Almost five.

Every newspaper in the state ran a story about the fire. It even made the wire services. Fifty people lost their lives and a dozen more went to the hospital with various cuts, burns, and broken bones. The news people said they were lucky anybody survived at all.

Lloyd McPherson hadn't felt lucky.

The fire started on the outside of the building and effectively trapped everyone in the ballroom from the start. At first no one noticed. It was Thanksgiving, and the Steadman was hosting its annual black-tie charity dinner and dance. Champagne. Party favors. The works. The orchestra had been playing an arrangement of "Woodchopper's Ball" that had two thirds of the couples in attendance on the dance floor. The large hearth at one end of the room—so big you could roast an entire pig in it—crackled and snapped while the celebrants whirled and glided across the room.

Blanche Lee was the first to notice that something was wrong. She noticed the moment the window next to her shattered from the heat outside. An eighteen-inch dagger of glass pinned her to her chair and claimed the first casualty.

Marge Newland, Blanche's newfound friend and fellow antique shop aficionado, screamed as the shards of glass fell around her. She watched her companion die in horrible slow motion. Time was molasses thick, and through it all Marge could neither move nor breathe. The scream siphoned all the air from her lungs, and the effort to refill them was thwarted by panic. She started to hyperventilate.

At the same time Marge screamed, Joe Ramey burned his hand on the door that lead to the outer hallway and on to the main building. The massive oak door blistered his hand, but his yelp of pain had been lost in Marge Newland's scream. Later that night Joe would tell district fire chief Walt Richards about the ensuing pandemonium after himself rescuing five people from the blazing ruin.

All Lloyd remembered from that point on was trying to get himself and Carrington out of the building. When the severity of the situation hit home, the herd instinct took over and the occupants of the room all headed for an exit. Joe waved them away from the door that had devoured two layers of skin moments earlier, and the crowd shifted toward the next exit. Caught in the crush, he and Carrington had been swept along with the tide. Stumbling, sweat-soaked hands slipping but never completely losing contact. They scanned the room for another way out.

When the line that fed the gas jets in the fireplace ruptured, the orchestra was as good as dead. The resulting explosion unfolded a fan of solid blue flame that covered the entire bandstand. So intense was the blaze that the lead trumpet player's valve oil bottle erupted in his hand and created a blue-hot formal-length glove of flame. Elbow to fingertips. His screams were never heard.

Overhead a beam exploded, and several others ignited as if by an unseen hand. The crowd, very much like stampeding cattle, finally found an exit and began to trample one another in an effort to leave the microcosm of hell. Pushing and shoving. Trampling anything and anyone in their path.

It was at that point the beam above Lloyd started to fall.

His first instinct had been to pull Carrington to safety, and he had pulled with all his might.

He had pulled against the tide of terrified humanity.

He had pulled against the tide of the inevitable.

In the seconds that seemed to stretch into months he saw her face. Saw the look of horror on that smudged, perfect face. Somehow her cheek had been cut, and the blood seemed to have been painted on in a long thin line from ear to chin. Then time suddenly sped up, a demon train on its way to oblivion. He remembered screaming her name, remembered being shoved deeper into the crowd, remembered the feeling as their fingers slipped apart. And he remembered the beam falling. Flame brushed oak, close to a thousand pounds of flame and timber, came crashing down with an ear-splitting roar. He remembered thinking at the time it sounded like a victory cry. In the end, it had killed four people. Carrington and three others.

He could remember screaming and trying to wade against the frightened, cow-eyed mass of people, but he couldn't remember how he managed to get out. And at this moment, watching the world through a haze of tears, he didn't know how long he had been in the Steadman parking area.

Lloyd switched off the Jaguar's engine, unbuckled his seat belt, and got out of the car. The last half hour was a blur. He still thought about that night often enough, but it had been a while since the memory had been that vivid. Was that an omen? A message to retreat for a while longer? He didn't know. Couldn't bring himself to think about it now.

The first thing he noticed when he entered the lobby was the sameness of it. It hadn't changed one bit. The wood, the furnishings, the plants, even the smell. Brass polish and heart pine. It was as if the Steadman had never burned.

The sound of the bellman's voice jolted him back to reality. "May I be of service, sir?" A voice accustomed to helping travelers caught up in the spell of the Steadman. No impatience. Just waiting to do his job, a job he had no doubt performed since the Steadman's opening.

"No. I mean yes. I need to check in. My reservation is in the name McPherson."

The bellman took the lone suitcase. "Of course, Mr. McPherson, we've been expecting you." He bowed ever so slightly. "Please follow me."

Lloyd was escorted to the front desk where he was greeted like an old friend. "Mr. McPherson," the desk clerk said. "I trust you had an enjoyable drive." He nodded to the bellman. "Take Mr. McPherson's case to his room."

He turned to tell his escort he would be glad to handle his own bag, but the bellman and his suitcase had disappeared.

"Mr. McPherson, here is the key. You will be in room one thirty-nine. If there is anything else you need, please don't hesitate to ring the desk." Lloyd turned and accepted the brass key. He looked at it, trying to find the answer to a question as yet unformed.

"Mr. McPherson, is there a problem?"

"No. No, I was just—" He looked at the desk manager. "Just trying to get over how perfect everything is. It's almost as if the Steadman never, well, never—"

The desk manager smiled. "I know. It is quite astounding what can be done when you want it badly enough."

"True enough I suppose. It's funny though." Lloyd looked at the key again. Noticed how the light rippled across the polished brass. "I didn't realize you had rebuilt the entire complex."

The desk manager, smooth, polished wood voice, smiled. "Well, you have been rather preoccupied, if I may be so bold." The smile changed ever so slightly.

"No," Lloyd answered, "you're absolutely right." He pocketed the key and stepped back from the desk. "I think a few days here might actually be just the thing I need to—"

The desk manager cut him off. "Of course. We understand completely. This cannot be an easy journey for you." The smile slipped away. "So sad. So tragic and so sad."

Lloyd nodded but said nothing. Another sound had captured his attention. A sound he really hadn't expected. It was music. Big band music. He looked around to his left then back again. "You really have made a comeback." He looked in the direction from which strains of "I Can't Get Started" flowed.

"Maybe you'd care to have a drink and listen to the orchestra for a while before you turn in, Mr. McPherson. I believe you will find it beneficial."

Lloyd started to refuse the suggestion and go straight to his room. The trip had been long and he wasn't sure he was ready to go in the ballroom just yet. He was just now becoming accustomed to the idea that he was here and having a conversation with the desk manager. In fact, he realized he had not had his credit card imprinted or even inquired about the man's name.

He turned to raise the issues with the desk manager but was stopped short. The blond man behind the counter extended his hand, and Lloyd shook it automatically. "Now, Mr. McPherson, you go right in, order a drink, and make yourself comfortable. Don't be concerned about your room. We will take perfect care of you. And should you need anything, ask for me personally. My name is Paul."

The room seemed to tilt slightly, and he followed the tilt toward the room where the orchestra played. He turned back just long enough for Paul to say "Go ahead in, sir. This is the reason you came."

Before he could respond his hand was on the brass door handle and he was inside.

The room was exactly the way he remembered it. The long mahogany bar to his right was polished to a high sheen. The brass rails and sparkling glass and crystal were reflected in the long mirror behind the bar created the illusion of a huge double bar. And the single bar was plenty large for the room.

The tables were arranged in clusters around a pristine dance floor, recently polished to a high gloss. There were already about fifty couples in various sections of the room. The orchestra played as if there were a New Year's party in full swing. The band leader threw a two-fingered salute in Lloyd's direction while giving the downbeat for "Satin Doll."

"How many in your party, sir?"

Lloyd turned to the woman who addressed him. Her platinum hair and fair skin was a perfect contrast to her night-black dress. "Just one, thank you."

"Will anyone be joining you later?"

Lloyd cocked his head as if he hadn't understood. "No, I'm alone this evening." That's the truth if I ever told it, he thought as he was escorted to a table close to the bandstand. When he was seated, the platinum vision in black took his drink order and went back to the bar.

For the first time since his arrival Lloyd had a chance to really look and take everything in. It was the same. From the exposed beams right down to the design in the carpet. It was exactly the same. Like the desk manager had said, it was amazing what you could do if you wanted to badly enough.

If only that were really true.

His thoughts were interrupted by a movement at his right elbow. "That didn't take very long," he said as he turned to take his drink.

"No, not long at all," Carrington said in response.

Carrington.

The room shifted, slightly out of focus. Lloyd could see nothing except the face of his beloved Carrington.

Carrington was dead.

Impossible. She died here.

Heart hammering. Hard to breathe. Room spinning.

Lloyd's heart jackhammered his ribs. Cold.

Oh, dear God, he thought. I'm losing it.

He closed his eyes and tried to bring his breathing under control. Calm. Deeper, deeper. There now. He opened his eyes. The specter of his dead wife was gone. Stress, he thought. That's what it is. I just came out too soon.

He turned to pick up his glass. God, he needed a drink now.

"Lloyd."

The sound of his name turned his spine to ice.

Carrington sat across from him looking for all the world the way she had looked the day they first came to the Steadman.

He looked at her. Saw without fully comprehending. The face was the same. The same delicate nose; the same bright green eyes. The same porcelain skin. It was Carrington.

It couldn't be.

"What's happening to me?" Lloyd asked no one in particular. A last attempt to hold his emotions in a safety net. "What's happening?"

Carrington smiled. "Don't you know? Really?"

Lloyd slid his chair back and jerked his hands away from the table as if it had carried a two-twenty charge. "This is not happening. It's not." A tear formed in the corner of one eye. "It's not."

The smile changed ever so slightly. "Yes, it is, Lloyd. This is happening. Everything here is perfect. Just the way you wanted it."

The words were lost on him.

"How? I mean . . . I . . . ." He looked around the room. The orchestra played—had never stopped playing—while couples danced, or sat and listened. Ice tinkled in glasses. Smoke from a dozen cigarettes ambled toward the ceiling.

Smoke.

Fire.

Then.

Now.

"No. This is wrong. All wrong."

"Why?" she asked. "It's what you wanted."

"What I wanted?" He turned to face what had once been his partner in life. "What do you mean, this is what I wanted?"

"Lloyd, I know you've been hurting. Every day since—"

"No." He cut her off and shook his head. "I came here to come to terms with what happened." He sent a less-than-steady hand to fetch his drink.

"Is that really why you came?"

The bourbon was tasteless. There was no reassuring jolt of initial fire from throat to belly. He looked at the glass. Then at his wife. "What?"

"You came here hoping to find it had all been a dream. You wanted the impossible to happen, and now it has." She held out a hand. "Now you have to accept it."

He moved his chair toward the table. Hesitated. His heart was a thoroughbred straining against the gate.

"Carrington?"

The tear traced its way down his cheek. Many more followed the path it blazed.

"Carrington . . . how . . . I mean . . . how did . . . ?"

"You did it."

The words hit him with the force of a sledgehammer. "How did I do this? How could I possibly?"

"If you want something bad enough." She smiled again. The smile he had seen a thousand times. The smile that brought the reality of the situation home.

He reached for her hand. "It really is you. You're here." Now it was his turn to smile. "It's impossible, but you're here."

She nodded. "I told you so."

He looked at her. Really looked at her. He couldn't help himself. She was exactly as she had always been. Perfect.

He released her hand and wiped the tears from his eyes. The orchestra played and couples swirled around the floor. But as far as he was concerned, there was no one else in the world but Carrington. His Carrington. It was absolutely impossible and absolutely true. He stood and walked around the table.

"Can I hold you?"

The orchestra played a slow Glenn Miller tune. Carrington stood.

"Yes."

Lloyd took her in his arms. Savored the feel of her. He buried his face in the soft junction of her neck and shoulder. Pulled her closer. All the memories and all the suppressed feelings rushed back in a solid wall of emotion. She was here. They were together. And she felt

"If you want something bad enough."

different.

He held her tighter.

She didn't respond.

He held her at arm's length. "Carrington, what's wrong?"

She smiled again. The same smile he had loved for years. The same? Almost the same.

"Just then when I held you. Didn't you feel anything at all?"

"No. We don't feel anything here."

He bit his lower lip. Partly habit and partly for the pain. He needed to clear his head. "What do you mean, you don't feel anything here?"

She motioned for him to sit. "When I passed over I saw the fire, the smoke, the crush of people. And I saw others around me watching the same thing. Then there was nothing for a while. I knew what was happening, but it didn't matter."

Lloyd's head was spinning. The orchestra continued to play and the couples continued to swirl. Then he realized what had bothered him from the moment he walked in. With the exception of the desk manager and the hostess, no one had spoken. The couples at the tables smoked and drank but never uttered a word. The orchestra played but there was no banter between songs from the band leader.

"You see, we know everything we need to know here. This is a different level of existence, so the physical amenities of the other existence really aren't necessary."

"If you don't have any feelings for me, then why did you come back?" The tears started again but this time there was no trickle.

"Lloyd, I didn't come back. You came to me. What you see is the essence of who I was. Much like it was frozen in time. We do not age, we do not feel. We know what we need to know. We exist, and existence is enough."

He attempted to understand. "Then this is Heaven?"

"No."

"Is it Hell?"

"No."

Lloyd felt the first stirring of anger push his fear off to the side. "Then where are we?"

"We're at the Steadman. Your Steadman."

The black dawning of complete realization struck him full and hard.

"Carrington, you said there were others watching the events of that night with you. Do you mean these—"

She nodded.

He began to shiver. The air had grown suddenly cold and the fire in the hearth provided no warmth. He watched the couples swirl soundlessly. The orchestra played on, no longer burned by the inferno, no longer feeling the music. Just shades of musicians playing shades of feelings now forgotten.

"If what you say is true then I'm going back home. If I can't hold you—the real you—then I won't settle for the substitute. I just can't."

She took his arm. "You can't leave."

Another smile. Mirthless. The memory of a smile. "Those who haven't crossed over know so little. You assume it is always those from this side who cross over. Hauntings you call them." She paused.

if you want something bad enough, you can make it happen

"Sometimes one of you crosses over to here. That's what you did." She sounded so matter-of-fact now.

"There is no front desk. No Steadman. And tomorrow or the day after someone will find your car parked where you left it. In front of the charred foundation of what used to be the Steadman Resort."

Lloyd's breath caught in his throat. The room grew colder. The band played louder. He took her shoulders and shouted to be heard above the orchestra. "You mean I'll just stay here, never age, and keep company with a room full of what used to be?"

"Not exactly. You'll age, but since time has so little meaning here, you will age slowly. But you will never die." She smiled that damned smile.

The horror of the situation bloomed, a blood rose opening in his mind. He would age beyond ancient with the specter of his fondest memory eternally before him. Never changing. Never caring. The realization was too much. He pushed what was the love of his life aside and raced toward the nearest exit.

He turned the brass door handle and rushed toward the lobby and his waiting car.

The room was exactly the way he remembered it. The long mahogany bar to his right was polished to a high sheen. The brass rails and sparkling glass and crystal ware reflected in the long mirror behind the bar created the illusion of a huge double bar. And the single bar was plenty large for the room.

The tables were arranged in clusters around a pristine dance floor, recently polished to a high gloss. There were already about fifty couples in various sections of the room. The orchestra played as if there were a New Year's party in full swing. The band leader threw a two-fingered salute in Lloyd's direction while giving the downbeat for "Satin Doll."

"How many in your party, sir?"

Lloyd turned to the woman who addressed him. Her platinum hair and fair skin were a perfect contrast to her night-black dress.

He could not speak. Undiluted dread clutched his throat with fingers of cold glass bone.

"Will anyone be joining you later?"

He heard a soft click as the door closed behind him.

"Yes."

Worst Fears

Rick Hautala

Laura Griffin, who is my absolute closest friend, says to me, "Do you realize what you sound like?"

I hardly notice the dampness of the wooden bench we're sitting on outside The Book Shelf on Exchange Street.

It's a gorgeous late September afternoon. A rain shower passed through an hour or so ago and is moving off to the east and out to sea. The setting sun is shining at a sharp angle from underneath the retreating edge of the cloud bank. Seagulls circle high in the sky, bright white dots against the gray, swift-moving clouds. Wisps of steam rise like phantoms from the rapidly cooling street and sidewalk.

It's getting late, and shops are closing, so the street isn't nearly as busy as it was during the day. Still, a few people stream silently past us—one or two couples, a few moms with babies in strollers, groups of teenagers and college kids, and some professional people out running last-minute errands before heading home from work. As warm as the autumn day is, though, it can't come close to stopping the shiver I feel deep inside me.

"Yeah," I reply after swallowing hard. "I know exactly what I must sound like, but I—"

My voice cuts off sharply.

I want to say more.

I want to tell her what I'm really thinking, but I know that I have to ease into it. More than any other of my friends, Laura knows perfectly well what I've been going through ever since my—well, ever since what happened to my husband, Jimmy.

"Did you ever go see that therapist I told you about?" Laura asks.

I shake my head and say, "I didn't think she could really help me."

Laura's brow creases with concern. I know from more than fifteen years of friendship that her concern is genuine. Her dark eyes glisten like wet marbles in the gathering twilight. A maple tree arches over the bench we're sitting on. Shimmering drops of water dangle like tiny jewels from the tips of each leaf. The air has a clean, fresh-washed smell.

Laura looks to me like she's about to cry, but I can tell that she's holding back her tears so she can help me.

I feel nervous. My stomach feels like it's filled with cold jelly. I want to reach out and hug her, if only for the solid, warm reassurance of a human touch, but I hold myself back. Even sitting right here beside me, she seems so far away. I can't bring myself to touch her, no matter how much I want to.

I need to say what I have to say first.

"I—I know it sounds crazy, like a . . . like it's from a nightmare or something, but I swear to God it really happened."

Laura's concerned frown deepens. She runs her teeth across her lower lip, sawing back and forth as she considers what I've said so far and what she should say to me.

It's almost like I can read her mind and can tell what she's thinking.

She's thinking that my situation is much more serious than she thought or than I can recognize. She's thinking that, maybe, I might even need to be hospitalized or something.

"Tell me exactly what happened," Laura says mildly. "Don't leave anything out."

I hesitate, trying to gain at least a shred of composure. Usually I can stay pretty much in control of things, but after everything that's happened lately, I'm not so sure anymore.

Blinking my eyes to fight back the warm gush of tears, I tilt my head back and look up at the top stories of the brick and granite buildings across the street. In the slanting orange sunlight, every detail stands out in painfully sharp detail. The buildings look almost ethereal against the backdrop of the dark, rain-laden clouds. I can easily imagine that they're not real . . . that they're just projections against the darkening sky.

I look around, tracking one of the cars as it creeps past us down the street. Its tires hiss on the wet pavement, sounding like a nest of snakes. No matter where I look, everything seems to be lost in a dim, dreamy haze.

"It seems so long ago, but it was . . . just last weekend—last Friday night," I begin, almost choking. I don't like the way my voice sounds so tentative, as if someone else is speaking through me.

"We were—I was—Jimmy and I went out to eat . . . at Costello's. It always been one of our favorite places."

Laura crosses her right leg over her left and shifts an inch or two closer to me. I think she's thinking that I'm going to fall apart completely real soon now, and that she has to be ready to grab me, hug me, and tell me that it's all right, that I can cry all I want to as long as I need to.

"We were sitting downstairs, over in the far corner," I tell her. "I was trying hard to pay attention to Jimmy, to what he was saying, but I couldn't stop staring at this man who was sitting at a table diagonally across the room from us. He was far enough away so I only caught a glimpse of him every now and then. Jimmy was going on and on about how his boss at the radio station was driving him crazy, but I'd heard it all before, plenty of times, so I guess I just sort of tuned him out. I thought that—"

A sudden wave of emotion grabs hold of me, and my voice falters.

Looking fearfully over my shoulder, I glance up the street in the direction of Costello's restaurant. Its arched doorway looks dark and foreboding. I can't see any lights on inside, which creates the impression that the restaurant has been closed for a very long time.

People passing by seem to sense this too, and hurry their steps until they are past it.

I look back at Laura, but it's hard to see her clearly in the gathering gloom. Tears are welling up, warm in my eyes.

"So he caught you looking at another man and maybe got a little mad—is that it?" Laura offers. "Did you guys have an argument?"

Biting my lower lip, I shake my head and barely whisper the word, *"No."*

Finally, after I catch my breath, I continue.

"It wasn't that at all. Jimmy had already said several times that he thought I looked really distracted, and that he was worried about me. He mentioned more than once that he thought I looked pale, kind of sickly. I finally couldn't stand it any longer and told him what was bothering me—that I thought I recognized the man who was sitting across from us, but that I couldn't for the life of me remember from where. It was bugging the heck out of me."

"Did you eventually figure out who he was?" Laura asks.

I nod, but even the slightest motion sends a ripple of shivers up my back.

I look around at the people passing by on the street. I can't get rid of the feeling that they all look so . . . so unreal. I'm convinced that I can see right through some of them, that their shadows are more real than they are. A city bus roars by. The sound of its engine seems to come at me from all sides, filling the air like the long, rolling concussion of thunder.

"What happened next?" Laura asks.

Her voice sounds so loud and vibrant and close that it pulls me back. I shake my head. Closing my eyes, I rub them hard enough to make bright, swirling patterns of light shift across my vision.

"I . . . I saw someone else," I reply, even though it takes almost all the air out of me.

Suddenly fearful, I open my eyes and look at Laura again if just to convince myself that she's really there. I am unable to speak for several seconds, but Laura doesn't push or prod me. She just sits there, looking back at me with all the patience and understanding in the world.

"A woman walked in with a man," I finally say.

My voice almost breaks, and when I lick my lips, they feel as dry and rough as sandpaper.

"They looked like they were in their late twenties, maybe early thirties. Both of them were nicely dressed. Healthy-looking people. Jimmy kept right on talking, not even noticing that I was tracking them as the hostess led them over to a booth near us. When they sat down, the woman sat facing me. Sitting in the darkened corner, I felt almost invisible, so I could take the time to study her face."

"And that's when you recognized her?" Laura asks, obviously already knowing the answer.

"Yeah," I say.

The word sounds like a dry gulp.

"I was positive that I knew her, but—just like the man sitting across the room—I couldn't remember where I'd ever seen her before."

Feeling desperate and alone, I want to reach out and grab Laura's hands, but I hold myself back.

"Honest to God, Laura," I say. My voice is trembling terribly. "It was the weirdest sensation I've ever had in my life—like a feeling of . . . of déjà vu that wouldn't stop. I felt sort of like I was experiencing someone else's memories or something."

I sigh so heavily that it hurts my chest. The sun has set by now, and shadows are deepening around us.

"I . . . I just don't know what's happening to me."

Laura recrosses her legs and leans forward, planting her elbow on her thigh and covering her mouth with her left hand. She stares back at me for so such a long time I start to feel uncomfortable. I don't like the way her gaze makes me feel as though she can see right through me.

I suddenly feel a powerful impulse to get up and just run away—from Laura, from everything. I find myself wishing that I could dissolve, just disappear into the rush of activity around us, but everything seems so distant.

Besides, I know that Laura won't let me do that.

She's always been the kind of friend who doesn't let me get

away with anything. And she's always been there whenever I've needed her.

"So then what?" she says in a voice as airy and light as a spring breeze.

It sounds to me almost like we're talking in a vacuum. All the other city sounds around us seem strangely muffled and distant compared to the closeness of her voice. When a car passes by, less than ten feet from the bench where we're sitting, I almost can't hear the soft whisper of its tires on the wet pavement.

"It . . . it wasn't until Mr. Nolan came into the room that I finally realized what was going on," I say.

Laura shakes her head, her liquid brown eyes clouding with confusion.

"I don't know who Mr. Nolan is," she says mildly, but her voice is also strong enough to urge me on.

"He was my high school English teacher senior year at Gorham High School."

Laura nods, her whole demeanor saying *Yes . . . and?*

I find it difficult to breathe. The blood in my veins feels like it's turning to ice. Every nerve in my body is numb, like I have pins-and-needles all over.

"But you see—" I finally say. "Mr. Nolan is . . . dead."

I can hardly hear myself speak, and it's dark enough so I'm having trouble seeing her face clearly, but I can tell by Laura's reaction that she heard me. When she looks at me and silently mouths the word *dead,* I nod like a marionette whose strings have been cut.

"He died of lung cancer more than twenty years ago, a year after I graduated from high school."

The worried expression on Laura's face cuts me deeply. I can see the concern she feels for me, but I can also tell that she's realizing just how bad off I really am. I know that she's thinking what happened last week has totally unhinged me.

I want desperately to tell her that this isn't what's happening. Even considering the circumstances, I still feel pretty stable, but I can tell that, no matter what I say, she won't believe me.

If our situations were reversed, I wonder if *I* would believe *her.*

"You're sure it was him?" Laura says, no longer able to disguise what she's really thinking behind a low, calming voice. "It wasn't just someone who looked a lot like him?"

I bite my lower lip and shake my head firmly, blinking my eyes rapidly to force back the tears. A thick, salty taste fills the back of my throat, almost choking me.

"No, I *know* it was him. Without a doubt. I'd recognize him anywhere."

I look around, suddenly afraid that I must be shouting and drawing attention, but the passersby seem not even to see me.

"And then," I say, "when I looked back at the woman who had walked in earlier, I realized that I knew her too. She was Gail Grover, my roommate from college, freshman year. But you see—I read in the alumni magazine maybe five years ago that Gail Grover had died in a car accident out in California."

Laura has nothing to say. She just sits there, looking at me with total patience and understanding, but I know that she's thinking I will probably have to be hospitalized.

"And the other man—the one sitting across the room—I finally realized that he was Frank Sheldon, a longtime friend of my father's."

"And he had died too, right?" Laura asks.

I hear something crackle in my neck when I nod. "Yeah. He used to fly small-engine planes and take aerial photographs of people's houses, then go door to door, trying to sell the pictures to the homeowners. He took me up in his plane a few times when I was a little girl. I remember being really scared. I was maybe ten or eleven years old when his plane crashed somewhere in New Hampshire."

Laura lets her breath out in a huge sigh. She uncrosses her legs, folds her arms across her chest, and leans back against the slats of the wooden bench and just stares straight ahead as if I'm not even there. Before long, I can't take it any longer, so I say to her, "And there were more."

Laura looks at me with a faint, distant light in her eyes. She looks dreamy and far away in the twilight. The streetlights have come on, and some of the shop windows glow with soft, lemon light.

The maple tree we're sitting under throws a long, angular shadow across the sidewalk and up the wall of the store across the street from us. Somewhere in the distance, I can hear the high, winding wail of a siren. It sounds a bit like someone crying in pain.

"There were other people in the restaurant—lots of them—and all of them were people I had known before and who had died."

Laura's expression doesn't alter in the slightest. She just sits and stares at me, but for some reason I can no longer tell what she's thinking. I have no idea if she believes me or if she thinks I'm lying to her. In some ways, I decide, it doesn't matter because at least I'm finally talking to someone about it!

"I saw my cousin—Rachel Adams. She died years ago, when she was fourteen. She drowned swimming in the Royal River out behind the house. And my Aunt Lydia was there, and all four of my grand-mothers and grandfathers, and Mrs. McMillan—Edna McMillan, the old lady who used to live next door to us when we lived out on Files Road."

The whole time I'm talking, Laura is just staring straight ahead, but I can tell that she's still listening to me. The muscles in her jaw rapidly tense and untense. I can see and almost hear the rapid throb-bing of her pulse in her neck. She takes several shallow breaths as though trying to calm herself.

"It sounds like an absolute nightmare," she finally says, still not turning to look at me.

"It *was!*" I shout, and this time I notice that a middle-age man wearing a three-piece suit who's walking by turns and looks at me like I'm a crazy person. He gestures and starts to say something, then, still looking mystified, shakes his head and continues on his way. His footsteps echo hollowly in the darkness.

"It was like . . . like having to face all of your worst fears all at once," I say in a low, trembling voice. "I had no idea what was hap-pening, but I finally couldn't stand it any longer, so I got up and ran out of there. Jimmy called after me, and I stopped and looked back at him to see him scrambling to get up and come after me, but I was out the door and on the street before he could catch me."

"Did he catch up with you?" Laura asks.

I shake my head sadly.

"The heavy wooden door slammed shut behind me, but he never came outside. The night was cold and dreary. The street was slick with rain, but I ran as fast as I could down the street. I was terrified that all those dead people had left the restaurant and were coming after me."

Laura sighs and clicks her tongue as she shakes her head. I can see tears streaming down her face. They glisten on her pale cheeks like quicksilver. She swallows with difficulty and then turns to me.

"So what happened after that?" she asks.

I open my mouth, but before I can say anything, I realize that I don't remember what happened next. Whatever it was, it feels like the memory of a dream that's fading away fast, like fine beach sand sifting through my fingers.

"I . . . don't know," I finally say.

Huge chunks of memory seem to be missing, like the faint tracing of words that have been written on a chalkboard and then erased.

"I remember running down the street, heading this way, toward Exchange Street. I was thinking that I'd parked my car around here somewhere. I remember seeing the city lights reflecting in the rain on the street and sidewalks. I remember hearing the clicking sound my shoes made. The sound echoed like gunshots from the buildings on both sides of the street. I wasn't paying attention when I crossed the street, and a passing car almost hit me. The driver blasted his horn at me, but I didn't care. I just kept running. And after that, I . . . I—"

I shake my head and sigh again.

The soft, steady rush of wind still smells fresh with rain. It whisks my voice away.

"—I can't remember where I went or what I did after that."

"Try . . . *try* to remember," Laura urges.

The mild tone in her voice has returned, and it soothes me, at least a little. When I look at her again, I see a warm glow of friendship and trust in her eyes, and I think—for just an instant—that everything might still be all right, as long as I have a friend as loyal as Laura.

"The next thing I remember is . . . being back at my house. It was dark, and I'm pretty sure it was still raining, although my hair wasn't wet and there was no other evidence that I had been outside. No wet raincoat or anything. It was only once I got home that I realized—like I was remembering it—that Jimmy was—"

My voice chokes off again, but Laura completes the sentence for me.

"Dead," she says.

For a shattering instant, I have the unnerving impression that my voice is coming from Laura. I'm aware of the darkening street around us, of the shops and passing cars, of the people drifting by in slow motion, but they all appear to be impossibly distant. They're no more . . . or less . . . substantial than the memory I have of all those dead people in the restaurant.

"Yeah," I say. "I remembered that Jimmy was in a . . . a car accident and that he had . . ."

I can't finish the sentence because I still can't bring myself to say the word *died*.

Saying it would mean that I had to accept it.

I hear Laura whisper softly, so close to me.

"Good Lord," she says. "I wish there was something I could do to help you."

She sighs again and shakes her head from side to side. I can hear the whisking sound of her long brown hair brushing against her shoulders. Tears are streaming like tiny rivers from her eyes, but—surprisingly—I don't cry.

I can't cry!

I think I must have used up all of my tears over the last few days just getting through Jimmy's funeral.

"So what you're telling me," Laura says, "is that you think, even when you were sitting there in the restaurant with Jimmy, that he was already—"

This time, even Laura can't say the word that echoes hollowly inside my brain.

Dead!

I close my eyes and shiver as I nod.

The rushing sound of the busy street around me fades away even further, and I am swept up by an incredible sinking sensation of being alone . . .

Utterly alone.

For a timeless instant I keep my eyes tightly closed. I feel lost in a dark, directionless void that seems to want to absorb me, but I struggle to focus on the tiny, flickering spark of my own identity.

When I speak again, my eyes are still closed, and I hear my own voice booming inside my head like the rumbling roll of kettle drums.

"I don't know what to think anymore," I say.

I can't help but notice how different my own voice sounds when I listen to it with my eyes closed.

"I'm absolutely positive that what happened in the restaurant really did happen. I saw all those dead people there, Laura. I know I did. I even saw Jimmy! I know what you're thinking. You're thinking that it has to have been a dream or something, a . . . a hallucination."

I squeeze my eyes shut even tighter.

The shifting patterns of light behind my eyelids intensify. Jagged lines of light and darkness spiral inward like razor-lines whirlpools.

"You're the only person I've ever mentioned this to," I say, feeling the heavy vibration of each word in my throat.

"I can't explain what happened. I have no idea what it was or what it could mean, but I do know that . . . somehow . . . Jimmy was reaching out me. He was trying to . . . to contact me . . . to comfort me . . . like you're doing now."

My hand is trembling as I reach out, feeling for Laura's hand to grasp and hold. The emotions that are swelling up inside me are almost too much to bear. I feel as if I can't breathe, that a huge iron band has been wrapped around my chest and is steadily squeezing . . . squeezing . . .

"Laura!" I call out.

My voice is a long, wavering moan.

A thin sliver of panic stabs me when I open my eyes. For a terrifying moment, I can't see a thing except the dark street and hints of darker motion all around me.

"Don't worry. I'm right here beside you."

Laura's voice sounds impossibly far away.

No matter how desperately I reach for her hand, I can't touch it.

"*Laura!*" I cry.

As my vision adjusts, I look into the dense darkness of night that has descended. A thrill of fear runs through me when I see that the bench beside me is empty.

A faint puff of warmth, like someone's breath, blows gently into my ear, but it doesn't come close to stopping the terrible shiver of fear and loneliness that is trembling inside me.

I look around at the city street and see that it is empty too.

Deserted.

The sun has long since dropped below the western horizon, but its light still edges the underside of the clouds with a baleful red glow. Ink-deep shadows reach out like grasping hands from across the street and between the buildings.

I realize that I am surrounded by dense silence, and that I am absolutely alone . . .

The Willcroft Inheritance

Paul Collins and Rick Kennet

I had been mistress of Willcroft for three years before an error in judgment caused my ruination.

Until then I had had worse, but more manageable problems to concern myself with. The running of a large fruit plantation and a house so big and detached from the common circle of society is not a simple undertaking.

How I remember the way the seagulls wheeled and cried above the cliffs the day I first arrived here. And my thinking it a welcome. Today I would see it more as a warning of the lonely months I would spend in this house whilst Reginald, my husband, was on the other side of the world, pursuing his shipping interests. Salt in the wind holds more potential for adventure than does dirt under the fingernails. So it was left to me to organize the labor, the buying of saplings and bulbs, the timing for seeding and pruning, watering and caring of the flower beds and fruit trees upon which the viability of the estate depended every bit as much as upon my husband's seafaring.

In the winter of that third year of my marriage to a man mostly absent, subsidence in the servants' quarters in the south wing caused a wall to partly collapse. The house had stood solid on its headland perch for over one hundred years and had never been in need of major repair until now, the worst of all times, for most of the money at hand had already been appropriated in anticipation of the season's harvest.

Then an idea came to me—a disastrous notion I see now in hindsight, but then the thought seemed the shining salvation from my predicament. A quarter mile west of the house, in a rocky paddock not used for anything save the grazing of occasional livestock, stood the ruins of an older house, a broken wall, a tumble of stones, and something that may have once been a chimney fireplace. It was from here that I told the tradesmen to take their stone for the repairs, and over the three weeks the work took to complete I watched the outline of this ruin slowly diminish.

The night of completion was blustery and cold and I had the lamps lit and the curtains drawn. I was seated at my husband's bureau, making a start on tallies and accounts, when a timid knock came on the study door. I fear I answered with a snappish "Yes?" for after all this time figures are still not my friends, and at the end of the day it takes a while for me to approach them in the right frame of mind.

The door opened and Mrs. Flute took one small step into the room.

"Beg your pardon, Mrs. Willcroft, but Jane tells me . . ."

"Jane?"

"The new maid, mum."

"Yes?"

"Well, she tells me there's someone getting about in the south wing."

"Getting about? Can you be more specific, Mrs. Flute?"

"I mean someone what ought not be there." She said no more, but stood regarding the floor whilst her fingers, clasped before her, flexed in an agitated fashion.

"Work was finished there today," I said. "Perhaps it's a late workman making some finishing touches?" But the explanation rang false in my own ears. No tradesman should be in the house without my knowledge, certainly none at this hour. "Mrs. Flute. I hope you're not lending credence to what some young girl, a new girl in a new position, probably on her first night away from her mother—"

"Oh, no, mum. I wouldn't have been bothering you if I hadn't sent Flute and a couple of the stable lads to see for theirselves."

"Come to the point. What did your husband find? Is there some-one in the south wing or is there not?"

"That's just it, mum . . . they're not certain. But they hear things, and the dogs . . . they afeared too."

I caught up the lamp from the bureau. "Come, then, let us see who is 'getting about' the south wing."

The smell of new paint and woodwork still hung in the dark of the south wing. Flute, the head gardener who had been in the em-ploy of my husband's family some twenty years, and one of the sta-ble boys preceded me holding up lamps. There was nothing to see in the short distance its light penetrated. As if by common consent, we halted then, and as our footsteps echoed into silence there came to my ears the faint sound of chipping from the far end of the corridor.

"It's but a late workman," I said. The sound of a chisel working stone was unmistakable: The sharp *chink* of the hammer striking the chisel simultaneous with the crunch of bitten stone was mo-notonously rhythmic in the quiet of the night. "Who is it there?" I called aloud.

But no answer came from the dark. The chipping of stone went on steadily. Steadily and *delicately*, as if by a hand performing fine work.

"Go and see who it is, Flute," I said.

The gardener looked at me doubtfully. His face was grotesque in the shadow from the lamp. "Can I take the boy?"

"No," said the boy.

"Yes," said I.

They crept forward with lamps held well before them. The chip-ping continued unabated.

"Hello?" called Flute. "You there . . . hello?"

I followed them for a few yards, conscious of my position, but also of needing to set an example.

The chipping stopped as Flute and the boy, surrounded by their ring of light, reached the end of the south wing without coming upon anyone. Then all at once a shadow flickered across the light cast upon the wall, a hideous shape only partly human with great squares of light shining through it. It carried something like a book, dark and oblong in its one arm. It danced through the light and was gone.

Flute and the boy hastened back with many backward glances. That night the servants refused as one to sleep in their usual quarters, and so camped down in the kitchen with a good fire burning until morning.

The sun came out of the sea to show a sky rough with black, sullen clouds. A ship almost on the horizon battled a white-flecked seesaw ocean, with coal smoke streaming back flat from its one tall funnel. The wind swept over the clifftops and rattled the windows and nodded the trees. I went out into the bluster and examined the outside of the south wing. It was, in truth, the first chance I had had to examine at close hand the workmanship of the builders. I was not altogether pleased with what I saw. Here and there bricks were ill matched, and their varying shades of white, dark gray, and even stark blue, gave the wall an unhealthy, diseased appearance. Nowhere, however, were there any signs which would explain last night's noises.

The corridor of the south wing was a dismal place even at noonday, which was the next time I ventured into it. I had the absurd, perhaps even the macabre notion that a workman had been trapped inside the walls and had been trying in vain to break out.

In the shipping industry there are sometimes rumors of riveters being inadvertently sealed up within the spaces between double hulls. Those aboard the *Great Eastern*, so my husband has told me, are often troubled by inexplicable hammering from belowdeck, and one wonders what might be found when she is eventually scrapped. With these thoughts in mind I tentatively tapped the walls with a small hammer. In truth I was scared should my tapping receive a reply. But no answering sound made itself known within that dismal corridor, though I tapped at various places and heights. I left then to return to my husband's study. A feeling of having tempted providence was with me until I reached the lighter, warmer, more human parts of the house.

Once more the staff refused to sleep in their allotted quarters, but simply made their beds in the kitchen and servants' hall. All but the stable boy who slept in the loft and probably thought himself lucky. As for the rest, they would not hear of approaching the south wing after dark. I went alone then to the south wing that night to see or hear whatever might manifest itself.

As I feared, as I half hoped, the sound of the chisel tapped and echoed along the dark, stone corridor as I approached.

Chip, chip, chip, in a familiar rhythm, punctured by silences equally spaced.

"Now we shall see," I said in order to feel brave, and strode forward confidently, plunging into the dark and the *chip, chip, chip,* with my lamp held high and my heart in my mouth.

It was a shadow, a shape only half solid, and it sprang as the lamplight reached the farthest corner. It twisted like so much rag about me in a macabre solo dance, thin and full of holes, a thing of broken outline; it flailed one arm and the wink of light on a sharpened edge flashed past and was gone with a chink of metal into stone; a rushing cold and all was gone, leaving me staring down an empty corridor, and listening to an intense silence.

I foresaw trouble. Ghost stories travel. Staff had already begun to leave—Jane the new maid had given immediate notice, and the stable boy had run away in the night—and would be difficult to replace. Field laborers would become impossible to procure. I could deal with fruit blight and wall subsidence—but ghosts! A thing so insubstantial had the potential of utter ruin.

"It's the stones, isn't it?" I said to Flute the following morning. "You've lived here two decades. What story pertains to the old house?"

"Only vague whispers, mum."

"Such as?"

"That it were burnt down when its master—Mr. Willcroft's great-great-grandfather—threw a lantern at something what came to presage his death."

"And what 'something' was this?"

"Well, mum, there's always supposed to be a ghost walkin' in every old place—"

"Nonsense, Flute. What walks, creeps, dances, beleaguers the south wing is *not* a supposition!"

Flute blinked his surprise at my outburst. "Beggin' your forgiveness, mum, but save for wild stories a nurse will tell the children around the evenin's fire, there ain't nothin' to say 'bout the ghost from the old house."

"Except that it comes to presage death in the house?"

The old man looked down at his scuffed boots. "I know it ain't my place to say, but the master's family ain't always been the good folk they are today."

"Yes?"

"It's just that way back in the years some wild things were done. The ghost, so they says, were a stonecutter in the employ of the master's ancestors. One day this stonecutter made some such mistake in his work as to enrage the old gentleman to striking him a fatal blow with his own hammer."

"And that is when the ghost of the stonecutter began to haunt the old house?"

"No, mum. Not for several more years when it appeared to the man who had been the cause of its death, and then to warn him of his coming death. It happened a month later in a hunting accident. From then on it has appeared to . . . well . . ." He paused, then added, "So they says."

"What," I began, thinking aloud, remembering the unfinished appearance of the apparition, "if we were to bring more stone from the old house?"

Flute looked up sharply as though panicked by such a thought.

"I'd say there's naught to be gained from such a folly, mum," he said miserably.

"Then what if we were to tear down the wall and return the stone to the old site?"

Flute's eyes went wide. "Mum, the orchards have tied up the money, and it is wiser spent there, if I may sound to presume."

"You do. But go on."

"The ghost, or whatever it be, harms no one. We has tampered enough, and I says we should leave it be. The orchards need the money, mum."

"And shall you and the rest of the servants sleep in the kitchen from now on?"

Again Flute found great interest in his hob-nailed boots.

"That will be all, Flute," I said.

That night I had a most peculiar dream, if dream it was. I felt myself rising above my body, and for one moment I was horror-stricken with the thought that I had died. Yet leaving my burdens behind felt so melodic that I simply relished this newfound freedom and let myself go wither I would. In this incorporeal form I drifted through the walls and rose up the stairs, drawn inexorably to the south wing.

I could hear nothing, of course, and despite having no tactile feelings, I knew I would be cold and desolate in this place. My "self" was everywhere, yet nowhere, a pinpoint of luminescent confined to a bodiless intelligence. I saw the ghost then. A hunched thing of some substantiality, methodically chipping away at a tombstone. I willed myself closer, more out of curiosity than of desire to see what was written there. The specter regarded me with eyes set within its jagged, unfinished face, twin deep hollows born not of age or death but of something more bestial and bitter.

I glided within its sphere. Our ethereal bodies converged, and as we did it pushed the tombstone close into my face and I saw.

There was a shock as though I had been caught in a whiplash. It flung me back into my earthly body.

I sat bolt upright in bed and screamed.

*   *   *

"You heard what I said, Flute!"

"But, mum . . . the money . . . the time . . . the trees!"

"Money is no object. Time is short and the trees can wait under such circumstances."

"Beggin' your pardon, mum, but the master should be informed if you wants to do such a thing."

"No!" I cried, alarmed. "No, he must not hear of this until I know for certain what is written on that damnable tombstone. Gather what field workers you have managed to muster; promise them extra wages if you must, but have the west paddock ruin broken down, moved, and piled against the south wing as soon as possible."

He hesitated but momentarily. "As you wish, mum." He nodded curtly and left the study, muttering in his short beard.

I stared at the door for some time. The insolence of the man. He thought me mad. But I had seen a name being cut into that tombstone, which was still partially a void. The thought it would eventually be my husband's name drenched me with anguish; the thought it would be my own filled me with a fear that impelled me to know, and the only way to do that was to complete the ghost.

Within a week the ruin had disappeared from the west paddock and had been piled close in pyramids about the south wing of the house; every block transported by cart, every stone, fist-size rock, and sweeping of dirt. The fruit trees, as Flute had intimated, had begun to suffer through neglect, but I did not care.

Each night, as the work progressed, I ventured into the south wing with a lamp and as much courage as gnawing uncertainty would grant me. But the specter failed to manifest itself. Then on the night the day work was completed my persistence was rewarded for I saw it again in its far corner, chipping carefully away at the stone. I approached. It turned and I saw the face of a young man that still lacked part of the forehead. This puzzled me for an instant, making me think that week of toil with the ruin's stone had been in vain, that it had not completed the ghost as I had expected. It was then I realized that the ghost *was* complete, for it included in its countenance a hideous hammer wound. The thing grinned at me and seemed to mouth the word "soon." As before, the tombstone was pushed up into the lamplight, and at this the vision began to fade.

But not so quickly as for me to miss what was partially written there: "Reginald Willcroft, accidentally killed aboard . . ." and a date only four days hence.

"It must be done, Flute."

"Mrs. Willcroft, please. The plantation will not survive more neglect!"

"Oh. Don't you see, man!" I said, flinging my arms upward and wildly pacing the path beside the south wing pyramids. "If we take away the rock and stone we will undo our wrong. We brought it here in the stone, and we shall be rid of it likewise. I have seen it for what it is: not merely a harbinger but an instigator. All must be torn down and removed within four days. You will see to this at once, Flute."

"But the planting, mum. What will the master say about the—"

"Mr. Willcroft will thank me for what I am doing. Now go."

So he went, shaking his head, and I watching him with scorn. Was he so thick he could not see?

Summoning Mrs. Flute, I sent her into town to send a telegram to my husband, via his shipping office in London and to be lodged at his next port of call, imploring him to leave his vessel at once lest the ghost's threat come to pass.

Later, while watching from the study window, I saw the woman, accompanied by her husband, leave for town in the cart. Why, I wondered, was Flute going with her? He had work to do here.

By the time I got outside they were far down the drive, and though I called and called they did not heed.

There was no one working to remove the stone at the south wing. In ones and twos the staff existed the house, carrying their belongings. "What is this?" I demanded. "Gather those able and we shall pull the wretched building down ourselves." They too did not heed, but only afforded me pitying glances or looks usually reserved for growling dogs.

I stared at their retreating backs until I was alone in the grounds of Willcroft. Alone with the house and its ghost.

I rushed to the gardener's shed. I threw tools out through the door in my fervor to find something with which to bring down the piles of stone, demolish the wall.

The sledgehammer felt heavy in my hands, but my resolve was stronger. I hefted the thing two-handed and hurried across the courtyard. Within moments I was battering the wall with all my strength, praying that I might at least dent the entity's power and let it know fear.

At sunset I heard from within the south wing the beginning of that familiar, that hateful *chip, chip, chip* of chisel against stone.

Late in the night a carriage came hurtling down the drive and I wept with joy. Flute hadn't deserted me after all. I puffed with exertion and let the sledgehammer fall from my now blistered hands. It would soon be a powerful weapon in Flute's gnarled hands.

Grim-faced, Flute jumped from the carriage. Two members of the constabulary strode purposely by his side.

"Flute?" My voice sounded childlike. Confusion rode me like a dervish.

"That be her," Flute said.

"We'd like a word with you at the station, Mrs. Willcroft," one of the constables said, taking me gently but firmly by an elbow. "We have a telegram from Mr. Willcroft."

"I don't understand, Flute. A telegram from my husband?" I looked from one man to the next, but saw nothing but pity. And perhaps a little fear.

"We have an order for your arrest," the same constable continued.

Before I could demand an explanation, they manhandled me to the carriage and manacled me to the rear seat.

"Flute!" I screamed. "The south wing! Tear it down before it's too late!"

Flute stood stock still with arms akimbo as the carriage rattled down the drive. My screams were meaningless things.

As midnight approached, I watched the sky turn to a deepest black, heralding the coming storm. I had stopped screaming by then, had stopped pummeling at the brick walls of the outhouse where I had been incarcerated.

Even here, many miles from Willcroft, despite the rattle of the rain on the outhouse tin roof, I can hear that jarring chisel cutting the last of the tombstone inscription.

Only now it sounds more like nails being driven into my husband's coffin.

Seers

Brian Stableford

𝕸iss McCann was glad when she saw that the new people in number two had girls. She felt comfortable with girls, but not with boys. She'd been one of three sisters herself, never had a brother. In her experience, boys nowadays were rude and worse than rude; Colin from number eleven swore at her constantly, even though he was only ten, and she had a strong suspicion that Terry from number fifteen and his acne-stricken friend Jason from Smallwood Street had been responsible for the break-in she'd suffered last year. In the old days she could have had a quiet word with a young burglar's parents, but these days the parents were as bad as the kids. Terry's Pete and Liz didn't even say hello when they went past, and she'd long since given up saying hello to them. These days, even the people who did return her hellos tended to say it shiftily, as if they'd much rather not.

Mr. and Mrs. Number Two would probably have said hello in their own scrupulous fashion, coming as they now did from the posh side of the street, but they never passed by in a manner that permitted hellos. They were a two-car family—which was only natural, given that number two had recently been converted into a double-garage house—and they never seemed to go anywhere on foot. He had a silver Saab and she had a dark-red Citroën. Not that Miss McCann disapproved of that; at least they were *sensible* cars, not showing-off cars like the ones the last-but-one Mr. and Mrs. Number Two had had. She hadn't been at all surprised when they got divorced—but you had to feel sorry for the kids, even for the boy.

For the first couple of weeks, Mrs. Number Two ferried the girls to school in the Citroën, but then she stopped. By that time Mrs. Forde next door, who knew Mrs. Parris the cleaner, had found out that Mr. and Mrs. Number Two were called Mike and Milly Sandall, and that the girls were Natalie and Gwen. He worked for a firm of building contractors whose offices were in Hammersmith, although he spent a lot of time on sites scattered across three counties; she worked in the Halifax—or what had been the Halifax when it was still a proper building society—in Wokingham. The reason Milly had stopped driving the girls to school was that she had to drop them off half an hour early in order to get to work on time and they'd convinced her that it was safer—or nicer, anyway—to walk there in their own good time than to hang about in the playground.

Miss McCann started saying hello to the girls even before they started walking to school, because they'd always walked back, but it wasn't until she started seeing them mornings as well that they relaxed into the routine of it. She could tell that Natalie was only replying because she'd been brought up to be polite to old ladies, but Gwen actually smiled sometimes. It was easy to see that Natalie was the star of the family and that Gwen walked in her shadow. It wasn't because Natalie was older or prettier, simply that she was star material, while Gwen . . .

From the very beginning, Gwen reminded Miss McCann of herself. Among Miss McCann's sisters, Linda had been the star while Jennie had been the sergeant-major. Miss McCann didn't know quite how to characterize herself. Being a seer didn't count, because that wasn't a family thing at all; it wasn't something that defined her relationship with other people, merely something within herself.

Miss McCann didn't suspect Gwen of being a seer at first—smiling was no clue at all—but after a while, she began to get an indefinable inkling of it. Maybe it was something in the way Gwen looked round when she and Natalie walked past the graveyard in the shadow of St. Anne's, or maybe it was something in the way she faded a little when Natalie criticized her in the presence of other schoolfriends while they were walking home, as Natalie sometimes did when she thought Gwen wasn't being bright enough or brave enough in her manner and her conversation. One way and another, though, Miss McCann soon picked up the impression that Gwen was even more like her than she had thought at first. It didn't bring them together in any measurable way, but there were the smiles, and if ever Miss McCann saw Gwen when Natalie wasn't with her, there were a few brief words of the kind of conversation which was somehow full even when it was empty.

Miss McCann hadn't known that there was anything to see at number two, of course. She'd been in every odd-numbered house on the street at one time or another, but she'd never been in two, four, or six. The odd-numbered houses two-up-two-downs blocked into a single terrace, and the fact that the neighborhood estate agent had started referring to them as "artisans' cottages" whenever one of them went back on to the market didn't fool anybody; the even-numbered houses had been built between the wars, when commuters and dormitory towns had first been invented, to house people of a very different kind. The two sides of the road didn't mix, except for Mrs. Parris the cleaner. Mrs. Parris had never said anything to Mrs. Forde about goings-on, but that wasn't surprising; Mrs. Parris couldn't see for looking, even with her bespectacled eyes. If any of the people who'd occupied number two during the last fifty-odd years had ever seen anything, they'd sensibly kept it to themselves.

It would have been sensible of Gwen to do likewise, and sensible of Miss McCann to let her, but that simply wasn't the way things went. It wasn't anybody's fault.

It was only natural, of course, that Gwen should bring her questions to Miss McCann. It wasn't just that she said hello to Miss Mc-Cann, and smiled; it was the fact that Miss McCann was the oldest inhabitant of the street—the only rock that had resisted the tides of time and fortune since the dismal days when the street had only had one gently hissing lamp, fueled by coal gas, and the middle of the road was perpetually perfumed by horseshit.

Gwen was subtle about it, of course. She was fourteen, after all. Even in Miss McCann's day, girls who hadn't mastered all the arts of misdirection by the time they hit fourteen were entitled to be regarded as freaks of nature. She began by leaning on Miss McCann's gatepost one warm Sunday afternoon, watching her while she watered the begonias in her windowbox. She made five dutifully innocuous remarks before casually springing her trap.

"Did anything ever *happen* in our house, a long time ago?" she asked.

Miss McCann put down the watering can and wiped her hands on her apron. "What sort of thing?" she asked, although she knew perfectly well.

"Anything. Anything unusual, that is. Natalie heard that there might have been a murder, or a suicide . . . but she might just have been trying to scare me. She does, sometimes."

Miss McCann was sure that Natalie hadn't said anything of the sort, although that the last part was probably true. Jennie and Linda had often tried to scare her, and had often succeeded.

"No," Miss McCann said positively. "Nobody was ever murdered in that house, and no one ever committed suicide. If they had, I'd have known about it."

"But somebody must have died there."

"Why must they?"

"It stands to reason," was all Gwen could come up with. "It's been there for ages. Not everybody dies in hospital, even now."

Miss McCann knew perfectly well how many people had died in number two, but she also knew perfectly well that it wasn't a relevant issue. Dad had died in her own house, and had spent an intolerably long time doing it, but she'd never caught a glimpse of him since. Dying in a place obviously had nothing to do with it. Nor had being buried—ghosts were occasionally to be seen in St. Anne's churchyard, but they weren't the ghosts of the people in the graves. She had no proof, but she was pretty sure that they were visitors.

That didn't signify anything either; when *she* went visiting, she wasn't mourning or "paying her respects." She wasn't sure what she *was* doing, but it wasn't either of those things.

Later, Miss McCann reflected that it had been a mistake to think about the graveyard, given the way that one thing could lead to another, but at the time she was thinking about Gwen, and about Gwen being a seer, and about the possibility of helping her just a little.

"I've got to go to St. Anne's," she said to Gwen, ducking the question about people who had died in number two. "You can walk with me if you want. I'll just get my coat."

"It's not cold," Gwen pointed out. Gwen wasn't wearing a coat. "Anyway, you've missed church." Mike and Milly didn't go to church, unless you believed what Mrs. Forde said about the Safeways on the trading estate being a Temple of Mammon. They probably went there on Sundays because it was crowded on Saturdays. Most once-a-week car-shoppers had stuck to their old habits in spite of the relaxation of the Sunday trading laws.

Miss McCann didn't go to church either; it had seemed such a precious freedom to be able to stop, once Dad was gone. That, at least, was one thing Mum had never cared about.

"I'll get my coat anyway," Miss McCann said. "It's just habit. When you get to my age, habits set in. You don't have to come with me if you don't want to."

"I want to," Gwen said. "I want you to tell me about the house— about people who lived in it a long time ago."

Miss McCann took her coat from the peg. Later, she was to wonder whether she'd hung up her common sense in its place, but at the time she thought she was building herself up to be kind.

Miss McCann was careful while they walked along the avenue, and while they walked through the churchyard. Gwen asked a few more leading questions, but she evaded them easily enough. When they got to the graves, though, she immediately took a different tack.

"That's my mother and father," she said, pointing out the twin headstones. "That's my Aunt Bet, and over there by the tree's my grandfather Bill Weatherly. There's three more Weatherlys over there, including Bill's brother Fred and his wife, and there's supposed to be a dozen more farther over, only the stones have gone. Even gravestones don't last, you know. Everything fades away, given time."

"Why aren't there any more McCanns?" Gwen wanted to know.

"Dad came from Ayrshire, settled here for the work. He was on the canal, then on the railway. Always in transport, he used to say, and never made but one journey in his life. Not true—he was in the war, went to France, was wounded at some place called Chemin-des-Dames . . . Primrose Path, he always used to call it, the way others used to say Wipers and Passiondale. He was spotting for the guns, caught a stray shell from behind. Always said he still had shrapnel in his shoulder, but it was just his imagination, and lingering pain that came out in the rain like rheumatism. I never knew what to call it until that war in the Middle East a few years ago. Friendly fire, that's what got him. Didn't stop him outliving Mum by twenty years, though—look there, see: died August 4th, 1969. Would have been eighty if he'd hung on till October. Mum was fifty-six. High blood pressure. Worry, she said. That's got a different name nowadays too. Stress, they call it. *Distress*, I call it. She was a holy terror, was Mum. There's no more room there now, of course. Time was Dad wanted to keep the plot next along, but Jennie wouldn't have it. Jennie was my elder sister—she had three of her own, but they're all grown up. Lives in St. Albans. Linda went to Australia, back when it was fashionable. Sends Christmas cards. Linda was the middle one, the pretty one. Probably still is. I bet she dyes her hair."

Gwen endured this long speech with the infinite patience of one well used to deferring to adults desirous of making long speeches, but she was quick enough to return to her own agenda. "Is there anybody here from my house?" she demanded.

"Not one," Miss McCann was able to tell her truthfully. "All those Weatherlys were people who stayed put, but there aren't any people who stay put anymore. They move on, and on. Everybody in the street bought their houses but me. I'm the only inheritor. Nobody ever lived in my house except my family." She hesitated, but only briefly, before saying: "Sometimes, I think they're still there. Sometimes, I see Mum out of the corner of my eye. Not Dad—but he was a McCann. It's really a Weatherly house, see—around here is the place of the Weatherly dead."

While Miss McCann was driveling on she was looking into Gwen's eyes in search of some sign that she'd touched a chord. What she saw was that she'd been rumbled. Somehow, Gwen knew that she knew. It wasn't as simple as one seer recognizing another, nor as consoling; it was altogether more anxious than that.

"I got Natalie to swap bedrooms," Gwen said unhappily. "Let *her* see it, I thought. Serve her right. But she never did, and I *still* do, even though she couldn't possibly have died in *both* rooms. She's following me, and it's not fair. I can't tell Natalie, because she'd laugh, and I can't tell Mum and Dad because they'd make a fuss of *understanding* and send me to the school counselor. I thought at least you might know who she was."

Miss McCann noted that Gwen didn't seem particularly surprised that her elderly neighbor was the kind of person who saw ghosts. She was evidently certain that her parents were the kind of people who didn't, couldn't, and wouldn't see ghosts—or even entertain the possibility of their being seen, in any real sense—but she obviously took it for granted that Miss McCann was cut from commoner, more superstitious clay.

"How old is she?" Miss McCann asked. "Have you noticed what she's wearing?"

"About your age," Gwen told her. "Mostly, she wears dark green. Something heavy, but not thick like velvet. I don't see all of her, but she's not *transparent*, like some people say ghosts are. Not solid, but . . . well, as if she were *flat*. And there's something weird . . . you know people say about paintings that their eyes can *follow you round the room* . . ."

"That would probably be Mrs. Trevithick," Miss McCann interrupted her. "Lived in number two way back, during the second war.

Son in the navy, daughter a land girl over Twyford way. Both lived through it, married—daughter right there in that old monstrosity. Nice woman, but always a bit feeble. Thirty years earlier she could have been a full-time invalid, but that wasn't respectable any longer. Nerves was what they called it then. Hadn't invented hypochondria—or if they had, they hadn't told old Dr. Ross."

"Old" Dr. Ross, she remembered with a pang, had been ten years younger than she was now when he had his heart attack. An ugly man, but not as ugly as the "old monstrosity" of a church. She'd never been able to understand why they built it like that when St. Luke's over the river had been built ten years earlier and looked *much* smarter. It hadn't had anything to do with money—something called the Gothic revival. She sometimes heard strangers cooing over it: church-spotters, she always called them, by analogy with the young lads who used to hang over the railway bridge agitating over engine numbers in the days when the trains ran on steam.

"Did Mrs. Trevithick die in the house?" Gwen asked, still relentlessly barking up the wrong tree.

Miss McCann stared down at her mother's grassy grave. She couldn't remember the time when it had been freshly dug, nor ever having seen flowers on it.

"I've known a lot of people said they'd seen ghosts, Gwen," Miss McCann told her, speaking as softly as she could. "Most of them were fools or liars, but not all. There's others like you and me. Some of them think it's a gift and call it *second sight,* one or two think it's a curse—but they're all just fools, feeding on their own pride or their own fear. The only thing I ever learned from listening to them—the only thing there was to be learned, unless I'm the fool— is that each and every one of them borrowed the stories and the explanations that suited them best, to make sense of what they saw. I can't say whether I'm much different. I like to think that I am, but I dare say the others thought the same. What I can say, though, for sure, is that haunts have nothing to do with murders or suicides, or even deaths in the house. That's all storytelling and dressing up, to make things seem more interesting. It's like fishermen talking about the ones that got away—everything has to be *more so,* or it doesn't seem worth talking about. Everyone who sees ghosts wants to make them more than they are, but if you'll trust the word of an old woman you can take it from me that they're just *echoes*."

"Echoes?" said Gwen, sounding like an echo herself. She was facing the east wall of the church, and the word bounced back off it, almost as if the old monstrosity had a sense of humor.

"They don't do anything and they don't mean anything," Miss McCann went on. "They're just things left over, which some people can see and others can't, but which don't mean a thing. Understand what I'm saying, Gwen? *They can't do you any harm.* Flat is what they are, all right: flat like shadows, like rainbows, like the colored sheen on oily rainwater running in the gutter. A trick of the light. There's no need at all to be frightened, and no need at all to tell anyone else what you see, if you don't want to or if you think they won't take it right. It doesn't *mean* anything. It's just echoes."

On the whole, Miss McCann was pleased with the speech. It was the best she could do, and she didn't think anyone cleverer could have done much better. In 1955 or 1935 it might even have worked a treat, but Gwen was a child of a new generation and she probably did Shakespeare at school. Miss McCann looked into the girl's contemplative eyes, and she could see the judgment contained there.

Methinks the lady doth protest too much.

Whenever she heard that line quoted in a TV show, always as a joke, it sent a peculiar shiver down Miss McCann's spine.

"What happened to Mrs. Trevithick?" Gwen asked, still searching for something that would make sense *for her.*

"She and her husband bought a bungalow in Bournemouth," Miss McCann told her. "A retirement home, they call it these days. I never heard any more of them after that. Died long ago, I should think, but not here. Nowhere near here."

"So why is she haunting me?"

Not "haunting the house," Miss McCann observed, but "haunting *me.*"

"She isn't," Miss McCann told her, trying her damnedest not to protest too much. "She's just an echo. She's not even a *she*, not really. It's an image, not a person. It can't see you, you know. You must believe that. Even if the eyes do seem to follow you around the room, they can't see you. There's no intelligence there, no mind at all. Please believe me, Gwen—I know there are some people who say different, who believe different, but *I know*. It's just something left over from the past, like a piece of old newspaper or a thread of old cotton. You can see her, but she can't see you, any more than she could if she were a photograph you kept on the bedside table."

Trying her damnedest hadn't worked. Perhaps the great looming mass of St. Anne's was defeating her dogged attempt to achieve matter-of-factness. She could see Gwen's staring eyes reading between the lines.

Or could she?

After a long pause, Gwen said: "Will I see ghosts wherever I go, from now on?"

"Perhaps," Miss McCann told her reluctantly. "I don't know. It's said that some people lose the gift, but I don't know."

"A puberty thing, you mean," Gwen muttered. Milly must have talked to her about *puberty things*, as carefully as she could, but Gwen still spoke the words in a shamefaced whisper. She couldn't help it.

"Maybe."

"Are you a miss because you never got married, Miss McCann?" Gwen asked. She blushed as she said it because she knew it might be a direly undiplomatic thing to say, in the circumstances—but she wanted to know, so she blurted it out anyway.

"I've heard it said that some girls lose the gift when they marry," Miss McCann admitted, treading on eggshells. "I think it happens, sometimes. I certainly didn't stay single because I wanted to keep it. I had to look after Dad when Mum became ill, you see. It was expected. Spinsters and maiden aunts were two a penny in those days—it wasn't such an unusual thing to be. Someone had to look after Dad, and I was the one. Jennie was always going to leave home as soon as she could, and Linda . . . well, she was the pretty one. I was always bottom of the heap, you see: the extra one, the one that turned two's company into three's crowd. My house is only a two-up-two-down, you see. We didn't have separate bedrooms like you and Natalie. We were always in one another's pockets, always about one another's business, always running poor Mum ragged and being shouted at, always crammed in like wriggling sardines, always . . . well, let's just say that you and Natalie have *space*, in a way we never had. You're *separate*, in a way we never were. It's difficult to explain, but it was always going to be the way it was. Someone had to look after Mum and Dad when Mum got ill, and then look after Dad, the way Mum would have if the worry hadn't killed her, and go from spinster to maiden aunt to old maid. Nobody decided—it all just *was*. It doesn't have anything to do with my being a seer." *Not in the way you mean, anyway*, she refrained from adding.

Gwen digested as much of that as she could, and seemed to have taken some consolation from it. At any rate, she didn't want to dwell on *puberty things* any longer than she had to. She'd grabbed what reassurance she could on that score.

"Are there ghosts in there?" Gwen asked, pointing at the gloomy facade of St. Anne's.

"Sometimes I see them out here," Miss McCann said, "but they're nothing to be afraid of. All you have to do is look away. All you'll ever have to do is look away. You don't have to let it make any difference to your life."

Gwen looked up at her, weighing the words; she nearly said something else, but she thought better of it. Perhaps she thought she'd given away far too much already. Miss McCann wondered if she'd still smile next time she said hello.

"Let's go back now," Miss McCann said. "Your parents might be wondering where you've got to." She no longer thought that bringing the girl to the graveyard had been a good idea, but what alternative had she had? Where else could they have gone to talk between themselves, except indoors?

Later Miss McCann wondered whether it might have been better to say nothing at all, to have stood her ground in the narrow space between the gate and the door, answering the girl's questions in such a bland way that Gwen would never have guessed. But how could it be better, in the long run, for a girl like that to go on thinking that she was all alone, that she might be mad, or that the ghosts might indeed be haunting *her*? Wasn't it better to offer what reassurances she could? Wasn't it better to try to help her understand?

Such doubts took a little of the taste away from her evening meal, and made it difficult to concentrate on the TV—not that that mattered, given that most TV shows were designed for people who weren't concentrating, especially the ones she habitually watched. It wasn't until she got into her nightdress, though, and took herself off to bed that she really began to worry.

She'll be all right, she told herself. *She's a bright girl, from a sensible family. Things aren't the way they used to be in the old days. She probably has boyfriends already. She certainly has her own space, her privacy. Anyway, kids these days take things in their stride. Drugs at the school gate, computers, holidays in Florida, school counselors, GCSEs. How can a few leftover images, glimpsed from the corner of an eye, get in the way of all that? She can cope. I'll be here to talk whenever she wants to. She'll trust me. In the end, she'll see that what I tell her is the truth, the whole truth, and nothing but the truth. She's bright enough. She'll be all right.*

All the while, Mum was hovering just out of sight, just beyond the scope of the corner of her eye. Miss McCann couldn't see her at all tonight, and she knew perfectly well that what she'd have seen, if she'd seen anything at all, would be just a stray image dislodged in time, just a meaningless trick of the light, whose inescapable gaze was utterly blind, utterly devoid of sense or censure.

Even so, she couldn't help but mutter, as she turned over to face the wall and huddled within her blankets: "It's all right, Mum, I'm not doing anything. I'm not doing anything at all."

And even though the house was empty, with nothing left inside it but space, and even though the words were true, and had been for as long as she could remember, she couldn't raise her voice above a whisper.

Even in the soundless privacy of her imagination, she couldn't raise her voice above a whisper.

Unexpected Attraction

Matthew J. Costello

𝕴 guess the house—at first— underwhelmed her.

Connie took one look at the Revolutionary-era structure, surrounded by overgrown sumac and chaotic brambles that looked on the verge of storming the boxlike domicile, and she said, "Puh-lease."

"You don't like it?"

I phrased it as a question, but there wasn't any doubt.

Connie had no trouble communicating her likes . . . and dislikes.

After I stopped the car, she made no attempt to get out.

"*This* is the best you could do?"

"For the money . . . yes. It meets a lot of our criteria. . . ."

"Like what—filled with wormwood and dry rot? More animals *inside* than out?"

I tuned to her, seeing her pretty face locked into an impassive, fortresslike expression, daring me to mount an assault on her negativity.

"You haven't seen inside. It's amazing. It was built a year after the Revolution."

"By the winners or the losers?"

"And the floors. You love natural wood, and these floorboards are half a yard wide."

"Be still my heart."

I dared to reach out and touch her arm. Touching didn't come so easy for us. That's why were were here, after all. To see if a bit of seclusion could make our marriage work, to get the pieces back into place.

Oddsmakers in Vegas would have called it a long shot.

There was another reason, though. We were down to one income—hers—and the loft and the city "lifestyle" had to go. This dilapidated rental was our best, and last, shot.

"At least take a look at it."

Only then did Connie turn and look at me. There was no change in her expression. But she was playing fair. I imagine that she felt much as I did . . . the play was over and this was just the epilogue. Connie and Mark's final breakup.

I pictured the next few weeks, the slow disintegration, the inexorable eroding of the last vestiges of a marriage. It happens. Sure, just like you can find yourself kicked out of Goldman Sachs and absolutely nobody in Wall Street wants you.

This was a mercy mission for Connie. Let's not give Mark *all* the bad news at once.

Sure, I pictured the next few weeks.

Needless to say, I got it all wrong.

I liked the house. The floorboards were as described (though the cracks between the planks were big enough for one of those plump black ants to crawl through with ease). And, as I enjoyed pointing out to Connie, structurally the house was in tiptop shape.

"Right—at least it has indoor plumbing," Connie said, in what passed for wit in our Revolutionary abode.

Of course, she expected me to work on the place while she commuted into Manhattan scoring our one paycheck.

And I did make some attempts in that direction. I loved the kitchen, dominated by a giant hearth that could easily accommodate a roast pig, were one available. The dining room was a dismal and dark room, and the small oak table that sat in the room looked better suited for deals with Beelzebub than elegant dinners.

It was upstairs that I found myself spending most of my time. The master bedroom was the same size as the other two rooms. "Master" was a completely arbitrary designation.

The upstairs rooms had small windows and screens with gaping holes to accommodate whatever flying insect might like to come in for a visit or a nibble. There was no upstairs bathroom, but there was an oversize linen closet . . . at least we assumed it was a linen closet.

My head nearly brushed the ceiling on the first floor. Upstairs, my hair *did* actually touch the ceiling, making me feel like one of those amusement park bumper cars clawing at the electricity on the roof.

For some reason, I liked it up there, and not just when I was sleeping.

While waiting for the SNET to come and set us up with phone service, I walked from room to room, listening to the creak of the wood, the sound of my steps, enjoying how wonderfully *old* this place was.

I made plans to paint. To strip some wood. To replace the screens.

I did none of it.

Connie came home. We ate quietly together. We talked about her work. And she, after the first week, tactfully avoided any discussion of my day.

What was there to say?

Honey, I looked out the south window and saw two chipmunks arcing around. Or, I started a fire in the hearth and, hey, it *works*. We can cook in it. I mean, for those times when we don't want to use the stove. I'll go kill a wild turkey, or maybe I'll trade with the Pompsqautch Indians for some elk meat.

I guess, if I had been able to afford therapy, a trained outside observer would have pointed out the obvious.

You sir, are de-pressed. You are down for the count. You are non-functional. I recommend daily sessions, and no, you may not call me at home. And by the way, is your lovely wife available for an illicit affair? I mean, since you, quite obviously, can't—

Connie went to bed early nearly every evening. After all, she did have that 6:37 train to catch.

I was up until midnight, sometimes trying to watch the two pitiful Connecticut UHF stations we could get on our TV. (We both had decided that cable was not an option. It was a way of punishing ourselves, or me at least, for having no work and no money.)

By the time I went to bed, Connie was a dark sleeping (need I say unresponsive) shape in the small dark bedroom.

In a way, it was like living alone.

But like they always say on the *700 Club* . . . you're never really alone.

At least, *I* wasn't.

The first time it happened I was dead asleep.

And I heard something.

Now, we've all heard noises in the night. Some odd sound that wakes us up, stirs us out of the world of dreams and nightmares to that wonderful place known as 2:30 A.M.

First you lie there, waiting. It was nothing, you think. There was no sound.

I can go back to sleep.

That's what happened this night.

And since sleep was the place I felt most content, most at home in the universe, I had no problem burrowing quickly back to REM land.

Which is when I heard the fatal *second* noise. Now, this is, of course, the noise that throws all of one's switches. At the second sound you have to admit that, hey, there *was* a noise. And, golly, said noise was loud enough to wake me up. And more . . . I'll have to listen *very* carefully now, to determine—in a scientific fashion—just what the hell the sound was and where was it coming from.

It's raccoons at the garbage.

Or it's a squirrel on the roof. Or it's the wind, that pesky wind blowing shit at the house. Sure, that's what it is.

Except, with the third sound, I knew that—no, it wasn't the garbage, wasn't little feet on the roof. No, this noise was someone walking around downstairs.

Inside the house.

My body felt icy. My assorted limbs seemed not to belong to me. There was no way they'd move if I gave them the order. No, they'd rebel. Hell, no, Captain, we're not moving your lazy ass out of bed and downstairs.

I hoped that there would be no fourth or fifth sound. I'd could go back to a monitoring state. I wouldn't have to really *do* anything.

But there was another sound, the slow groaning creak of one of those giant floorboards.

The mad killer was downstairs. Soon to come up, where he would slowly torture me while raping Connie . . . or slowly torture Connie while raping me.

I gave the bad news to the troops.

I slid my legs out from under the sheets, down to the cool floor, wishing I had a baseball bat and a flashlight. And having neither, I slowly made my way to the hall.

My own creaks sang out a warning that, I hoped against hope, would send the mad killer running. God, no, the killer would think: Someone is coming. And they have feet!

Halfway down the stirs, I devised a plan.

When I was nearly at the bottom, I would call out.

Hey, you. I'm here. You better go. 'Cause I'm here.

I'd wait then, give the hapless multiple murderer time to run out the back door . . . so I could get to the phone and call the trusty Connecticut State Police.

And that's what I hoped would happen.

I stopped four steps from the bottom. And God, did they make houses dark back then. And why hadn't we put in some night-lights . . . the gloom was positively stygian.

I hesitated. Who wouldn't hesitate? In the manner of an old London bobby, I called out "Hel-lo . . ."

Which is when I saw her.

Now, before I proceed to detailing what happened in the next few minutes, a few words of background may be in order.

My relationship with my wife had, for many, many weeks now, perhaps months, been completely free of the shackles of any physical demands. In other words, I was, in a rather diffuse and disoriented way, quite horny.

Did that put me more on edge, make my nerve endings fire a bit too fast in the darkness and gloom of that boxy house? Sure it's possible.

But what happened next, really happened, I assure you.

A woman *appeared*. She was dressed in a flowing gown—of course—a gown that was nearly a sheer and gossamer as her flesh. She glowed like a lightning bug on a July evening.

And I wasn't scared.

Who'd be scared looking at someone so beautiful? Later I'd learn her name (Monica) and her sad history. I'd learn how her husband killed her one night for a suspected and falsely accused infidelity . . . and how she has wandered the house ever since.

But that night, that sweet first night, there was no time for talk.

She embraced me in all her firefly brilliance, and, despite a slight chill, I felt her touch. It had been many miles between such caresses.

"I've been watching you," she said. (Yes, she spoke, in a voice that sounded as normal as yours and mine, except for a slight Kathleen Turner huskiness that was, well, absolutely thrilling.)

Her gown rippled behind her as she led me into the living room where, on the aforementioned plank boards, I had an experience, that I'm sure, few have dreamt of.

I was in love. Immediately. And with love comes complications.

The big complication here was my wife.

The marriage was over, that was obvious. We had even launched a preliminary discussion of how we'd proceed—in a civilized way—to legally ending our relationship. And that all seemed fine for me.

Except for a small problem.

I had no job, no income. I was completely dependent on Connie. And worse, Connie was now having trouble at work. Her position looked as if it might shortly be excessed. She explained that we'd have to leave this Revolutionary abode, split up . . . she probably back to the Big Apple, job hunting, and a life. As for me, where would I go? My Uncle Henry's bee farm in Somers?

As I said, love brings complications.

My paramour, my dream goddess, the woman who now meant the universe to me on a nightly basis, was unfortunately trapped in this house, locked here by some act, some chain of events that we never had time to get into in any detail (at least not in those early, heady days).

And Connie, an organizational juggernaut, proceeded with the plans for the divorce and for our forced imminent departure from the house. During the early evenings, when I'd leave the house to give Connie some "space," I began to panic.

As each night brought new heights of wonder, as skin touched ectoplasm, as I became totally lost in a sea of otherworldly caresses, I told Monica about the problem.

"I'm going to lose you," I said (not once questioning the intelligence of talking to a ghost).

Her face changed. Here was, er, a spirited woman who didn't brook frustration well.

"No," Monica said. "I *can't* lose you. You've become everything to me."

I nodded. Monica was everything to me. But then, I didn't have much. The only difference between Monica and me was that she was dead. Other than that, we were both without any worldly ties.

Except for Connie.

Now, usually in a situation like this jealousy might rear its head. But that wasn't a problem here, No, there was no love between Connie and I . . . just my terror that I'd lose the house, and with the loss of the house (and, God, maybe new people moving in) therein lay my terror.

Once Monica said, "Maybe some nice man will buy the house."

"No," I said. But Monica drifted away. She'd float in the air in the most disconcerting way, a symbol of her sudden change of mood. When she got really annoyed, I'd watch her glow fade, until she was no more than a dusky near-smoke hanging in the room, like air mites caught by the moonlight.

"You will lose me," she said coldly, matter-of-factly.

Then she was gone, letting me ponder such a fate.

The solution, surprisingly enough, came from me.

"What if," I said only weeks before the house was to be vacated by me, "what if Connie died?"

Now, I had never killed anyone. I was not a cold-blooded person, but you have to understand the adolescent intensity that possessed me. It was, I imagined, what being hooked on crack as like. I'd do anything to keep Monica.

Monica smiled when I mentioned the idea. After all, death held no terrors for her.

"Explain," she said, brushing my longish hair off my forehead, seemingly pleased with my brainstorm.

"Well, Connie and I both have insurance, *tons* of insurance. What if something happened to her, what if she died?"

Monica drifted closer, the living cloud. Her ghost fingers caressed my cheek, then trailed to my lips. "Go on, clever boy."

"If Connie died, I'd get the money. We've done nothing to change beneficiaries, not yet."

"And you could buy this house!" Monica grabbed my feverish head in her two cool hands and planted a big kiss on my lips.

(Only then did I think that she seemed a bit too poised to embrace the idea, as if she had thought of it and only had to wait for me to catch up.)

The kiss sealed the idea. Then we needed a plan, and organizing the details consumed the next few nights . . . until the fateful evening arrived.

The day of the "event," I took an especially long afternoon walk, all the way to the Gas & Go near the Merritt Parkway. I bought some sugarless gum and a jumbo cup of café ordinaire, noir. It was going to be a long evening.

Which began, as most evening did, with Connie going to bed after a dinner of wilted lettuce and cherry tomatoes drowning in balsamic vinegar and the oil from thrice-squeezed virgins (or so ran my joke, which drew not even a smile from my soon-to-be ex-wife).

And while the idea of Connie's death originated with me, the plan was—mostly—Monica's.

"You live out here all alone," Monica purred. "Such a *lonely* house surrounded by dark trees. Wouldn't it be terrible if an intruder came one night, knife in hand . . . someone who'd leave muddy footprints, someone who'd steal some jewelry—"

"And the credit cards!" I improvised. Beautiful Monica nodded.

"And you are asleep downstairs . . . while the intruder makes his way up, to your wife's bedroom . . ."

"A-and he goes in and Connie wakes up, screams, and—"

"The terrible intruder with a knife panics and—"

Monica waited for me to pick up the ball. But I had a bit of trouble with this part of the story.

Monica repeated, "And he panics and—"

I licked my lips. I nodded.

"And the intruder kills her?" I said.

Monica clapped her hands. "Bravo! And on the way down, you wake up, and now *you* get stabbed too . . . but only enough to show how brave you were, to deflect any attention."

"You'll take care of that?"

Monica nodded. At that moment, I had the odd feeling that aspects of this setup weren't actually novel to her. But I was beyond questioning. Outside of the insurance policy, Connie meant nothing to me . . . while Monica meant everything.

That was the plan.

Or—so I thought.

Around 2 A.M. Monica *appeared*, gliding down the stairs to the living room.

She smiled at me.

"Your wife is asleep," she said.

I nodded. The knife, with a very sharp and very big blade, lay next to me. I wore my winter gloves, puffy mittens that were more suited for skiing than wife-slaying. But they were all I had.

"It's time," Monica said. She leaned forward, her gown seemingly more translucent for the occasion, and as goosebumps rose, she bathed me in surprisingly warmish kisses.

Primed and pumped, she pulled me to a standing position. "Soon there won't be anything to keep us apart."

I smiled.

I started up the steps. Now the moment became truly absurd . . . as I became the "dangerous stranger" walking up the steps, murder and mayhem on his mind. The boards on the steps creaked, begging for a gallon or two of linseed oil. I held the knife in my bear-paw mittens. The knife would be deadly . . . if it didn't slip out of my clumsy gloves.

I reached the hallway.

Monica was right behind me. I could smell her perfume, an intoxicating scent that ebbed and flowed, as if my ghost lover used it as a leash.

I breathed deep. The heady scent fortified me.

I started for the master bedroom.

I'd be less than honest if I didn't confess to some nervousness about phase two of the plan, namely my getting myself gingerly stabbed by the self-same imaginary "intruder." Monica said she'd take care of that, that a ghost can only hurt a living being when they *want* to be hurt (which neatly explained why Monica—who had nothing to lose—couldn't take care of Connie for me).

Still, the idea of getting cut by the same blade that would soon end my unfortunate wife's existence made me take those last few steps a bit more slowly.

Until—as in the "Tell Tale Heart"—I lingered by the doorway and peered into the black hole of a room.

I smelled Monica behind me.

Then, her lips close to my ear . . . "Go on . . ."

I whispered. "I can't see a damn thing."

The lips again, almost nibbling on a bottom lobe. "You *know* where she is."

Sure, Connie would be in the middle of the blackness, wrapped up in the sheets, a lump that would be hard to miss.

"Go on," Monica urged again.

I gave the door a push. And it creaked. I paused, letting my eyes adjust to the darkness, wanting to see if the creak made the lump— only now coming into view—stir. And when it didn't, I gave the door a final push, and the hinges gave out their last warning.

"Now!" Monica hissed.

And I ran into the room, raising the knife, the apprentice killer in action.

I fell on the bed, jabbing the blade down into the very center, where the lump would be curled unsuspecting.

When the bedroom light came on.

The lump on the bed was only pillows.

I turned.

And there was Connie, standing by the far wall, holding a small handgun aimed right at me. The first question I wanted to ask her was, "Hey, where'd *you* get a gun?"

I realized that this all looked pretty bad . . . the knife (now enmeshed in the bed springs), the mittens, the skulking around. I wanted to say, "Connie, I have an explanation for everything."

But I didn't have any explanation.

Monica was nowhere to be seen. So I couldn't use her as an excuse.

But I didn't have a lot of time to think about the embarrassing nature of my predicament.

The small gun that was aimed right at me exploded once, and then again. I felt all sorts of weird pain in my chest and midsection. Connie didn't shoot a third time.

I think she recognized that she didn't have to.

I didn't die immediately. I had a few minutes of blurry-eyed consciousness. Which, all things considered, was the only plus of the evening.

And what did I see in those precious few moments?

Something completely amazing and, I must admit, totally unexpected.

Connie stood there, smoking gun in hand, looking ever so much like a very noirish '40s gun moll. The gunsmoke hung in the air while she waited—I thought—to be sure I didn't need another lead plug to be down for the count.

(I had, up to then, given absolutely no thought as to the reason she seemed, well, *ready* for my entrance, and ready to kill me. But then with two big openings in my body, gushing ye olde vital fluids, I had more important things to think about.)

But in the last few blinks of earthly awareness, I saw the bluish smoke hanging in the air . . . and then, from the doorway, that gunsmoke was joined by something else equally gossamer and smoky. I couldn't turn around, but I could smell it. The perfume was painfully familiar.

And then I did get to see Monica drift close to Connie, wrap her arms around her, pull her close—and final image—give Connie a long, lingering kiss.

I had been set up in a not-quite classic lovers' triangle.

But then the curtains were drawn.

For a certain period.

The next thing I saw was the master bedroom. It was night. But I immediately knew it wasn't the same night. There was a full moon hanging out the window and, yes, sports fans, two bodies in the bed, at rest, I'm glad to say . . . though I imagined that they might have trysted the night away.

I moved closer to the bed.

My first thought was that it seemed as though considerable time had passed. How did I get here? Was this a dream? There were no bloodstains on the floor. They probably had been cleaned up after the police investigated Connie's quite reasonable charge that her demented husband tried to stab her.

Then I noted how I moved. There was no need for "steps," though my feet did kick and pump.

No, moving was easier . . . now that I was dead.

I realized why.

I held my hand up to my face—just to be sure. And I saw that my hand wasn't quite opaque. No, I could hold it up to the full moon and see right through my hand.

I was a ghost.

And having been given this second lease on life, I wasn't about to waste it.

In the stillness of that summer night, I tried my vocal chords to see if they still worked in this new incarnation.

"Good morning, campers! Sa-a-a-y, it's a beautiful evening here in the afterlife, and we're here twenty-four hours to bring you the very best poltergeist effects that money can buy!"

Connie shot up in bed and screamed.

I guess my reappearance was unexpected. Then Monica, a sister at heart, popped out of the bed like a doughy loaf of bread toasting to a golden brown.

"Go the hell away," Monica snarled, obviously understanding what was happening here.

I shook my head. I glided to the ceiling and stretched out, face-down, right over the bed of my unfaithful spouse. Monica hissed. Connie screamed and threw things—to no avail.

Me, I had a great time . . . until Connie left days later. My unexpected resurfacing obviously was enough to cool her ardor—and convince her that she didn't want to use the insurance money to buy the old rat trap of a haunted house.

I was a tad disappointed at that . . .

Until I realized that now I had *eternity* to drive Monica crazy.

And that gave me something to look forward to every night.

Mi Casa

Kathryn Ptacek

Anita Rodriguez stared out the window, but could see nothing but her reflection, almost watery in the glass. Dark hair pulled back severely, dark skin, dark eyes . . . dark, dark, dark . . . everything was so dark.

And darkness had come prematurely to the northern New Mexico mountains, blanketing everything with a wintry breath that even now puffed against the house, trying to get in.

She saw no other lights outside. How could she? The house was so far away from others that it might well have been the only one in the county.

Shivering, she turned away, the old lace curtain fluttering back into place. She hitched her shawl up around her shoulders, then settled on a low bench and picked up the book she had been trying to read for the past hour. She was still on page one.

Tears blurred her eyes. Swallowing rapidly, noisily, she studied the large room, almost Spartan in its simplicity. Whitewash covered the adobe brick walls, and there were only a few pieces of furniture: a plain bench, a chair with a high leather back, an immense double-doored wooden cabinet dating from the colonial Spanish days, and a weathered table with a carved *santo* atop it. The floor displayed a

Southwestern pattern of inlaid Mexican tiles in vivid turquoise and salmon and canary and beige. Two doors: one to the outside, one to the rest of the house. Light came from the pierced tin wall sconces, once holding candles but now electrified, and the *horno,* the rounded fireplace in the corner, where piñon logs crackled as they burned. From the hallway she heard the steady ticking of a clock. The door frames and windowsills, inside and out, were painted blue.

To guard against evil spirits, or so the tradition claimed.

But nothing would keep the spirits—the remembrances—out of the house. The pungent fragrance of the burning piñon alone was enough to make her cry, without all the memories crowding her tonight.

Softly the clock chimed, and she recalled the day her father had presented it to her mother. He had saved all year for it, this tenth-anniversary gift, and he was so proud of the beautiful walnut veneer grandfather clock with its silver embossing. And her mother's eyes had welled with tears and—no.

Why had she come back?

To escape?

Hardly.

Yet that was the precise reason Jerry had urged her to return home—to get away. Her mother had finally entered a nursing home, and Anita had wept long hours since, even though she knew there had been no choice.

"It's not really your decision any longer, hon," Jerry had said as he comforted her in his arms. He kissed the top of her head.

Anita had nodded against his chest, knowing he was correct; that she had done the right thing. And still the guilt and unhappiness flowed through her.

She could no longer do anything for her mother, who had lain so still in the bed with eyes closed, rarely responding to anyone's voice, nearly comatose, but not quite. Monitors and machines beeped, hissed and hummed, while tubes snaked and coiled out of the woman, and after a while Anita couldn't separate in her mind what was really part of her mother, what wasn't. Sometimes she thought she remembered her mother having the tubes coming out of her skin years ago, back when Anita was a child, but she told her-self that was nonsense. It was, wasn't it? But the memories from be-fore were fading, were changing, and she didn't like it.

Anita had done what she could to make her mother's life easier, and her brother and sister were not willing to help. In fact, they had proved quite vocal, informing her that they didn't want the old woman living with them. Their conversations had stayed with her all too well.

"Old woman?" Anita had said, not believing she'd heard the scorn in her siblings' voices. "That's our mother there."

"That's a shell," Raymond had said, his voice devoid of emotion. His eyes would not meet hers. "Nothing more, Nita."

"No," she'd whispered.

"Face it," Anna had said, "that hasn't been our mother since the accident. You know that—God knows, we've been telling you that for a year now. But you never listen to us; you never have, even when we were kids. It's for the best, you know."

"But—"

"No," Raymond had interrupted, holding up a hand. "We've al-ready heard all the arguments. There's nothing new you can tell us. And face it, Nita, you'll be better off with her in the nursing home. We all will. We can get on with our lives now."

After that, Anita knew they were right, that it was time for the professionals to take over, time for her mother to go where she would get around-the-clock treatment. It was time. Long past time.

Time . . . the clock ticked away. One, two, three, four, and she found she was breathing in rhythm with the pendulum. She held her breath for a moment, tried to break the rhythm, then almost laughed at the absurdity.

Time . . . one part of her wondered if she should have kept their mother just a little longer. What if she had abandoned her parent too soon? What if it had only taken a few weeks more, a month, two or three even . . . Time . . .

No. It was the right time; and she hadn't abandoned her mother. She hadn't. Really.

Even though she felt as if she had.

And so here she was, getting away to rest in her mother's house, getting away from the situation. The irony, of course, was that it was all she could think of.

It was all her life had turned into. Waiting for her mother to live, to die, to do something other than lie there so still.

No.

She wouldn't worry about her mother and the nursing home any longer. It had been done; the act was completed. There was no turning back.

The door and pane rattled against the force of the cold wind. The curtain trembled ever so slightly, as if something had breathed against it.

The clock ticked and ticked and ticked . . . ticking away her life, she thought.

She concentrated on the book, forcing herself to finish the paragraph and go on to page two. But again her mind wandered; her eyes lifted, glanced at the dark oblong window.

Something white pattered against it. She rose and glanced out, and saw snowflakes.

That was the problem with coming to this old place set in the foothills of the Sangre de Cristos, east of Santa Fe. Winter came so early here, painting the slopes white long before it ever reached the capital city. It was only mid-September, and yet it might as well have been the depths of December.

She had not thought she could take the time off—after all, she was a legislative assistant and the legislature was in session right now—but somehow Jerry had arranged it. He insisted she needed the time away, and her boss had agreed, and so she had come home.

To this house.

She remembered when there had been much more here, in this room—when it had been filled with the playful shouts and gleeful laughter of three energetic children, and the cheerful calls of their mother from the kitchen for them to wash up and come to dinner right away.

She remembered when Raymond, not more than nine or ten

years old, had drawn in bright red Crayola a picture of Father Martinez from the parish church on the wall; it had not been a flattering representation, but all their mother had done was chuckle and suggest that perhaps he might wish to use paper next time.

She remembered her mother sitting by the window the night they had learned that their father had walked out on them and would never be back. She, not even eleven, had gone to her mother and put her arms around her, her head resting on the dark one below hers, and the others had come to them and held their mother as well. So long ago.

Years before she had gone to the legislature, years before Raymond had bought his art gallery on Canyon Road, years before Anna had moved down to Albuquerque with her second husband.

Years before they had grown apart.

Tick, tick, ticking away . . .

She shook her head, sighed, then started when she heard a sharp bang in another room. She hurried down the darkened hallway and into the end bedroom—one of the casement windows had blown open, and the lace curtains stood straight back from the wind gusting snow across the sill. She rushed over and locked the window, batted away the damp curtain as it slapped against her cheek, then fetched a towel from the bathroom to wipe the snow up before it melted.

When she finished, she looked around the room, with its blue and white quilt on the wide bed, at the intricately carved pine chest set against one wall, at the painting of a Santa Fe church she had done when she was a teenager and had thought she wanted to be an artist. The room was so . . . bare . . . bare of furniture, of belongings, but not of memories.

Again she could close her eyes and recall so easily those days when her mother had let them climb into bed with her, and the three children had piled up onto its softness, then burrowed under the quilt while their mother told them tales of talking rabbits and squirrels. How warm and cozy—how safe—it had all been.

She forced herself to return to the front room, where she stood before the fireplace and held her hands out to the flames. She was so cold; maybe this would help.

The ticking sounded louder now.

Wind pounded against the door, and she stepped closer to the fire, as if seeking protection. Of course, that was nonsense, she thought when she realized what she'd done.

She shouldn't have come out here this time of the year, she told herself, not for the first time since her arrival. She should have waited for spring; but she couldn't. She'd had to get away now, before the weeks grew into months, the months into years, into decades.

Something white drifted across the floor, and she whirled around.

A snowflake.

It had sifted in through the crack under the door.

Ice crystals had formed on the window too, and she wondered how long the storm would last. Hours, perhaps; maybe even a day or two. She didn't worry about being stuck here, though, because Jerry knew where she was. He would come for her, if she needed him, if she couldn't get out in the morning.

Jerry. She smiled at the thought of her husband, then sat on the bench again to read. Another page gone by slowly, then she looked up as more snow drifted into the room.

The windows were not as tightly closed as they could be, she knew. Or rather, the old wood frames were warped from cold and heat and age; there was nothing to do but replace them, and perhaps she and Jerry could do that in the spring, when it was warm again.

It hadn't always been this cold, the house; once it had been warm and open. *Mi casa, su casa,* her mother had always proclaimed to friends and strangers alike. *My house is your house.* And their mother had never turned anyone away in all the years she had lived here.

Not like Anita. Anita had turned her mother away.

No, she told herself sharply as she bit back tears; she had not turned her mother away. Her brother and sister had done that; Anita at least had nursed her as best she could. And when it had grown too much, she had sought help. There was nothing wrong with that.

Was there?

Mi casa, su casa.

Yes; she had told her mother that very thing when the old woman had come to live with them after the accident, the accident that had left her paralyzed along one side and nearly speechless and her mind rambling, a wreck of the once-smiling and pleasant woman who had raised three children by herself. But it was Jerry's and her house, and her mother's.

And then, when the situation had grown too inconvenient, she had turned the old woman away.

No!

She shook her head, denying.

Mi casa—

There was a deep roaring, like a dark train barreling a hundred miles an hour or more along a steel track—the wind had become a gale. The walls of the house seemed to reverberate from its power, and she wondered if they and the roof could withstand the escalating wind, this blizzard. Surely, yes, because they had withstood so much else before.

Snow formed a powdery semicircle inside the door, and the windowsill was white. A trickle of water from melted flakes inched down the wall.

The temperature in the room had dropped in the past few minutes, and she shivered, then rubbed her arms briskly with her hands, but nothing would warm her. Not now.

The ticking of the clock dropped to a whisper, as if the clock were winding down. Slowing, slowing, slowing . . . as if it were more the beat of a heart than a clock now.

Anita admitted it at last. She had in fact turned her mother away. Had abandoned the woman when she needed her family most. She had.

But coming here had been the right thing. This would make it all right. This waiting at the house. She knew it would.

Slower . . . slowly . . . the ticking . . .

She smiled. Nothing ever changed. The snow would come in, as it always did, and in a minute she would get another towel from the kitchen, and she would wipe it up, knowing even then that this small action was futile. And she would look once more out into the darkness, and behind her the fire would burn, and the wind would scream.

The snow would continue falling, collecting slowly around the house in gigantic drifts.

And she would sit down and read again.

And she would listen as the wind screamed and the roof shook. She would.

Just as she had every night for the past five years.

She would wait. Wait until her mother joined her, and once more there would be warmth and laughter, the two of them together.

My house.

Syngamy

Nancy Holder

The ghosts of ghosts floated around Belle, sighs that were not breaths and never would be; the notion, the *thought* of touching or being touched a weaker thing than the phantom memory of a caress. She sat alone in the haunted waiting room and stared at the London *Times*.

It seemed that in a place called Gombe, on the shores of Lake Tanganyika, a mother chimpanzee had recently died. The eminent researcher Jane Goodall watched it happen and, scientist that she was, did nothing to prevent it. The mother, who had been named Flo, died beside the lake, her body falling half in the water, and all the other chimps grieved, and then moved on.

All save her son, a horribly spoiled six-year-old who had been named Flint, a terror who stomped and threatened and had no friends. He climbed into a tree and watched his dead mother's body rippling at the bank, and would not move, and died of grief.

That was what was in the *Times*. She was shocked that it was here, in this waiting room; they should censor the papers in fertility doctors' offices.

Her hands shook as she laid the *Times* on the coffee table. It was dark in the room; the paneled walls were dark, and the light from the lamp on the table beside her struggled watery as a tear. Two large burgundy leather couches stood amid highly polished antiques—one would not find such things in a fertility clinic back home. In America, the furnishings would trill with cheerfulness, hope, and good health, despite the reality that the patients felt broken and ashamed. There would be pastel prints on pastel walls of New Mexican Indian women in shawls, or of nothing—flowers, vague landscapes, like a hotel room.

There would not be stories of unending filial love moving beyond the grave.

The ghosts that were not quite there swirled; outside, fog weighted the ivy and weathered brick and ran in rivulets down the arched windows. There were no windows in the waiting room, but Belle heard the dripping. She didn't know how she would drive home. What condition she would be in afterward. Dr. Samuels, not she, had requested this consultation. *To discuss your case.*

To discuss the ghosts, the ghosts of eggs and sperm and embryos, who even now did not sigh or breathe or touch with the slow sound of raindrops, teardrops, the beads of perspiration on Belle's clammy forehead.

But she must have hope. She swallowed and held her own hands, the left one comforting the right. No one understood how little hope it took to keep her going, keep her from dying, because even after all the failures, there was always something left: a new treatment, a tiny scientific breakthrough that might make it happen this time. And if anyone could make it happen, it was the famous Dr. David Samuels.

He was why they had moved to England: stories had traveled over the Atlantic of experimental treatments, controversies, major, startling successes. Since Belle's husband was British and could live wherever he wanted as long as an airport was near, it had made sense to make the pilgrimage. She had given up everything else: university position, friends and family, who had not languished, who had not locked themselves into houses and died of missing her. They didn't understand at all: *Your life is so full. At least you have Richard. Why don't you just adopt?*

When they said these cruel and unthinking things during her low times, she felt foolish and self-deluded. Perhaps she was absurd to want a child from her own body. Obsessed. Maybe God had decreed that miracles were for others; other women could have what they wanted, something as simple as their own successfully conceived infant. Something they put little value upon because it was indeed so miraculous, and therefore could not comprehend the depth and need of Belle's desire to be like them.

But: *Syngamy.*

On first meeting, her desperation, shame, and hope filtered her impressions of Dr. Samuels. She had long ago learned to discount the personality of any reproductive endocrinologist: Jocular or cold as the grave, only results mattered. Dr. Samuels had been British and polite, his hands resting on her chart (*I have read it, I have learned opinions and new approaches to offer*). He bore the same air of self-confidence she had seen in her other R.E.'s, crackling, alive: *I can make you pregnant. I shall.* Thus, whatever small need in her still required the reassurance of dealing with another human being and not the vicious fates, someone who appeared to care and to believe, was fulfilled.

But then he had spoken to her of syngamy, and she had fallen in love—not so much fallen in love but become very focused, keen, and hyperalert—as only a dying patient can focus on a physician in whom she has placed her final hope.

Give me children else I die, Hannah begged Jacob, the prophet of the Bible. Though no one understood it—not her mother, nor her best friend, Chris, back in Massachusetts, nor even Richard, her husband—she was dying for lack of a child. The hunger gnawed away at her like a terrible, incurable disease. She could feel it, feel the sickness, and wondered if that was why she so constantly and consistently failed to get pregnant: Perhaps babies knew they could not live in her.

The door that separated the waiting room from the warren of examining rooms opened. Victoria, the nurse, stood before her with her soft, calm smile, and said, "Mrs. Relling?" After all this time, Mrs. Relling, when in America she would have been Belle from the start. The aristocracy of medicine in a democratic land, the doctor a king, the patient, his vassal.

Nervously Belle picked up her purse and stood. For a flash she felt despair—*I was a university professor; I was vibrant, clever, beautiful*—and then she moved on numb feet across the room. The nurse waited with her calm smile. Yes, she had once told Belle, not smiling, yes, she, too, felt the ghosts. But not to worry, Dr. Samuels could work wonders. Belle knew Dr. Samuels's success rates; his staff had no need to puff him up or lie about him. He could work wonders. He often did, for others.

"Good afternoon," Victoria said warmly. Belle tried to respond, but was afraid to move her face, else she would burst into tears from nervousness.

They went down the hall. The British darkness of early evening made the plaster walls close and unfeeling. On her first visit to the clinic, she had almost asked Richard to turn the car around. A Victorian-Gothic monstrosity dotted with turrets and arches, it was too bizarre, too old, for their high-tech purposes. In Belle's mind she had seen unclean instruments and cackling, mad scientists, women on examining tables writhing in pain, and no babies. How wrong she had been, how American in her prejudice.

Now Dr. Samuels rose as she came into his office with its ivy and griffin-footed table lamp, the hunter green appointments. His laptop computer was identical to her husband's.

There were more ghosts in Dr. Samuels's office, but she wasn't sure he ever felt them. His walls of diplomas, like his eyes, proclaimed, *I can, I shall, make a baby live in you.*

He waited until she had seated herself—ever polite, ever gracious—and then lowered himself into his chair, placing his hands over the enormous folder she knew to be the second of her medical charts with him, her case so frustrating and intriguing that now she had a history set in volumes. As always, his fingertips lightly touched the center of the folder, as if it were a Ouija planchette that would divine the remedy to her condition.

"Right," he said, and she smiled tightly, putting aside her terror and depression as best she could to give him her full attention. "I hope this was a convenient time for your appointment."

"Yes." She couldn't swallow. "Fine."

"Good. I have a new idea." He shrugged boyishly; he was given to boyish shrugs. He was younger than she. It seemed everyone was. Most of the ghosts in his clinic were hours old, days. None was older than three months. "It's a bit odd."

Relief sent the tears down her cheeks. He had it now, whatever it was that would work. She hastily grabbed some tissues—he kept them ever at the ready—and daubed her eyes. As she did so, he made a sound, perhaps a whisper of sympathy. The curtains moved: wind, or ghosts.

"What? What's your idea?" Trying hard to keep the eagerness out of her voice. It was horrible to be dying of this kind of insatiable hunger. It mortified her.

"Well." He leaned back in his chair and made a steeple of his hands. They were pale and clean. She imagined them in his latex gloves, herself with him in the operating room. Richard in the waiting room, pacing endlessly. How many times? Two years' worth. And before that, two years in the States. Four years of hoping, dying a little more each time, then revived just enough to endure, to persist.

Dr. Samuels opened one of the drawers and pulled out an audio cassette tape. He laid it on his hunter-green ink blotter. "It's a subliminal conditioning exercise," he said, shrugging again. "A new study has suggested that listening to this tape twice a day raises the statistical success rate for in vitro fertilization by ten percent. That's for fresh cycles."

Her brows shot up. In the barren land she inhabited, ten percent was significant.

"There were flaws in the research," he said, cautioning her. "And of course it's controversial in the extreme." He looked modestly proud. "But I had someone run me off a copy. I figured, Why not?"

Why not, in her case, the hopeless one? "What's on it?"

Leaning back farther now, cocking his head. "Oh, I imagine

success phrases, you know, that kind of thing. You can't hear any of it. It's possible you might be able to use a similar tape, one you might buy in a shop. But I should like to duplicate the conditions of the study as closely as possible." He made his steeple again. "You would be my guinea pig."

And would he give her a discount? she wanted to ask boldly. Would he do something for her if this, too, failed?

But she meekly slipped the tape into her purse and said, "Twice a day."

"Yes. To duplicate the study." His phone beeped. "I know I can share this with you. You're an extremely motivated patient." He picked up the phone. It would be the receptionist, giving him a means to end the appointment. Belle pushed back her chair.

"Come back when your menstrual cycle begins," he said, re-placing the handset. "We'll get to work."

In the car, she sobbed through the rain and fog as the euphoria of the visit wore off. A cassette tape! Was she so beyond his medical help that he had to resort to humoring her with gimmicks? She was dev-astated beyond words.

Give me children else I die. So isolated with this terrible need. Haunted by it. Possessed. She pulled over and sobbed until she was almost sick, and then she drove home.

Richard was not in their small and very old Mayfair apartment, but the ghosts were. As she moved through rooms that had once been part of a large Victorian mansion, she felt babies and dark-haired boys and redheaded teenage girls who had no idea what their parents had been through to fail to bring them into the world. Her throat was tight, her stomach clenched. How had she come to this?

Mary, her cat, mewed, greeting her, and she quickly picked her up, trying to warm herself. She remembered then that Richard had told her he would be very late. He worked for a Danish company that sold computerized mixers and ovens to restaurants. Tonight he was dining with a Saudi prince. They put aside their wives if they did not produce offspring. Or got another one; they could have up to four. Vast numbers of children were a visible symbol of their wealth and vigor.

Efficiently she fed Mary, cooked pasta and bread, and got herself a glass of wine. She was not at the moment on any fertility medications; she could drink. The exterior of her own building was streaming with water, heavy, oily London rain. Where once she had imagined herself lush and fecund, now she was perpetually cold and feeble, like an old hag.

She ran the bath—the ancient building had been wired for electricity in the Fifties, though the plumbing was probably over eighty years old—and set her wine beside the tub. Just as she started to take off her clothes, she remembered the tape, and got it and her Walkman. The player ran on batteries; listening to it submerged to her neck would not be dangerous.

So she did so, hearing, pleasantly, some jazzy music. She imagined someone whispering into a microphone while the music played. *You can. You shall.* Is that how it worked? Good thoughts fusing with your doubts? She closed her eyes and drank her wine.

And thought of a place called Gombe, and a dead mother floating in a lake, and babies dying of grief, and lives that were not.

"God!"

Her eyes flew open as she leapt out of the bath. The water was ice cold. The room was freezing. Mary the cat sat curled on the bathmat, watching her, panting mist.

The Walkman clattered to the tile floor as Belle swore and grabbed a towel, her robe. Her feet stung.

A baby was crying.

"Yes?" she said loudly, halting her movements. "Hello?"

It was most definitely a baby. The walls of their flat were very thick; they never heard their neighbors. They were all quite elderly, looking as old as the building, and none had a child living with them.

The cat watched her. Belle's towel was cold, and yet the towel warmer was on. Belle frowned, trying to make sense of it while the baby sobbed pitifully on. It sounded colicky. It must be visiting next door, never mind the thick walls.

Stepping into slippers, she left the bathroom and placed her hand on the radiator in the hallway, jerked it back. It was searingly hot, and yet the room crackled, frigid. The entire flat was fused with cold as she navigated from room to room, teeth chattering, listening to the baby as it cried and cried.

She wandered through the flat, listening, shaking. After a time she fell to her knees in front of the fireplace in the front room and gathered up newspapers and kindling. Her mind flashed with the thought, *If that baby were mine, it would never have to cry like that;* but such thoughts were so doggedly common to her—*if that little girl were mine, I would never yell at her; if that handsome young man were mine, I would never resist kissing his cheek*—that it scarcely registered.

The baby cried. She lit a match and held it to the balls of newsprint and kindling, anticipating the warmth. The fire lit. The smoke rose—

—and fell, trailing out toward her in a thin stream, and then a thicker one.

Coughing, she waved her hand in front of her face. The smoke blossomed back down the flue.

"For God's sake," she said. She went for the broom and jammed it up the flue. There was no obstruction.

Belle opened a window and tamped out her fire with the poker. The baby began to keen. She dialed the police.

"There's a baby in distress," she said, coughing, after identifying herself and giving her address. "I think it's being hurt. I—"

The crying abruptly stopped. She jerked. The clerk on the other end said, "Madame? Hello?"

"It was crying just now. It just stopped," she fumbled. After a few confused moments, the clerk promised that someone would come by her building to check.

And then her front door opened, and her husband was home.

The house was instantly warm.

He said, "What's all the smoke?"

*   *   *

The policeman never came that night. Belle watched Richard, in very old clothes, crawl into the fireplace and scan it with his flashlight. He said, "There's a ledge in here. Did you know that?"

"No." She tried to look, her mind racing ahead to things that could suddenly block a chimney, then fall dead onto a ledge. Birds, small animals. She tried to swallow, could not.

"Oh, God." His voice was low and tense.

It's my cat, Belle thought, and cried out, "Mary?" in a panicked voice.

"Belle, ring the police again."

"What is it?" Her voice was shrill.

"Don't look, darling. Go and call the police."

It was the skeleton of an infant. The police inspector, though concerned, shrugged when he spoke to them. "Sad to say, this sort of thing happened upon occasion back when this house was built. Servants, you know. Girls. They would lose their positions if it were found out that they'd gotten themselves in a family way."

Belle couldn't imagine that a woman could hide her pregnancy and deliver without anyone ever knowing. She herself stared compulsively at round bellies. "But you'll investigate this," she insisted, her voice raspy and terrified. She was sick with the thought that a baby had died last night in her fireplace, its flesh somehow consumed as she listened to its weeping.

"We'll date the bones," he assured her. "They look quite old."

Her husband put his arm around her and she began to cry.

The skeleton proved over a hundred years old, Victorian remnants of infanticide. It had nothing to do with her.

"No," she murmured later, alone, teeth chattering, listening as a baby sobbed in the fireplace. The skin on her face burning with the cold.

The sobbing, long, low, devoid of hope and chance and future. She knew this feeling; it shook her spine and spread through her veins like the horrible disease it was: the cold grief of the hunger.

Richard, who never heard the weeping, worried about her, but still he kept his late nights that became later and later, and then went on a business trip to Spain. She had the sure sense that he did not go alone.

Another death.

But the tape was on the stereo, and she thought of syngamy:

"That perfect moment," he had whispered, "the beginning of life."

Syngamy: the next step beyond sperm and egg, when male and female components join into one body, twenty-three chromosomes merging with twenty-three others, a new being. The uniting magically invisible when peering through a microscope, where seconds before the individual genetic gifts from man and woman were clearly visible. A blanking-out of smooth, pale matter, like a veil. "A mystery," Dr. Samuels had said hoarsely, with real awe, "that we are not allowed to see."

Syngamy.

"Sing to me," Belle whispered, tensing with anticipation as she turned on the tape.

And the dead baby sang in the freezing apartment where she lived, or existed, alone nearly all the time now.

"Sing to me, my syngamy," as she stopped eating, and rarely slept, as when Dr. Samuels phoned her and said, "Mrs. Relling, why haven't you come to see me?"

"I've been listening to the tape," she said, to please him, and to stall him.

"The tape." He cleared his throat. "I had forgotten about that. The nature of that tape, it's rather unusual."

"Indeed," she told him, holding out her hand to see its transparency, the near translucence of her skin. Her bones, left behind, left on the shore at the water's edge.

"You haven't had your cycle?"

"No." She had forgotten about that, put that all behind her.

"I think perhaps you should come in and we'll do some tests."

"Oh," she said, and then, "the tape . . . I think the tape is working."

"Oh, dear." He paused. "It's really dreadful. I honestly didn't know about it when I gave it to you."

"I'm sorry?" She was hyperalert, waiting for the revelation.

"Well, there was a study with rats. If the population was threatened . . . if they thought they were dying off . . . I didn't know, Mrs. Relling, when I gave it to you." He was repeating himself. "It's most embarrassing."

She smiled gently into the phone. "Did you think to frighten me? Tell me if I didn't get pregnant I would die?"

"No, no. If the rats believed there were fewer of them, or soon going to be, the researchers believed they would be inspired to reproduce."

"So it's the recording of a baby?" she asked boldly, afraid. "A dying baby?"

"Ah, no." He cleared his throat. "It's ridiculous, of course. I'm sorry."

"But it *is* a person dying," she guessed.

"If you will return it, I will make amends." Financially, he must mean, since there was no other way for him to do so.

The room filled with the weeping. Her womb seized. She felt inside the familiar cold, the deadness of it. She whispered, "Syngamy. It was you who told me about the mystery," and hung up the phone.

The baby sobbed and Belle opened the windows to the tiny balcony of their flat. The rain poured down, a thick, ancient London torrent. It washed over her, blurring the lights below: It was nearly Christmas, the season of gifts, hope, and the fulfillment of dreams:

As the sobs came in waves, she climbed onto the rail and held open her arms. Not one moment of hesitation. As she fell, a short scream, and then the barrenness of her life smashed away in a sharp cold, union of the pavement. She thought one last thought, *I am syngamy. I can, I shall, become the mother of the dead.*

The Walkman crushed beneath her pelvis, her crushed reproductive organs. The tape—on which was recorded, not messages of hope but the death throes of a woman in labor; she could hear that now; they had taped a dying pregnant woman!—the tape skidded across the soaking lane, to be picked up by a translucent, ghostly hand, the other hand cradling a translucent, ghostly infant.

The face that gazed happily down upon the child was the pinched, tired face of a young girl in a Victorian maid's uniform, who turned to Belle as Belle lay dying on the road. Mother and baby disappeared.

In that moment Belle shrieked in agony, as even this child, even this one, was taken from her. As she lay in the gathering puddles, she closed her eyes and knew herself to be in Gombe, where a child dies of grief for its mother, where dead mothers are cherished.

Then, as light as smoke, as weightless as a sigh, she rose and held out her empty arms. Tears that were not rain streamed down her face and she lurched forward, then broke into a run, into the iciness and the unfairness and the betrayal of her infertility; even ghosts were taken from her, even the ghosts of ghosts.

She ran, unsure of her direction, running only out of a clawing hunger that propelled her, compelled her.

Ran; she would not rest until; she ran, starving. By any means, by whatever must be done. By wishing harder or weeping more incessantly, by haunting.

By a push down the stairs or a pillow over a small, pink, and beautiful face in the dead of night as no one suspected, no one saw her, no one would ever thwart her again.

Ran.

Give me children else I die.

Else I never die.

𝕳aunted by the 𝕷iving
(𝕺pelike, 1928)

Thomas E. Fuller

𝖂ith a start, the old woman looked up from her frugal meal. There had been a noise; yes, she was certain of it. The old woman was very familiar with her house, knew every creak and sigh it emitted. All were so familiar to her as the grim whisper of her own breath. This noise had been different, alien. But strain as she might, she could not recapture it. It was gone, gone as so many things were gone.

She was alone in the kitchen. Ordinarily, when Laura was there, she ate in the great dining room, supping in solitary splendor at the head of the fine mahogany table the Colonel had purchased for entertaining. After all, it was necessary to keep up appearances, even if only for the servants. Or, in her case, for the servant. But Laura was visiting her family over in Tallassee and, with her gone, the old woman preferred the homely little white table in the kitchen. She liked to think she was being thrifty but the truth of the matter was that without Laura, the dining room made her feel . . . lonely.

"Laura. Every six months, as regular as rheumatism, she insists on taking three whole days off and visiting her worthless daughter and

her horrible family. Then I will be forced to listen to the latest comings and goings, births, marriages, and deaths of people I do not
know and could not care less about. Ungrateful creature. And after
all I have done for her! Laura knows how important she is to the
smooth working of this house—she just does it for spite. And every
time she does it, we have the same argument: Laura will 'suggest'
that she have someone else in to do for me and I will 'suggest' that
she'll do no such thing.

"The very idea is revolting. Some outsider, some nasty little slip
of a girl, burning the toast and ruining the eggs and undercooking
the roast—it is enough to give one apoplexy! And of course, who
knows what the wretched child would be into the minute my back
is turned. This house is filled with things, valuable things. And mysteries. The thought of common country hands pawing through those
carefully hoarded secrets and treasures are more than a body can tolerate! So here I am, alone in my own house with nasty lukewarm
soup, Laura's slovenly prepared cold chicken, and my own dark,
grumbly old thoughts. But there are compensations. I, of course, do
not pay her while she gads about the state of Alabama. That almost
warms up the soup."

The soup was lukewarm because the kitchen was so abominably
hot. It was miserable enough normally, but even with the one burner
on, the stove had nearly driven her out of the room. Moisture pooled
on her forehead and dribbled down her back, but the old woman
could never be said to sweat.

"Horses sweat, men perspire, and ladies glow."

The old woman glowed excessively but was damned if she was going
to allow an appliance, an appliance *she* had paid for, thank you, to
force her out of her own kitchen. So she sat there eating. And
glowed. While around her the great old house creaked and groaned

in the way of old houses everywhere. It had been built fifty years ago
after the Colonel came back from the War. Actually, he hadn't so
much built it as he had engulfed it. Somehow—it wasn't considered
wise to inquire too closely into the method—he had managed to
hold on to the family money and, in the poverty-stricken aftermath
of the Lost Cause, decided to flaunt it.

"That ramshackle antebellum pile his daddy left him wasn't grand
enough for the Colonel. He wanted it huge, wanted its bulk to own
the countryside the way his money owned the folks. So the ele-
phantine new façade was erected, complete with a set of new rooms
and hallways that swallowed the front of the old house. Then the
Colonel expanded out from the sides, new wings and additions, all
frosted a blinding, glistening white. Took him five years but in the
end the house *was* the Colonel, nothing left of his Daddy at all.
Then, when he had built his snowball monument, he set out to fur-
nish it.

"And the first piece of furniture he looked for was a wife. Me."

The old woman gently dabbed her brow with a fine lace handker-
chief and smiled. Her family hadn't been as lucky as his. Oh, the
bloodlines were as good, better even, if the truth be told, but the
War had taken everything and left her with nothing but herself.
But that, as the common folk said, was a gracious plenty. She had
been a little thing but pretty and generously endowed for her size.
She had set her sights on the Colonel long before he had devoured
his own past, stalking him the way a fox stalked an arrogant rooster.
And in the end, she had allowed him to sweep her off her feet and
stage the most grandiose wedding ever held in the First Baptist
Church of Opelike, Alabama.

"Oh, my, but those were the Good Years and they had stretched
into decades, decades! I discovered I had a natural head for business,

for figures and things. And I liked it. The Colonel—he thought this was 'cute' and decided to indulge me by grandly turning the household accounts over to his 'little Lady.' Then the farm. Then the sawmill and the mercantile and the cotton gin until he had little to do with them at all. He would ask for my 'advice,' nod sagely, say he would consider it, and then do exactly whatever I suggested. As a result he acquired quite a reputation for his business aplomb and I shrewdly made sure no one was the wiser. None of their business, anyway."

Then there was the second discovery, and it was, in the end, the most powerful and powerless of her talents. She found that she had an almost limitless capacity for the conjugal act in all its varied forms and functions. In public she played the proper Southern Lady, gracious and aloft, a delicate flower that the slightest touch might destroy. In private she drove the Colonel wild, holding off on her favors until he was half crazy and then driving him the rest of the way with their lovemaking. Many times he had ordered the servants from the house and then hunted her naked through the myriad halls and rooms and corridors and passageways, a fevered hunter on the trail of an elusive sexual fox.

The old woman smiled nastily to herself, exposing expensive false teeth. That memory was sweet. The others . . . weren't. She had been very good in her attentions. Finally, though, her breasts didn't ride as high as they used to and her bottom became noticeably wider and then all her talents couldn't keep the Colonel's eye from straying. And it did, to her humiliation and rage. The only consolation was that it killed him.

"I had come home from a trip to Montgomery. The house was empty of servants but alive with a hoarse screaming. It echoed through the rooms and halls, high and shrill, full of blood and fear. I found them in the master bedroom, *my* bedroom, his current tramp trapped under his cold lifeless bulk. Miss Carrie Whitmore was well gone into hysterics, and it hadn't taken much to terrify her into eternal silence. The beating with the Colonel's belt had also helped. I had whipped her naked out the front door. Never did know how she got home. Never did care. There were rumors, of course, but as far as the county was concerned, the Colonel had gone to his reward in the midst of a midafternoon nap. I cried at his funeral, the cold heartless bastard.

"One must keep up appearances."

And with his passing came the final discovery. She no longer needed the trappings of power, power alone was sufficient. So the dances and parties ended and the servants were let go and one by one the multitude of rooms were sealed off and the old woman reigned supreme in her shrunken realm.

"There it is again! That same soft whisper of sound, like musical wind blowing through the empty corridors of the house. I am not imagining it—it is there!"

The old woman looked out the kitchen window. There was still some twilight left, although with the heat lightning it was hard to tell. The weather had recently joined Laura on the old woman's list of ungrateful things. End of October and things mildewing. Disgraceful.

But nothing happened in the house without the knowledge and permission of the old woman. Something was different and would have to explain itself. So, with the false immortality of the arrogantly powerful, she rose from the table and marched to the kitchen door. Beyond it stretched the hall that led to the dining room and beyond that stretched all the other halls and rooms and stairways of the great house. She took her candle and stalked forward.

The candle was an interesting concept in itself. The house had been one of the first in the county wired for electricity, but the old woman begrudged it every kilowatt. Laura was afraid of the dark and so for Laura's sake the electric lights blazed. The old woman rose with the dawn and went to bed with the sunset; she had no need for the lights and feared absolutely nothing. So when Laura was gone, the old woman indulged herself and threw the big switch in the basement. Candles were enough for her and they were cheap. So alone and without fear, she marched into the labyrinth she and a dead man had created.

"The sound flows on before me, always just hovering on the edge of hearing. If I can just get a bit closer, just gain on it a little, I could recognize it. Music? Is it just the wind making music or is it something making music with the wind? Something familiar? Laughter? Footfalls? The candle throws jibbering shadows over the Colonel's ludicrously long dining room table and its uncomfortable high-backed chairs, glistens erratically on the polished silver and crystal in their locked cabinets. Useless vanity! Should sell it all and be done with it! There it is again! Just ahead! Just ahead!"

As she marched deeper and deeper into her own restricted kingdom, portraits stared down at her from the looming walls, two-dimensional relatives locked forever in their frames. The sound beckoned her on and she followed. And with the sound came something else, a subtle fragrance, soft and sensual that grew as she advanced into the cavernous dark. It had hints of both perfume and incense, as if the rooms had been recently splashed by the smoke of unseen censers. And yet there was a taste of corruption to it, of fruit left too long on the tree or flowers too long on the vine.

"Once the canning went wrong and the jars exploded all over the cellar, covering the floors with a sticky flood of fermented grapes and plums and peaches and filling the house with a sickly sweet reek.

This is the same kind of odor only more subtle—and infinitely richer."

The heat in the house seemed to grow as she advanced, a moist hot house heat that made the wallpaper damp and the candleholder slippery in her hand. A faint aurora flittered around the edges of the heavy tightly drawn velvet curtains, and she knew that outside the heat lightning still leapt and fretted through the air. That information was noted and filed in her meticulous mind to be snarled over later; now the sound and the heat and the fragrance occupied her utterly.

"The search finally led me to the landing of the grand staircase, overlooking the vast foyer of the house. I stood there, holding the dripping candle high over my head, allowing its flaccid light to illuminate as much as possible. I heard myself cackle. Silly gesture, as if that insipid glow could show me a sound or a odor! But it did show me something, something almost lost in the dank gloom.

"There, just at the edge of the candle's light, moved a pale ivory figure! It pirouetted across the empty floor, leaping gracefully from foot to foot. Thick, heavy darkness streamed out from its head, alternately revealing and obscuring but never completely hiding. I gaped at the silvered perfection of it, dimly aware of a thin line of saliva trickling down my chin. Then it turned its face full into the guttering light and I felt my very brain explode.

"I knew that face! No name came but I knew that face! How dare she! How dare that shameless tramp enter *my* house, dance naked in *my* halls! *How dare she!*"

She filled her lungs to bellow her indignation, and in that instance the figure vanished from the vague light, vanished into the baking darkness that flowed back into the heart of the house. And behind came the old woman, a frenzied Fury hurling arthritically down the polished oak stairs, stabbing her candle before her like a banner.

Or the glowing blade of a knife.

The chase should have killed her—but it didn't. Instead she seemed to draw strength as she hurried along. Ahead of her, always at the edge of the light, flashed the pale figure and its glittering black crown. Through rooms and down halls they went, up stairwells and corridors, past doors that hadn't been opened since someone had died so long ago. And as they moved, the hot moist air seemed to become thicker, like wet velvet, and the cloying smell of decayed perfume and praetorian incense grew stronger and stronger. And over it all the lubricious sound that had originally sent her forth soared and swelled.

The old woman was becoming confused. The house seemed to have joined forces with the figure and the sound and the smell and the heat. Rooms seemed to open onto rooms that they had never opened onto before. Halls moved in the wrong directions, and furnishings she had never seen before decorated the walls. Curtains writhed like bursting serpents, and there was an electric ozone taste in the air. She was gasping from running, but with each ragged breath her lungs were filled with the saturating aura of sour orchids and moldering fruit and this gave her a contaminated strength. She would catch the intruder, run it to ground like a depraved badger, then it would pay. It would pay dearly.

"Ozone. The whole house reeks of ozone! Its smell is worse than the other one! What's that? There's something rippling along the walls! Yes, a bluish quicksilver undulation like liquid neon. Laura must have left a window open and let the heat lightning in and now the house was infested with it! The rooms, they all seem so unfamiliar, that strange radiance twisting in on itself until features are beginning to form in the flashes! Oh, look, look! Grotesque, bizarre things with gaping mouths and eyes in all the wrong places, hoofs with fingers and beaks on human faces. They are all a jumble, flash-flickering around me! I will wonder about them later, they are unimportant now, now while that lush sluttish phantom flees with waltzing swirls before me and the music—yes, the music, it's music!—crests about me and that hateful overripe hothouse fragrance fills me with fires I haven't felt since he . . . since he . . . No! I'll kill her! I'll kill her!"

And then it ended, suddenly, in a blaze of lights. She had chased it into a room, a room that would have been familiar if it hadn't been for the burning little lights that surrounded them. Now this miniature galaxy silhouetted her quarry, the libertine brought to bay. But there was no fear in it; instead it undulated and writhed before her, shimmering in time to the decadent music. Perfect arms pushed the midnight cascade up over its head and the flawless breasts rose and fell with its breathing. Indignant shock ripped through the old woman and she prepared to smash that lush languid face with the heavy candle stick.

"I swing the heavy silver over my head and the hot molten wax splatters around me, burning my hands and face. I will cave her skull in like a brick through a rotten melon! I will bathe in the rich red pulp, drink it like a tonic. All the loss and loneliness shattered down to bone and blood and long black hair like mine used to be . . . like mine used . . ."

And the thick mane was pushed aside once more and for the first time she actually saw the half-hidden face, saw the soft grey eyes sleepy with sex under the hooded lids, the pointed strawberry tongue darting out to taste the sanguinary lips. The sharp white predatory little teeth. And she remembered other nights when the servants were gone, other nights when she had raced these convoluted halls, shadows like jungle beasts dancing on her naked skin, her long black hair like storm clouds streaming behind her. An elusive sexual fox fleeing the Hunt.

* * *

"My face . . . my face . . . so long ago . . . my face . . ."

And then she remembered what had hunted her.

The hand was on her shoulder, spinning her around, sending the room and its stars hurling like comets around her head. And as she spun, two figures swam past her. One was the suddenly familiar figure she had pursued with such unexplainable strength. The other was a vast billowing whiteness lit from within by the invading heat lightning, a billowing masculine cloud thundering up from the empty nautalus heart of the house. She screamed as she stumbled into its arms, and in that moment the sweet defilement of the dancer's incense was blasted away by a thick male reek of bourbon, bay rum, and cigar smoke. And the heavy musk filled her and the heat lightning cloud shimmered into something familiar, something hated and loved and, most of all, missed.

Part of her mind jibbered and cavorted like a demented monkey, but the rest yielded itself up with a deflating sigh. She felt her clothing fall away from her, sliding away like withered leaves from an aged oak. Behind her the ghost of her youth and passion still stroked the air with its perfect body, but in front of her the vast bulk of the Colonel had superimposed itself over the flickering cloud. She felt the sharp whispers of pain behind her breasts and through her malfunctioning heart as she opened her arms to it, but she no longer cared. The star haze was getting brighter and brighter and she toppled into it, her last thought as her demon lover embraced her that it was a shame they hadn't gotten the eyes quite right.

"I've missed you so. I've missed you both so."

And in that flaring light two figures danced with a third until the third seemed to melt away, like a wax doll on a stove. And in the end the second led the first away while the third, or most of the third, lay curled on the floor.

And when they were gone, the house folded back in on itself, collapsing puzzle pieces resuming their proper shapes and structures. Then it settled down to its specific function of guarding its mistress.

At least until Laura came home.

Dust Motes

P. D. Cacek

Why is it that all the architec-
turally overdone, Neo-Greco–inspired, Carnegie-endowed libraries
look alike?

The same towering canyons of words and ideas that press down
on the back of your neck even if you keep your eyes lowered to the
scuffed parquet beneath your feet . . . the same milk-glass lights,
cool green shades to minimize the glare, suspended over the
banquet-size tables on thin cords from a ceiling so high it could be
mistaken for the sky at twilight . . . the same windows, set high so
as to be unobtrusive, so the outside world might be forgotten by
those cloistered within . . .

. . . and the same shafts of dust-choked golden light that always
seem to spill into the otherwise dark caverns despite the time of
day. Or the month of year.

When I was younger I used to love the shafts of light—tiptap-
ping on Buster Brown shoes from one radiant beam to the next until
either my mother or the librarian would tell me to stop . . . or find
the one I thought the brightest and twirl in it, my skirt lifting unla-
dylike, until the dust swirled around me like a golden cloud.

When I was younger.

Now I only noticed the dust.

Why the hell did I think coming here would be a good idea? I could have just stayed home and drugged myself into mental oblivion with pain medication and the midday soaps.

Except I had already done that for the last eight months, ever since the tiny, hard pebble in my right breast turned out to be a monster I had never even dreamt of back when I could still see the golden light and make the dust dance.

Besides, home meant waiting for calls that had been well-rehearsed beforehand to cheer me up, with pity so thick it would sound like static on the line. Or worse yet, it meant waiting for the calls that never came from those who thought that by acknowledging me the cancer would somehow seek them out.

Either way it meant waiting for someone to remember I was, at least for the present, still alive. And I was tired of it.

Just as I was tired of *people* who still had the luxury of having time to wait.

When an old man in a pale gray suit brushed against my arm and looked as if he were about to say something, I moved out of the relatively bright foyer and into the book-lined twilight. The library was more crowded than I'd expected (or hoped) it would be on an early spring afternoon.

A covey of teenage girls in Catholic school uniforms whispered to one another at a small table near the Information/Check Out counter. Middle-aged women in housedresses and older men (although none as nicely dressed as my would-be friend from the foyer) moved idly through columns of bookshelves or sat at the row of tables . . . some reading bound volumes, some newspapers; some hunched over yellow, legal-size notebooks furiously scribbling away, some gossiping while others listened; some (those dressed in layers of mismatched clothes) sleeping, heads on folded arms.

An Hispanic boy of about twelve, obviously truant, slumped against the paneled wall near the history section and glared . . . at nothing in particular. Two women about my own age, one pushing a sleeping baby in a stroller with a squeaky wheel past the romance aisle, laughed.

Why not? *They* had their whole lives in front of them.

I could feel the sudden anger compete with the Valium I'd had for breakfast and self-consciously lifted my hand to brush the hair off my forehead. It was an old habit and one that hadn't died simply because I no longer had hair to push aside.

My fingers touched the padded crown on the custom-made bandanna that one of the "Cancer Specialists" had handed to me while a student nurse (young, bright, *alive*) shaved off the few wisps of auburn still rooted to my scalp.

"It will grow back," the specialist informed me, smiling while she checked off her good deed on the clipboard she carried, "once the treatments are over."

I remember that smile—forced, pitying, and more than just a little grateful that she wasn't the one being turned into a human cue ball. Or having to wear the god-awful flowered bandanna in public.

Or dying.

When I lowered my hand I noticed my fingers were trembling even though I couldn't feel it.

I tried not to listen to the sounds of my footsteps as I walked. They sounded hollower here than they did at home (or at the clinic) . . . less substantial.

A little girl wearing a starched white party dress was standing in the pool of dusty sunlight in front of the children's section; turning slowly, arms outstretched . . . the same way I used to.

Back when I still believed in the possibilities of "happily ever afters."

When her slow dance finally turned her toward me our eyes met . . .

. . . for only an instant . . .

. . . and then I moved on—quickly—ignoring the sorrow and pain I'd seen in her round green eyes the same way strangers (and friends) pretend to ignore the bandanna covering my head and the reason behind it.

Whatever problem the child was having, it was nothing compared to mine.

I got as far as the periodicals before stumbling and banging my right hip into a ladder-backed chair. The resulting sound, unlike my footsteps, wasn't hollow *or* insubstantial . . . it bounced off the high ceiling and echoed through the darkened corridors like a thunderclap. Three women at the far end of the table looked up from the magazine recipes they were copying and glared at me.

How dare I disturb them.

Breathing as slowly as I could so I wouldn't attract any *more* attention by panting, I pulled out the chair I'd bumped and let my body collapse into it. The seat had the same hard polished, butt-numbing shape I remembered so well.

Oh yeah, this was a *lot* better than curling up on the sofa in front of the tube.

The women were still watching me. I could feel their eyes, like cobwebs against my skin, as I reached into the pile of magazines the librarian hadn't had a chance to put away, and instantly found myself leafing through articles and ads geared toward surviving the first "traumatic weeks" of motherhood.

Right.

I forced myself—face relaxed, hands trembling only slightly, fingers itching to claw out the photogenically enhanced smiles—to keep turning the pages. Pretending

. . . that somewhere in the future I really might consider having children . . .

. . . and that I really *had* a future . . .

. . . and the bandanna was only a fashion statement . . .

. . . and everything really would turn out "happily ever after" if I just wished upon a star or found the end of the rainbow or could be awakened from this dream by a handsome prince on a white horse— as long as the prince didn't mind bald princesses with one breast who might never be able to produce heirs to the throne that is.

I got as far as a full-page ad showing a leggy "mother" in swirling gauze standing in a field of daisies smiling down at a nude baby in her arms while Disneyesque bluebirds and butterflies fluttered through a cerulean sky dotted with golden-edge rose-colored clouds. A white unicorn mare and her foal grazed in the cool blue mist just out of focal depth.

The ad was for a diaper-rash medication.

"A blatant attempt to capture the style of Maxwell Parish, don't you think?" a low voice suddenly rumbled from over my right shoulder. "Although I can't remember if he ever painted unicorns. I know he did angels, of course, but . . ."

The legs of my chair scraped against the floor (*again*) as I jumped and I could feel a newer, more improved glare-fest coming from the far end of the table as I turned.

Oh, God.

It was the old man in gray.

I frowned and honed the edges of my glare to the razor's sharpness that had served me so well in late-night bar encounters and drunken office Christmas parties. Once upon a time . . .

Go away. Leave me alone!

So naturally he came around to the opposite side of the table and sat down across from me. His chair didn't scrape.

"I am sorry to disturb you, but . . ." He had a clipped somewhere-back-East-with-money accent, but his voice modulated more for the daylight world outside the library than inside it. God, the women at the end of the table must really be having a hissy fit.

". . . you can see me, can't you?"

I *think* I nodded. Or maybe I just asked him what the hell he was talking about. Loudly. Either way he clapped his long-fingered hands and one of the women got up and stormed away.

"You can . . . dear Lord, you really *can* see me. I told the others someone would come . . . someday, but . . . You don't know what this will mean to them. You *still* can see me, can't you?"

He stopped talking and smiled at me, slowly lowering his hands to the tabletop. The polished wood showed a reverse image of the old man—deepening the gray silk of the jacket and the pink (*Jesus, he was wearing rouge!*) on his cheeks; and exaggerating the line of his square chin while making his pale blue eyes seem smaller and closer set than they naturally were. I found myself staring at the image instead of the man and slowly sliding my chair away from the table.

Crazy people have always frightened me.

And it was obvious that this old man, for all his East coast polish and implied wealth, was a well-bred loon. Asking me if I could *see* him . . . unless . . . Christ, I bet he was exposing himself under the table.

This time I didn't care if my chair scraped or not. I stood up quickly and took a step toward the exit. The two other women had already fled in the direction their companion had taken, when *he* stood up.

Right through the tabletop and its scattered display of magazines.

My back teeth clinked together when I sat down again.

I had seen stage magicians slice women in half, both horizontally and vertically, and one had even beheaded a woman and carried her head out into the audience where it winked and flirted silently on cue . . . but this didn't appear to be any kind of "illusion." The old man in gray silk and rouged cheeks had simply stood up *into* the table.

Only no one had said "Abracadabra."

And I was beyond applauding.

He finally noticed me staring and sat down quickly—his jacket front and tie disappearing into the wood, then coming out whole when he sat back in the chair.

"I am sorry," he said, straightening the line of his tie. "Please excuse me, it was just that I was so excited about finding you. . . ."

"Me?" I heard myself ask.

"Well," he said, still loud enough to attract the attention of every librarian in the place, "someone *like* you . . . who is caught between life and death. Straddling the cosmic fence, so to speak. What is it? Cancer?"

"Who *are* you?"

The old man nodded as if I'd just confirmed what he suspected and laced his fingertips together beneath his chin, sighing softly like a college professor confronting a student on a less-than-brilliant term project.

"And it must be in remission or you else you wouldn't feel well enough to be here. Yes, of course, that probably explains why we don't see many of the dying here . . . But, then again, why would somebody teetering on the edge of life want to visit a library? I would think it'd be torture, to see all the books you might never have a chance to read. Augh, horrible thought.

"May I ask why you came? Not that we're not grateful that you—"

This time I didn't mince words. And I didn't whisper. "Who the *hell* are you?"

He looked up and blinked. "Oh, my . . . I do get carried away sometimes, don't I. Think I'd learn after all this time." Squaring his shoulders, he leaned forward (shirt-front and tie sliding effortlessly into the table) and extended his right hand. "My name is Howard Roth and I've been dead seven years. High blood pressure, not enough exercise . . . you know the sort of thing."

He paused and cocked his head to one side, pale blue eyes blinking.

"Is there some—"

"—thing I can do for you, ma'am?"

The new voice took me by surprise and I yelped. Loudly. My voice rising to the shadowed ceiling and swirling through the dusty, golden light. When the echoes finally died, I heard chairs scraping and the sound of more than one pair of leather soled shoes heading toward the entrance.

Quickly.

I guess I'm not the only one who feels uncomfortable in the near vicinity of "crazies."

Part of me wanted to find the people scurrying away and tell them that I was perfectly sane . . . *dying,* but sane; but it was all I could do to swivel toward the woman in the matching vest and chino short set standing next to me. And convince *her.*

"Is there a problem?" she asked again when my eyes finally made the long journey from cinched-in waist to name tag (MS. MESSIE/ASSISTANT LIBRARIAN) to golden chain to golden hair and amber eyes.

My first impression was that she should have been draped over some tropical sea–drenched rock, modeling the latest in should-not-appear-in-public-without-liposuction swimsuit. God only knows what her first impression of me was . . .

. . . no, the tight almost-wrinkles around her peach-color lips told me that much.

"Yes," I said, pointing across to the old man despite the muttered instructions not to, "he's bothering me. Would you please tell him to leave me alone?"

"I really wish you hadn't done that." Howard Roth sighed. "They might ask you to leave."

"Me?" I turned and glared at him. "Why would they ask *me* to leave?"

But instead of answering, he shook his head and pointed to the assistant librarian.

The amber eyes had darkened and the lines had deepened by the time I turned around. I must have looked the same when I first thought Howard Roth was simply a crazy old man and not a—

"I told you," he said softly—but still loud enough for Ms. Messie to hear. But there was no indication that she could. Or did. "The *untouched* living can't see us. Please, we desperately need to speak to you. Tell her it was a mistake or a side-effect of your medication. Please."

"Um, ma'am," Ms. Messie said after another quick glance to what appeared to her to be an empty chair, "I really think I'm going to have to ask you to leave unless . . ."

"You mean you didn't *see* him?" I said quickly, ignoring Howard Roth's hollow *(ghostly)* groan. "The . . . man over by the newspaper rack. Oh, he's gone. But . . . he was *exposing* himself . . . I think . . . I think he might have gone into the *children's* section."

I'm not sure what it was—either the thought that a man would have to be a pervert to expose himself to a bald, *dying* woman or a quick mathematical rundown of the lawsuits that would occur if such a man displayed the "family jewels" to a minor—but the blond-haired, amber-eyed *living* woman actually mumbled an apology and hurried away.

The sound of applause made me turn around. Howard Roth was beaming like a proud father. A *dead* proud father.

"I am impressed, Miss . . ." The beam faded only slightly as he extended his hand the way he had earlier. "Dear me, in all the confusion I seem to have failed to ask your name."

This time I reached out to take his hand. And watched my fingers pass through his as easily as he had passed through the top of the table. Only the tiniest chill lingered against the palm of my hand. I don't know why this bothered me, all things considered, but for a moment I forgot how to breathe. When I finally remembered the air trapped in my lungs came out as a rush of words.

"Leslie Carr and oh, God, you really are a ghost, aren't you?"

Howard Roth, *ghost*, chuckled. "Yes, I am, my dear Leslie. Ah, Leslie . . . one of my favorite names. 'A queen, too, is my Lesley,/And gracious, though blood-royal,/My heart her throne, her kingdom,/And I a subject loyal.' James Wittcomb Riley. Do you know his work? No? Ah, I am sorry to hear that. Marvelous poet . . . I can hardly wait to met him."

"Shall we go?"

The chill that had touched my hand traveled up my arm and into the hollow left by my metastasized breast.

"Go?" I asked. "Go where?"

Howard Roth stood up and walked through the table instead of going around it. My, the things I have to look forward to.

"To meet the others," he said, stopping at the junction where periodicals met current events and holding out his hand.

The little girl in white came slowly around the corner and took his hand. No wonder she looked so out of place in the library. She'd been dressed for a funeral.

Hers.

If I had tried to stand at that moment I would have passed out.

"It's all right, Minka," Howard Roth said to the dead child, "the lady can see you."

A shy smile appeared at the corners of her mouth as she looked up. It was only when I saw her away from the dusty golden beam of light that I realized her cheeks had been rouged a shade lighter than the old man's.

Maybe her family had used the same mortician that worked on Howard.

I closed my eyes and covered them with a trembling hand. "Oh, God."

"Yes, it is sad when someone is so young. Minka was only four." He clicked his tongue and I felt the chill against the scar tissue on my chest burrow beneath the smooth, taunt skin. "A horrible accident, her mother had left her alone only for a moment in the tub . . . her baby sister had started crying . . . ah, well. She's been here fifty-three years—forty-nine years longer than she'd been alive."

My hand dropped to my lap with an audible thump. *Fifty-three years!* Here . . . haunting this place.

"What am I supposed to do?" I asked, leveling myself unsteadily to my feet. The chill, like the cancer that had invaded my body, had finally worked its way into my heart. I couldn't feel it beating.

Howard Roth patted the little girl's pale hand and smiled when he looked at me. They both seemed so real. So—how did he phrase it?—*untouched*.

Alive.

"Just listen," he said, then smiled at the little girl who had died decades before I was even born. "All of us here left life . . . unexpectedly; either by accident or violence or by simply ignoring their doctor's advice. My dear Leslie, we died unprepared and so missed the opportunity to relate that one incident which made our existence on this plane worthwhile."

Jesus, why hadn't my Sunday school teachers told me you had to pass a test to get into heaven?

"And . . . you want *me* to listen to these . . . stories?"

The ghost of Howard Roth winked at me. "Precisely."

I took a step forward and felt the chill race into my legs. "But why here? And why me?"

"I have already told you, my dear Leslie, why it is that you can see and hear us. And as to this place?" Another wink and he tucked the little girl's hand beneath his arm and began to walk them both toward the library's main room. "What better place to find someone to listen to stories?"

So I followed them, the ghostly old man and child as they moved through the living as silent and invisible as the specks of dusts dancing in the fading light, to a small alcove set far back along a section of shelved stacks labeled HISTORY/ANCIENT.

Where the rest were waiting.

My shoulder brushed against a thick volume covered in cracked red leather and toppled it from the shelf; but here, in this particular section, there was no one to notice.

No one alive, that is.

There must have been over two hundred of them in the alcove—standing ramrod straight or slumping comfortably against the shelves, a few even "sitting" at a small rectangular table near the back wall; talking quietly among themselves in voices hushed and calm . . . suitable for a library.

I leaned against my own section of books, listening to them . . . catching the occasional word or phrase (dull, mundane stuff actually—more concerned about the chances of a certain baseball team making it to the World Series and how much gas prices had gone up since that particular speaker's death than in questioning the cosmic joke that had *trapped* them here) . . . until, one by one, they noticed me.

"My dear friends," Howard Roth said, shooing the little girl toward a strikingly beautiful black woman in red serge, "this is Leslie Carr who, out of the kindness of her soul and despite great personal suffering, has come to listen."

I have to admit, that getting a standing ovation from ghosts was something I had never thought to achieve. Or even hoped for.

When the summer storm of applause trickled down to a few perfunctory claps, Howard Roth stepped forward and offered me his arm. Winking as I tried to balance my living flesh against his . . . and winking again at the little girl in white when she giggled at my obvious lack of skill.

"Who would you like to hear first?" he asked after I'd taken a seat at the table.

They huddled before me—silent, smiling; some with hands clasped in what looked like prayer, others sullen as if this was too easy a solution. I was like a queen, surveying her loyal subjects . . .

like that woman in the poem Howard Roth had quoted earlier. And then I saw the Hispanic boy who had glared at me when I first entered the library. He was slumped against a row of fat volumes he probably wouldn't have read even if he'd lived . . . the angry look making him look older than he was.

Than he *had* been.

When he died.

Yeah . . . I was queen all right. Leslie the First, Queen of the Dead.

Huzzah.

Without thinking, I brushed my fingers against the lock of hair that should have been there. But wasn't. At least *my* leaving wouldn't be unexpected.

Tugging the front of the bandanna lower on my forehead, I took a deep breath and jerked my chin toward the angry boy I had originally thought was only truant from school.

"Him," I told Howard in case there was any doubt, "the boy over there."

Howard nodded his agreement. "Berto, Leslie has chosen you first."

It was obvious by his reaction that the boy had seldom been chosen first for anything . . . except, perhaps, death. He suddenly stood taller, his backbone unkinking itself almost audibly as the angry mask slipped from his face. Beneath it lay the features of a frightened child—eyes wide, mouth partially opened, cheeks pale and sunken in, with no trace of rouge or mortician's craft. How long had making-up a corpse been standard practice? Since the '30s? The '20s?

Jesus, how long had he been here . . . waiting for someone to listen?

"Come along, Berto," Howard said, no trace of impatience in his voice—but why should there be, he had all the time in the world. "Tell Leslie what made you special."

Berto came forward, the cuffs of his trousers hanging over the tops of ratty-looking sneakers, his hands all but lost in the unhemmed coat sleeves. His death must have been unexpected . . . his family hadn't even had time to tailor a hand-me-down.

"I . . ." He stopped and cleared his voice like a child forced to recite at a school Founder's Day program. A breeze, possibly from some recessed air-conditioner vent I couldn't feel, began ruffling his oversized suit. "I . . . I saved a dog from gettin' drown."

That was it?

I don't know what I expected to hear—maybe something along the lines of his being a musical prodigy or being the sole support for his family or even having died while rescuing blind orphans from a burning building.

Just something . . . a little more *spectacular* than saving a dog from drowning, for God's sake.

But Berto didn't seem to notice my obvious lack of enthusiasm. He was smiling now, his face glowing. Christ, it really was *glowing!* And it wasn't just his face.

Dusty gold light, as if a window had suddenly been opened in the row of books, poured down over Berto—blurring the fine edges of his body as the breeze rippled and tugged at him.

"It was just a puppy," Berto continued, and I found myself leaning forward, straining to hear. It was almost as if the light, which was now so bright that it softened the lines of his body into a fuzzy blur, was doing the same thing to his voice.

Squinting against the glare, I pushed the bandanna away from my ears and held my breath.

"This man he was really mean n' he'd got this puppy n' was gonna drown it 'cause he didn't want no more dogs . . ."

The light became an incandescent flame with Berto as its white-hot core.

". . . so he puts it in this flour sack n' . . . throws it in the river back of his house only . . . I see it . . . n' go in t' get it. It . . . was a real . . . little puppy . . . but . . . I . . . saved . . . its

". . . life . . ."

The light blinked out taking Berto, whose one glorious moment of life had been to save a mongrel puppy, with it.

I felt the tears strike the back of my hands before realizing I was crying. It'd been so long—eight months exactly—that I thought I'd forgotten how.

"Thank you for Berto," Howard Roth said softly. "Who would you like to hear next?"

I didn't have to think. Swallowing hard, I pointed to the little girl in white who'd been waiting fifty years.

"A loving choice, dearest Leslie. Minka, you're next."

She was already glowing even before she stopped before me.

"I scare rat away from bebe sister." She giggled and was gone.

That fast. No muss, no fuss. As if the light was as eager for her as she for it.

Good-bye, Minka, I whispered silently to the empty air in front of me. *God bless.*

"Next," I said out loud, and smiled at an old black man in a shiny blue suit.

I went back to the library every day for a month—greeting Ms. Messie at the doors when they opened and bidding her a polite farewell when she finally made her way back to the HISTORY/ANCIENT section to kick me out each night. I know she thought I was crazy, but now it didn't matter . . . nothing mattered but the ghosts' stories.

Not that listening didn't take something out of me, it did. Sometimes I was so numbed by what they felt was the greatest moment of their lives (*"Ah returned dis twenty dollah bill ah found on da floor o'da market, ah did." "I shared the last piece of birthday cake with my brother." "I lit a candle in church for the homeless." "I got an A-plus on my last spelling test and a gold star and the teacher put it up on the wall."*) that I could barely stumble home.

But sometimes . . . no, every time, in that last moment before the light blinked out, I was able to feel some of their joy . . . their peace.

I don't know when I stopped being afraid to die, but I think it was about a week or two before I noticed that Howie (as he preferred to be called, probably because it made me laugh) and the remaining ghosts were becoming transparent.

"What's happening?" I hissed, dropping my Thermos of juice

and sack lunch to the table before nearly collapsing into a chair. "Why do you *look* like that?"

Howie lifted his hands and looked at them, turning them palms up, then palms down.

"What's different from the way I look?" he finally asked.

"You're—" Christ, how do you say this delicately to a ghost? "—a little, um . . . glassy."

"Glassy?"

I didn't think it was going to be that easy.

"You know . . . diaphanous, sheer, translucent . . . dammit, Howie, you're all fading."

He looked back at his hands. The others just looked worried.

"Are you sure, Leslie?"

I nodded. "Forgive the comparison, but all of you are starting to look like overlays in a B-rated horror movie."

Howie clasped his transparent hands together and brought them to his chin. "I'm so happy for you, Leslie," he said.

I shook my head. "What do you mean?"

"Don't you understand, my dearest Leslie? We're fading because you're slipping from the shadows back into the light. You're going to *live*, Leslie . . . and the living can't see us."

"Oh, God."

I leaned forward in my chair, my fingers wringing creases into the flowing skirt of the sundress I had chosen on a whim that morning. I *had* felt better in the last few weeks—stronger . . . Jesus, alive.

"Howie? Oh, God, Howie I can barely see you."

"It's all right," he whispered back, "we can wait."

"NO!" Now I *know* Ms. Messie must have heard that, hell, the whole damned library probably did, but I didn't care. All they could do was throw me out. Or try to. "Look, there still may be enough time. I can still see you . . . a little. It's like you're blending into the background. Quick, tell me your story, Howie."

"No." His voice was even softer than a whisper. "Miriam . . . first."

Miriam Horowitz, of the Bronx Horowitzes, glided forward and lowered her blue-tinted head toward mine.

"I . . . let . . . my . . . sister . . . marry . . . the . . . man . . . I . . . loved . . . according . . . to . . . our . . . father's . . . wish—"

And she was gone. But this time there was no heavenly luminescence. At least none that I could see.

"Hurry," I told the others, squinting as their outlines became more diffused. "I don't know how much longer I'll be able to hear you."

Their voices were barely audible, competing suddenly with other muted sounds I hadn't noticed before: the hum of traffic in the street outside, the rattle of book carts, the fluttering swish of pages being turned.

"Hurry."

". . . gold medal . . . in junior . . . Olympics . . ."

". . . read to . . . my son . . . every . . . night . . ."

". . . let my mother . . . pick out my . . . wedding dress . . ."

And on. And on. Their voices so soft I could hardly hear them over the beating of my own heart. But I listened. And nodded. And smiled when they ceased to be. And prayed that the light I could no longer see had finally come for them.

"Howie?"

The alcove looked empty. Emptier than I'd ever seen it.

"Oh, Jesus—Howie? Howie, where are you?"

There! A faint ripple in the air just to my left . . . like a heat mirage . . . no, like the swirling clouds of dust I used to dance with as a child.

"Howie, is that you?"

The faintest hint of a pale gray suit and bright blue eyes hovered in the air before me. He was smiling.

"You look like the Cheshire cat," I told him, "but I can still see you. Quick, Howie, tell me the one thing in your life that made you special."

His lips moved silently. God, no . . . not yet. Please, not yet.

"Say it again, Howie," I said, raising my own voice as if it were some sympathetic volume control. "Slower."

". . .—. . . said . . . my—Leslie . . . that . . . *this*—the . . .— proud of . . ."

"What . . . this?"

Very slowly, the ghost of Howard Roth lifted his hand and touched my cheek. The chill lingered for only a second but it was enough.

"... this ..." he whispered, and disappeared.

I don't know how long I sat there, listening to the hushed mutterings and shoe-clacks and fluttering of pages, but it seemed like a long time. Not as long as Howie and the others had waited, but long enough to accept the fact that I was going to live.

For a while yet, anyway.

And maybe . . . just maybe when my time did come, if I was caught unaware, someone would come to listen to me.

I left the library in slow, even steps . . . pausing only long enough in a beam of golden light to twirl the dust motes—and whoever might be standing there unnoticed—into a dance.

Of life.

Spectral Line

Robert E. Vardeman

𝕴'm getting a headache," Kandi complained from the backseat.

"Yeah, Mom," chimed in her twin, Randy. "I think I'm gonna puke."

"I told you to keep the windows rolled down," Marcia Browning said wearily. "Your dad said it was the muffler leaking fumes into the car."

"I seen the rusty holes," Randy said, his eight-year-old mind already diverted to the time he had wiggled under the car and had gotten oil all over his new sweatshirt.

"I *saw* the rusty holes," Marcia corrected automatically, her tiredness growing exponentially with the strain of coping with the penned-up kids and the rutted road. "And keep the windows open."

"The wind makes my eyes water," Kandi said.

"Enough of that griping," Marcia declared firmly. Distracted, she pushed back windblown strands of her long, unkempt brunette hair from her eyes. The drive along the deviously winding dirt road through the gloomy woods had been demanding, requiring her to concentrate when she was distracted constantly by her own worries.

"Is Dad going to be here?" asked Kandi.

"Of course not, dweeb," shouted Randy. Marcia glanced in the rearview mirror and saw Randy hit his sister on the arm. "Dad went away for good. He doesn't ever want to see *you* again."

"Is he dead?" Kandi asked the same question she had repeated a thousand times.

Marcia fought back tears. She wished she knew the answer—or how to deal with her children when they said such things. Four months ago Tom simply had . . . left. He had never given a hint anything was wrong with their marriage. She might have found righteous anger if he had been having an affair or even peace if his mangled body had been dragged from a car wreck. He had simply vanished, his only legacy an empty bank account and two young children asking unanswerable questions about him.

"He's gone, kids," Marcia said, brushing away the tears she had tried to deny, "and we're up here to forget all that. We're going to have fun."

"How? It'll be boring, and I don't like Laureen's kids," griped Randy.

"Nonsense. You, Steve, and Kyle get along just fine when you're together. I think it was mighty nice of Mr. Gulton to let us stay at his spare cabin."

"If they'd leave us alone, it might be," Randy said. "But they're not a quarter of a mile back along the road. I saw the sign for their cabin—and their dumb old car."

"That 'dumb old car,' as you call it, is a brand new Volvo and cost a small fortune," Marcia said. A flash of jealousy came and went. She and Laureen had been friends since college. For Laureen Gulton everything had gone perfectly. Phi Beta Kappa in college. A husband making a killing in real estate, two kids doing well in school and never in serious trouble like Kandi and Randy, never sick a day in her life. Marcia ground her teeth together unconsciously. How different it had been for her.

College had been a struggle, academics never really being Marcia's strong suit. But she had met Tom a year after graduating and for a while it had been fine. Randall and Kandace were healthy, even if the delivery had been difficult. Marcia rubbed her stomach, knowing they would be her only children. She had spent three weeks, on and off during her pregnancy, in the hospital being filled with mag sulfate and terbutaline and who knew what other drugs to keep the twins from arriving prematurely. The drugs had worked, but a C-section had been required.

With the two healthy children came an unexpected hysterectomy.

Maybe that was the start of the trouble with Tom. He had been besieged by bad things, small and niggling but wearing like water dropping onto a hard stone for years. She hated him for abandoning her, but she understood in a dark way. His struggling carpet cleaning business finally failed and working for the post office had changed him subtly. For the worse.

She took a deep breath, sucking in crisp, clean air laden with pine scent and the odors of a fresh, promising new spring. Then came a gust of choking carbon monoxide leaking through the floorboards. Tom had mentioned getting the noisy muffler replaced, but now there was no money. Driving with the windows down was easier than diverting her carefully hoarded salary from more pressing needs.

"There it is," cried Kandi. "What a dump!"

"Kandi," snapped Marcia, her patience at an end. "This isn't a resort. It's only a cabin. Laureen says it's nice inside. She put everything we'll need inside."

"If it really sucks," Randy said, echoing his twin, "we can burn it down and watch the flames."

The sandy-haired youngsters jumped from the car and raced to the porch. Marcia bit her lower lip. Ever since Tom had left, Randy's words, if not his actions, had turned more and more violent. He might need a psychiatrist to get over his father's departure.

Hell, Marcia told herself, *she* needed a shrink. But where was the money to come from? She shrugged it off. They were resilient. They'd get by. She would see to it.

"Hey, Mom, this is pretty cool. There's a bearskin rug on the floor and beds for each of us—I don't have to put up with Randy kicking me all night—and there's even a couple bags of groceries on the counter."

"Let's see if there's any cookies." With that Randy dashed into the cabin. Marcia sighed and got out their bags from the car. Let them rummage about. It was good of Laureen to bring food. Marcia would have to figure some way of paying back her friend.

After dumping the bags on the porch, she wandered toward the shoreline of Lake Veron and its cool waves gently lapping against pure white sand. She stopped just short of the water, staring at the endless parade of waves kicked up by the evening breeze. She inhaled deeply again, catching the sharp odor of fish this time. The tall, thin woman shivered a little. She and Tom had honeymooned in Orlando. This was needed worlds away from all that heat and bustle, cool and fresh and clean and not a soul in sight anywhere. Then she turned to study a wooded area a dozen paces from the lake.

"Who's there?" she called, startled. She spun about at a wet, squishing sound behind her and saw nothing. The wind might have brushed one limb against another. Mingled with the pines were white-barked beeches; their leaves shivered and quaked in the setting sun and might have caused the faint *sliding* sound.

"Who's there?" she cried again, seeing movement among the trees. A pang of fear passed and curiosity took its place. She walked briskly toward the densely clustered trees, her brown eyes fixed on a brightness bobbing about within the stand. She thought it might be a flashlight shining against the white bark, but when she reached to the spot she found only a few crumpled candy wrappers and stubbed-out cigarettes. She glared at this desecration of nature, then knelt and scooped up the offending debris.

"Marcia!"

She shrieked and slammed back against a tree trunk, hand going to her mouth.

"Marcia, I'm sorry. I didn't mean to startle you." Laureen Gulton stared at her with wide eyes. "Really! I'm sorry. Bill and I came over with the kids to see how you were doing. It was getting late, and we didn't want you stranded on the road."

"My car," Marcia said, her heart still racing wildly. "It made it up the road just fine."

"Bill's been saying he would grade the road and put up better signs for months now," Laureen said, still apologizing. "Are you all right?"

"It's nothing. I thought I saw someone here. I just found this." She held out the litter. "When will people learn to use litter bags?"

"Come on back to the cabin. Our kids are having a great time."

Marcia said nothing about Randy thinking the Gulton boys were, in his current favorite word, dweebs. Before she and Laureen had reached the porch, she heard their happy shrieks from inside.

"Hey, Marcia," called Bill Gulton from the porch. "Thought the Veronica Lake ghost had gotten you."

"What?"

"He's just kidding." Laureen nervously gestured for her husband to be quiet. He didn't notice.

"Am not," the man protested, a broad smile splitting his handsome face. "Well, yeah, about the Veronica Lake part."

"That's his pet name for the place," Laureen said, anxious to change the subject.

"It's Lake Veron," called out the two Gulton boys in unison. "Dad's always goofing around like that. Who was Veronica Lake again?"

"She starred in a lot of bad movies with Alan Ladd," Bill said. "And she was only four-foot-eleven-inches tall."

The four children let out squeals of disbelief, then chased around getting back into the cabin. Laureen and Bill followed them. Marcia started up the three creaky steps, then paused at the top. She jerked about, feeling as if someone were watching her from the direction of the lake. She thought she saw movement, then decided it was only afternoon sunlight slanting through a patch of fog.

Except there was no fog.

"I'll whip up dinner in fifteen," promised Bill. "Hot dogs and then we can roast marshmallows. You kids find sticks and . . ." His voice trailed off as he and Laureen started fixing the promised meal.

Marcia hugged herself and stood just inside the door, watching the sun slip silently into the lake. Shining reflections made her squint as the restless waves caught the bloodred rays of the setting sun, but none matched the curious shimmering white she had seen.

Marcia pulled her heavy coat closer and drew in upon herself. The wind howled outside and the fire in the stone fireplace had about burnt itself to embers.

"So," Bill said in a low, conspiratorial whisper designed to draw the children closer, "she watched her two little girls drown out in the lake."

Laureen swallowed hard, trying not to let the ghost story get to her. Bill told it too well. He was the perfect salesman, knowing when to lower his voice and when not to for maximum effect.

"What'd she do?" asked Randy in a hoarse whisper.

"She tried to swim out and save them. She dived deeper and deeper hunting them until she was gasping for breath. She swam until she was exhausted, but still she dived for her kids. Then, seeing how hopeless it was, she started for shore. But she didn't make it. She was too tired and heartbroken. She drowned. And now her ghost wanders Lake Veron hunting for two little kids, to replace her long-lost children. She might even be here *now!*"

Marcia knew what was coming. She hadn't spent most of her summers at Girl Scout camp for nothing. Bill still made her jump when he shouted.

"That's enough," she said. "It's getting late and Kandi and Randy will never get to sleep. Besides, such a tall tale might have scared them."

"It's not a tall tale, not exactly," Bill said. "A woman really did drown here after losing her kids. I made up some of the details."

"Bill, please," Marcia said, seeing how this revelation affected her children. Their eyelids had been turning heavier a few seconds before. Not now. They were wide-eyed.

"Ah, Mom, this is cool," Randy said. "I want to hear more. Is the ghost really yucky? Dripping slime, maybe with her skin all waterlogged and peeling off her bones?"

"Randy, to bed. You, too, Kandi." Marcia stood and smiled weakly at her friends when the twins paid her no attention. Bill shooed them off to bed. Marcia sighed. He was so good with the kids. He knew how to entertain them—and make them obey him too.

But now she was tired. So very, very tired. "Many thanks for inviting us up, but—"

"I know," Laureen said hastily. "You had a long drive from town. Come on, gang, back to our cabin. Hot chocolate and then it's off to bed with you," she told her family.

"Promise?" Bill gave his wife a lewd wink, smiled at Marcia, and herded his two boys from the cabin.

"Enjoy yourself, Marcia," urged Laureen. "We'll be around tomorrow. The kids can play and we can talk. If you want."

"It'll do me good." Marcia glanced after Bill, her thoughts jumbled. Laureen understood.

"He's got business in town. Won't be back till late afternoon. It'll be just us and the kids."

"Thanks," Marcia said, meaning it. She hugged her friend and closed the door after her. Separated from the bitter wind whipping across the lake by nothing more than the thickness of a door, she felt adrift again. Alone. Cold and isolated.

"Randall, Kandace, get into bed. Now!" She started for their bedroom when a sharp rapping came at the door. She spun around and opened the door, saying, "You forget something?"

No one stood on the porch. The tall brunette stepped onto the porch and glanced around. Wispy clouds hid the quarter moon, causing shadows to play across the porch like dark waves washing up from the lake. She frowned when she heard a mournful voice calling "My children . . ."

Striding quickly, Marcia went to one end of the porch and looked around the side of the cabin. A miniature tornado of leaves whirled there—and faint strands of the fog she had seen earlier caught in the wind slowly faded from sight as it blew into the woods.

Suddenly afraid, she ran back into the cabin and dashed to the bedroom. Both twins were curled up in their separate beds, looking like angels. She watched the slow rise and fall of the heavy comforters over them and knew they were all right. Still, she went to the window and made sure it was secure.

Outside, caught in the wind's feather grip, were more crinkling, dried leaves, but none of the luminous fog reappeared. She pulled the thin curtains shut and went to her bedroom. Through the night she kept awakening at the slightest of sounds.

"My children," she sighed around 4 A.M. "You'll be the death of me yet. I worry too much." Finally sleep possessed her and let her drift off peacefully until Laureen came banging at the door the next morning.

"All they want to do is sit around and talk," complained Randy. "It's boring."

"Yeah, I know," said Steven. He was younger than his brother Kyle by almost two years but stood a head taller. What Kyle lacked in height he made up for with a chunky, big-boned frame. "There are a lot of nifty places to check out around the lake."

"Veronica Lake," chimed in Kandi. The three boys looked at her as if she had turned purple and sprouted tentacles.

"Come on, let's go," urged Randy. He glared at his twin sister, glowering until she fell silent. She could be such a pain, especially in front of other guys.

"Hey, you kids, where are you going?" Laureen Gulton called from the porch of the cabin.

"Nowhere, just around."

"Stay out of the lake. None of you swims well enough to go in without an adult."

"We won't go swimming," promised Kyle, assuming his role as leader by virtue of his age. He was ten and a half.

"Enjoy yourselves," Laureen said, turning back right away to continue her deep discussion with her friend.

"Mom doesn't care what we do," Randy bragged. "Come on. You too, dweeb," he directed at his sister. The girl frowned but trailed along.

"Where are we going?" Randy asked eagerly.

Steve and Kyle exchanged a knowing glance, then motioned him closer. "There's a little finger of water a half mile off. Around it on the other side is an old boat. We can row onto the lake."

"We shouldn't—" began Kandi.

"What do you know?" Randy said, too loudly. How could his sister do this to him? She made him look like a brain-damaged wus.

"Come on, before Mom changes her mind," said Steve, glancing over his shoulder. The three boys hurried off, Kandi following. She caught up with her brother and the two Gulton boys as they rounded the inlet and started for a rocky point almost a mile from the cabin.

"Wow, look at that," Randy said, eyes widening. The leaky rowboat was held to a rock by a frayed rope. "I bet you could sail all the way across the lake in it. Want to try?"

Steve and Kyle exchanged their glance again, smiling.

"Your sister almost got us in trouble. She can prove she didn't mean anything by it," started Kyle.

"She can row out to the middle of the lake and come back," finished Steve.

"I don't know if she's strong enough," Randy said. "It takes a lot of strength to row."

"So both of you go out and come back. We dare you," said Kyle.

"Double dog dare," put in Steve.

"Okay, sure, why not?" Randy jumped to the rocky spit and worked to free the rope.

"Randy, no, I don't want to."

"I'll go by myself. You're nothing but a . . . girl," Randy shot back, giving his sister the worst insult he could think of.

"Well, all right," Kandi said, slipping on the slime-covered rocks to join her twin. "I suppose it is safe enough."

"This'll be fun. And when we get out a couple yards, we can laugh at *them*," Randy assured her. "It'll give us the upper hand."

"How?" Kandi asked, her tiny hands gripping the splintery sides of the ancient rowboat. She closed her eyes for a moment as the boat rocked from side to side, then Randy began straining at the creaky, balky oarlocks.

"Aw, you don't know nothing. Come on, help me row. These things need oiling." Randy and his sister sat side by side on the sagging board seat and carefully rowed. The boat lurched first one way and then the other until they coordinated their strokes. In only a few minutes they were twenty yards away.

"Wow, I'm sweating," Randy said, swatting at a mosquito buzzing around his ears. The boat rocked precariously from side to side, panicking Kandi.

"Stop it!" the girl cried. "This is scaring me."

"What, this?" Randy began shifting from side to side, rocking the boat harder.

"Don't make me fall out. And keep her away from me. I don't like her getting so close. *Stop her!*"

"What? Who?" Randy asked. He glanced at the ragged shoreline where Steve and Kyle waved at them. Randy waved back and then let out a yelp as the boat jerked hard. "Watch out, Kandi. You—"

His eyes widened in horror when he saw his sister bent halfway over the far side of the boat. Then her feet shot toward the bright blue sky. She slipped over the side and vanished beneath the surface, barely causing a ripple in the murky lake.

"Kandi!"

Randy got his feet tangled up in the mass of rope on the leaky bottom and fell heavily, making the boat rock even more. He flopped face forward and grabbed the edge of the boat where Kandi had been only seconds earlier. Peering over the edge he saw only choppy waves—and a faint blurred white light a dozen feet under water. It faded swiftly.

And there was no trace of his twin sister.

"I'm sorry, Mrs. Browning," the deputy sheriff said. "It's too late to do much more. First thing in the morning, we'll get a diving crew out and hunt for your daughter's body."

"But she might still be alive," Marcia said. She wondered at the curious emptiness she felt. No panic, no sorrow, no unrelenting pain.

Just nothing. Had she gone past the ability to feel any other emotion but shock?

"I wouldn't get my hopes up, if I were you. From what your boy said, she went straight to the bottom. It happens. Too damned often, it happens."

"And the other kids didn't see anything from shore either," piped up a man dressed in a slick yellow jacket carrying the marking of the County Coroner's Office. "The deputy is right. She's a goner—and not the first in Lake Veron. There are currents under the surface that are downright treacherous."

Marcia clutched her sobbing son close as the two left. Behind her stood Bill and Laureen. Where Steve and Kyle were, she didn't know. She thought Bill might have sent them back to their cabin, awaiting even more extensive punishment. He seemed so in charge, so sure of himself. Tom had always been a little out of control—just as she felt now.

"I didn't know she would fall overboard like that," sobbed Randy. "I tried to save her, but I didn't see her anywhere. Nowhere!"

"You shouldn't have gone out like that," Marcia said. The dark vacuum in her soul shrank and began to fill with determination. She had been passive too long. It was time to act, if the authorities wouldn't. But what could she do? She couldn't think of what to do. Perhaps Bill might be able to tell her.

"Marcia," said Laureen Gulton, shaking her lightly and breaking the circular thoughts rolling endlessly in her head. "The deputy thinks it would be best if you drive on back to town tonight. Bill's rented a room for you at the motel just off the highway. You know the one?"

Marcia nodded numbly.

"Here, Marcia, take this." Bill came over and shoved a cell phone into her hand. "Use it if you need help. Call us when you get to the motel."

"I don't blame your boys," she said, surprised at her words. It sounded to her as if someone else spoke.

"We're going to have a hard talk with them, believe me," he said.

"Come on," Laureen said, taking her husband's arm. "Marcia needs to get going into town. You won't be long, will you?"

"No, we'll be along soon," Marcia said. "When the sheriff and the others get out of the way."

"Call us," insisted Laureen.

"Mom, it was my fault," Randy said, wiping away tears with the back of his hand. He left behind dirty streaks on his cheeks.

"It was Steve and Kyle's fault," Marcia heard herself saying. But hadn't she just told Laureen and Bill she didn't hold their children responsible? Tears began leaking from her eyes at last, falling onto her only child. It was Steve's fault and his brother's and Randy's. And it was also hers. She had neglected her children and not been there.

"You remember what you told me when Dad left?" Randy stared up at her, his arms still tightly hugging her close. "That I was the man in the family. I screwed up bad, Mom. I'm sorry."

"Let's see if we can't do something about it," Marcia said. Moving seemed better than simply standing. "I want to go."

"To town?"

"To the lake. Kandi is still alive. I feel it in my bones. Not finding her body gives me some hope she might be sitting on the shore, all cold and scared. Don't you agree?"

Randy's sandy-haired head bobbed up and down. "I guess so. I never saw her once she went over the side. She might be anywhere."

Hand in hand they made their way through the dark woods. The fresh scent of fallen pine needles now seemed cloying, and every rustle made her jump guiltily. The soft sound of wind-driven waves against the shoreline caused gooseflesh to ripple along her upper arms until she wanted to scream.

"What's that?" Marcia's eyes widened when she saw a flash of white ahead.

"Somebody with a flashlight, maybe," said Randy. "The sheriff might have left a couple guys out here to hunt for Kandi." His words rang with the lie.

Marcia called him on it. "Do you *know* for sure?"

"No," her son said uneasily. "That just looks a lot like the light I saw. Down deep in the water. When Kandi disappeared."

She stiffened when a barely heard word echoed across the lake, a word she had heard before.

"Children . . ." came the faint moan. Then, more distinctly, in a tortured voice: "Where are my children?"

"Hurry, Randy, hurry. We must find whoever that is." She stumbled along, falling and skinning her knee. She hardly noticed. She scrambled up and rushed through the tangled undergrowth around the lake.

"Mom, wait, wait!"

"Come *on*, Randy. I see someone. That might be Kandi. It might be!" Marcia came to a level, cleared area and broke into a run. The light ahead of her flickered as if she viewed a dim lamp through a wedding veil. Low-hanging limbs cut at her face, but Marcia ducked and dodged and pushed through into the denser forest. Far behind she heard her son shouting.

"Mom, wait. I see her. She's out *there!* I can get her."

The faint radiance ahead of Marcia vanished, as if someone had clicked off the flashlight. She pulled up short, torn between finding the mysterious person ahead of her or seeing what Randy had found.

She turned reluctantly, going back to the shore. "Randy, where are you?"

"Here, Mom, out here! She's just ahead. I can get her. I can!" Loud splashing sounds sent a thrill of fear into her heart.

"No, Randy!" Marcia slipped in the mud along the shoreline and watched in horror as her son thrashed about in the water, thirty yards from shore. "You don't know any lifesaving." She kicked off her shoes and frantically worked at her skirt, tearing it with a loud ripping sound. Her feet were cut on sharp stones as she ran to the edge of the water and let the cold water slide up, past her ankles, to her knees, to her thighs, then to her waist. She pushed hard against the slippery lake bottom and began swimming with frantic strokes. The freezing water engulfed her completely.

"Hang on, Randy. Don't go any farther."

"She's so close, Mom. I can—"

Randy's words cut off, giving strength to Marcia's already powerful strokes. She kicked hard and rocketed through the inky water, spitting out the flotsam she sucked in as she gasped for air. Her lungs burned and her hips felt as if the joints were going to crack. But she never flagged.

"Randy!"

Marcia tread water for a moment as she spun in a full circle. Her son was nowhere to be seen. Looking down into the shadowy depths of the lake, the woman saw a glimmering. Faintly outlined by the light was her son. He turned up to her, first surprise and then fear on his face.

She dove. Kicking hard, she upended herself and swam fast for the light, her arms thrust in front of her. When she was sure her lungs would explode, her fingertips brushed across cloth. Cloth like Randy's shirt. Struggling hard, the blood pounding in her temples and her eyes bulging from effort, she dived farther until her fingers closed on the shirt front. Fumbling, she pulled herself down until she got her other hand tangled in the fabric.

The light she had seen vanished and triumph flared in her breast. She had retrieved her son, cheated death, gotten him back. Marcia broke the surface and gasped harshly for air as she rolled onto her side and pulled Randy up beside her. Only when she was sure his face was above water did she begin kicking for shore.

Laureen and Bill found her an hour later sitting on the beach, cradling her dead son in her arms.

"Come on, Marcia, I'll drive you into town," Laureen said as gently as she could. Her face alternated darkness and bloody highlights, the result of the rotating emergency light on the sheriff's patrol car. The ambulance carrying Randy's body had left ten minutes earlier.

"No," Marcia said. She had refused to ride in the ambulance. Being so close to her last child had ignited flames of cruel hysteria. One of the EMTs had given her a shot to calm her down. She wondered distantly why it wasn't working. Her guts were knotted tightly, her heart hammered like a smithy flattening heated metal, and she hardly contained the immense pain behind her eyes that threatened to explode outward.

She began to giggle at the image of her eyes expanding and then blasting into millions of bloody pieces like some cartoon the twins used to watch on Saturday mornings. Then she broke into tears.

"It's all right, dear," Laureen comforted.

Marcia jerked away and glared at her friend, her emotions mercurial. "All right? It'll never be all right. My children are dead, my husband ran out on me, I'll never have any more children again. What can make *any* of that all right?"

Laureen looked distraught. She opened her mouth, then closed it, struggling to find words. "How do I comfort you? I don't know what to say or do."

"There's nothing you can do," Marcia said in a monotone. She clapped her hands over her ears when an annoying ringing sound seized control of her hearing like an invading army.

"Sorry," said Laureen. "It's the cell phone." She quickly flipped open the phone. Laureen spoke quickly and quietly, shaking her head repeatedly.

Marcia didn't bother eavesdropping. It had to be Bill calling. No one else would cause such a reaction in her friend. She clung to herself, hands gripping opposite arms so tightly splotchy red fingermarks were left behind. This was about all the evidence she had that she still lived. Everything else had become so muted, as if she moved through a world filled with cotton candy, sticking on her flesh but not holding her.

Laureen continued arguing with Bill as Marcia stumbled a few paces away. In the woods behind the cabin shimmered a gossamer pillar of light like she had seen before.

She cocked her head to one side and heard distinctly, through the soft whine of wind caressing the profusion of tall pines, beeches and maple trees, "My children, my precious children. I love you so . . ."

"Wait!" Marcia groped in the direction of the flickering light.

On either side of the central brilliance floated smaller human-shape glowing splotches. She thought both turned in her direction, but the larger patch of luminance reached out and engulfed them.

"My children . . ." came the soft cry, this time carrying triumph.

Marcia started to follow when a strong hand on her shoulder spun her about.

"Marcia, don't wander off. You're in no condition," Laureen said irritably.

Marcia twisted about and stared at emptiness. Where the trio of glowing spots had been was now filled with the darkness possible only in deep woods far from city lights.

"Did you see it? Hear it? Her, them? Whatever?"

"Marcia, you're babbling. I've got to run over to the cabin for a few minutes. Come with me and—"

"No, no," Marcia said. Her eyes burned from the effort of keeping tears rubbed away as she tried to find the faint traces of light she had lost seconds ago.

"I've really got to go. Bill, the kids—hell, it's a mess. Look, Marcia, stay here and I'll be back for you in a few minutes. I won't be gone longer than ten. You understand?"

"I'll be here," Marcia said. "I won't go anywhere."

Looking more worried than ever, Laureen vacillated between abandoning her friend, even for a short while, and tending to family needs.

"Sit on the porch. Don't move. I'll be right back." With that, Laureen Gulton hurried off, disappearing down the unlit road leading toward her cabin a quarter mile away.

Marcia watched her friend until only darkness remained, then she turned in the direction taken by the ghost. It had to be the ghost of the woman who had lost her children to Lake Veron. Marcia tried to remember the details of Bill's story and couldn't. And it did not matter.

"Randy, Kandi," she muttered. "You're not lost. You can't be. Come to Mommy. Come to your mother." She followed the path taken through the woods by the ghost, reaching the spongy lake front.

She stood and stared across the water. The fragment of moon had yet to rise, but she saw the trio of shining figures plainly.

"Randy, Kandi," she said, her eyes fixed on her children. They were being led away by the ghostly woman, now no longer hunting for her own lost family.

She walked forward, stopping only when the water sloshed against her legs. The ghostly figures had vanished.

As before, the curious detachment descended on her, soon replaced by determination and sureness of purpose. She walked back to the cabin. After fumbling in her jacket pocket for her keys, she went to the car and climbed in. She had miles to go before she was done this night.

The engine coughed asthmatically, then caught. The loud roar ripped through the night. She floorboarded the pedal a few times to keep it revved until the cold engine ran smoother. Then she rolled up the windows and leaned back, eyes closed. She coughed a few times but her determination overrode physical comfort.

"Children," she sighed as she drifted off to sleep.

Marcia awoke to the sound of Laureen Gulton crying out. The car door opened with a loud squeak that did nothing to banish Laureen's hysterical shrieks. From a few paces behind her friend, Marcia watched Laureen turn off the ignition and pull out the body. It fell bonelessly to the ground.

Laureen began to give CPR, but Marcia knew it was futile. She was already dead.

Marcia turned and deliberately proceeded down the road toward Laureen and Bill's cabin. "Children," she whispered. The word came out a soft moan that mingled with the wind and echoed through the crowded, frightened trees. Not once did her ghostly feet touch the earth as she went hunting for a family to replace the one she had lost.

"Steve, Kyle . . ." She sighed heavily, then called with more determination, "Bill . . ."

And the City Unfamiliar

Russell J. Handelman

It was Eclipsion Sunday. Of that much, I was certain. I had come down to the city for Eclipsion Sunday, which should be tomorrow. I remember having marked it on my calendar, for this year, Eclipsion Sunday fell later than I could ever recall it having done before.

But what I could not remember was why I had strayed into this outer borough of the city. I squinted into the failing light at the blue-lettered sign on the lamppost, just making out Bullock Street. Had I ever been in this district before? Mostly I visited in the Heights, just across from the ferry dock. The buildings were different here, of soot-grimed brick, with heavy, black-framed windows. A few lights gleamed dully orange from the smeary panes, neither penetrating the growing dusk nor illuminating the rooms within. As I watched, the streetlamp suddenly glowed white, a pallid moonstone that shone for itself alone and cast no nimbus on the chilling pavement where I stood. Tattered shadows of pedestrians passed me by, hurrying home, I imagined, to dinners and then to gatherings, to await the arrival of Eclipsion Sunday.

Yet I did not see any enter the doorways I passed, as I continued walking along Bullock Street. I knew I must return to the city

proper, on its island bounded by the two rivers, where Eclipsion
Sunday would first be ushered in. I stopped once more, at the corner of Clermont Street, and peered up its steep grade. Clermont
was wider than Bullock, allowing rows of parked cars on each side
and still having room for both traffic lanes and streetcar tracks. A
streetcar rolled down the hill, rumbling and grinding on worn rails,
then stopped at the corner, its maroon and cream paint blending
into gray under the evening sky. I waited, but it did not move again,
although cars sped up and down the hill past it. Its windows were utterly lightless and its doors did not open. I was saddened by it and
hurried across the intersection, halting halfway down the block once
the streetcar was out of sight.

I felt that I was walking east, and that was wrong. The city was
west, and yet I was walking still away from it, or so I thought. I
glanced back along the way I'd come, searching the sky for the glow
of the city on its island. The sky was a curious hue, a deepening pur-
plish, like wine spilled on a white tablecloth, without a single star
visible. I searched without avail for the setting sun. Could it be that
late? I peered at my wristwatch beneath one of the useless streetlamps. It read quarter to five, and as I stared, holding my breath, I
waited for the second hand to move. I shook the watch and held it
to my ear. It could not be quarter to five; I had left home—when? If
I had taken a train into the city, then it would have been after five,
after work . . .

I did *something*. Of that much, I was certain. I worked, and left
a job to come to the city for Eclipsion Sunday, on the train, unless
I drove. I had a car—no, I had *driven* a car, once, perhaps. But if I
lived *in* the city, why would I have left it for this desolate street, in
a borough I seldom visited, when Eclipsion Sunday was about to
commence? I lived—my home was—

I swayed sideways, nearly falling, knife-jabs of pain spreading
from my twisted ankle. At some point I had begun walking again,
still away from the city, and fallen off the curb. I looked up to see that
Bullock Street had ended, split into two roads that veered off at
sharp angles. In the middle of the intersection stood another lamppost, indicating that the right was Dunscombe Place, the left, Eagle

Street. I waited a bit for traffic to ease up until I realized that no cars had passed for some time, then crossed Bullock to follow Eagle.

Eagle Street had looked brighter, somehow, with shop windows gleaming slightly in the fading light and pedestrians flitting batlike under the overhanging signs. After a few steps, I realized my mistake. This was solely a shopping district, closed for the night; no one lived here, and I was farther away from the city than before. It was time to think, to find a way to get back to the city. A taxi—that was it. Cars were passing by once more, surely a taxi would come. As I watched, one of the sleek-fendered, striped cabs for which the city was famous paused a few doors down to discharge a passenger—an old woman or child, unless it was a large dog, who immediately vanished into the shadows—and the driver switched on the red-and-green running lights to indicate that he was for hire. Now, if only I had money—I *did* have a wallet. I thumbed the thin sheaf of bills inside, squinting in the feeble glow of the taxi's headlamps. The largest I had was for two and three-quarters, the rest were even smaller. I pulled that one out, curious. The portrait on the left side was of a bearded man with glasses, the rest of the bill was curlicues and the denomination: 2 and 3/4. Along the top were three words, of which I could only make out the initial letters: U. B. S. The last word was short and looked like "Skye," or perhaps not. Whatever it was, it would not be enough for taxi fare all the way into the city. Maybe I could go as far as the ferry—the cab's lights went out. I walked over to the car and peered into its dim interior. My fingers brushed the hood; it was cold and filmed with dew.

I was mildly annoyed; still, a driver stupid enough to abandon his cab for the night in front of a potential fare was probably incapable of finding his way from here back to the city. And finding another cab at this hour—I peered at my watch again. Now it read two-ten. And the sky was the same color, burgundy bleeding onto linen.

There was nothing for me on Eagle Street. I began walking fast, back to the intersection, to try Dunscombe Place. I *was* lost. That is, I was lost, if I was unable to get where I was going, which was . . . I turned back and dashed down Eagle Street, stopping only where it came to an end at Fitzroy Road.

Here the houses were smaller, four-storied, each with a tiny patch of lawn and a great tree overhanging, fenced in by iron railings. Did I live in a house like that once? I seemed to know what I would find inside: molded plaster and polished hardwood, brass railings and red velour—I was far out of my class. These were not my people; mine were . . . in the city? I turned left and began walking along Fitzroy, across the street from the great houses. There were more of the grimy brick apartments on this side, and an occasional darkened storefront. And where there were stores, there would be a pay telephone. I could call . . .

I knew *somebody*. I had friends, family, co-workers, people I could call, who could give me directions, send a taxi, even come and get me. One of the cylindrical telephone booths was standing midway up the block. I pulled the door shut, slamming it repeatedly, but the light would not come on. No matter, I could dial by touch. I ran my fingers along the dial; odd, there were five holes, no fingerstop . . . and I remembered that I hadn't any coins. I put on the earphones and spun the dial, hoping to get an operator, but was rewarded only with a steady clicking, slightly metallic, like an old-fashioned alarm clock. I jammed the earphones back on the hook and stomped out. Another street would be crossing Fitzroy soon, maybe I could find an Elevated station there—then I saw her, lingering in front of an apartment-house doorway, unruffled by the bustling crowds.

It *was* Leonora. *And* she recognized me. Of that much, I was certain. There was no mistaking her slightly wide, lipsticked lips upturned in a slanted smile, eyebrows slightly raised over her green eyes, her auburn hair cropped pageboy fashion. And when she spoke, her voice was low, suggestive of hidden mirth:

"Well, hello. Who would have thought to find you here?"

I was puzzled, trying to place Leonora. I had not seen her for some time. We'd met after I'd stopped seeing Gabrielle—and while our times together had been at best pleasant, there had been clearly no future in continuing. It had been amicable, our parting, with no great sense of loss on either side. But she seemed genuinely pleased to see me, or so it appeared. I could never tell, with Leonora. And I had needed to find someone I knew. But I couldn't recall her living in this neighborhood, and asked as much.

"Oh, I've been here long enough. Come on, you'd best be coming upstairs." She smiled again and touched my arm. "Who knows, this time you may be in luck." She squeezed my arm and I felt warmth flood under my heavy coat, as she unlocked the street door and gestured up the lightless stairs.

"Well, what do you think of it?" Leonora waved an arm to encompass her apartment.

I lied about how much I liked it. The walls were bare-painted, with lighter rectangles where pictures had hung. A few chairs and sofas were pushed against the walls of enormous L-shaped living room, the only light coming from tiny shaded lamps on the end tables or from the streetlamp outside the narrow windows. My shoes grated unpleasantly on the varnished but grimy hardwood floors; I remembered Leonora's almost pathological hatred of any kind of carpeting, even the smallest throw rug.

Still, she was smiling as I unbuttoned my coat and folded it onto a chair, placing my hat on top. I turned to her, trying to match her crooked smile without leering, without seeming grateful yet still appreciative of what she appeared to promise. Leonora had turned away, though, stepping into the tiny front hall.

"The other guests should be arriving soon. We'll mingle for a bit, then . . ." She opened the door, and her voice dropped into muffled greetings to the visitors pouring in.

I stood, slightly baffled as the room soon became crowded, warming with the influx of bodies, the air becoming an almost palpable emulsion of perfume and shaving lotion and tobacco smoke. Leonora moved among guests clustered like blossoms, pollinating conversations with remarks or by shifting someone from one group to another. I tried to enter a group and stood waiting for some verbal entrée, but the talk was all of mutual friends and shared experiences; I was a stranger to all save Leonora. I drifted over to a window and glanced out at the still-unchanged purple sky. A peek at my watch revealed it to be nine-fifteen, which made about as much sense as it had earlier—or was it later? Still, I had found a place to rest, a gathering before Eclipsion Sunday, even if it was not where I had intended to be. I *knew* I was supposed to be somewhere else, but Leonora's party would do, even if I was temporarily as anonymous as I had been on the street before. And Leonora's hinting words and tone—

I was looking up then and our eyes met; she smiled her slanted smile and tilted her head slightly toward a half-open door at the far end of the apartment. My chest felt tight; it was hard to breathe. I was grinning, sidestepping my way through the gathered guests, nodding and murmuring meaningless politenesses that were as unheard as they were insincere.

Leonora pushed open the door with one hand while taking mine with the other. Her fingers felt smooth and cool; my head was hot and stupid as I stumbled past her into the bedroom. The windowless room was in keeping with the rest of her apartment, holding a single cot with a rough spread against one wall, with a dinette table and three chairs on the other wall; the only light coming from the tiny lamp on the table. A dark doorway across from the entrance seemed to lead to a tiny kitchen; I could see the faint gleam of chrome and white enamel.

Leonora spoke and I turned, quickly. "Well, are you through admiring the scenery? I *was* hoping you'd kiss me." She was sitting on the cot, leaning back on her elbows, eyes half shut. I managed to sit beside her, slipping one arm over her shoulders, and kissed her lightly on the cheek, moving my lips along to her mouth. She leaned back farther and I now lay beside her, our mouths together, listening to her breathe deeply as she ran one hand along my back. I was suffused with warmth; even more, a sense of belonging, of *place*, that I had not felt since— Dimly I wondered why I had never sensed this within her when we had been together before; had I deliberately blinded myself, in unconscious memory of Gabrielle? . . . I lifted myself on one elbow, breaking the kiss to gaze down at her; her lips were parted slightly and her neck was flushed, spreading down into her blouse. I ran my free hand along her side, my forearm just brushing one small breast as she rose up; I let her roll on top of me, closing my eyes as she kissed my face. I fumbled my hands under her blouse and began stroking her back in wide circles, when I heard voices. My eyes snapped open and I spun my head away from Leonora, to take in the still half-open door, through which some other guests had entered. They were seated around the dinette table, apparently oblivious, deep in some inaudible discussion.

I swallowed hard, mouth dry, waiting for Leonora to order them from the room. But she was disentangling herself from my hands, to stand at the foot of the bed with arms crossed, her trademark smile honed to a new keenness.

"Perhaps you're not going to be lucky, after all." She giggled with a sound of ice cubes crackling and turned to leave the room. "It might be better if you were on your way again." And she was gone, swallowed up by her party.

I felt chilled, my shirt damp with sweat as I stumbled back into the hot, stinking room, colliding unnoticed with Leonora's self-absorbed guests in search of my coat and hat. For an instant I saw her hair, visibly red even in the poor light, across the room as I flung open the heavy door and dashed down the stairs before she could make my humiliation the highlight of the event.

It wasn't until the inner door slammed and I was standing in the vestibule that I remembered that I hadn't tried to telephone anyone. Did I dare return to Leonora's apartment, to face certain ridicule or, at best, a sort of patronizing pity? The knob did not turn, and there seemed to be no call buttons beside it. Once more I stared at my watch, straining in the near-total blackness. The hands were barely visible; it was either eleven thirty-five or five of seven, and both made about as much sense. I stepped out into the street once more, grateful even for the purple-lit sky I had hated so much before.

I began walking along Fitzroy Road again, my quest forgotten as I turned over the events that had just unfolded. I had definitely not intended to spend Eclipsion Sunday with Leonora. Of that much, I was certain. Indeed, what had I seen in her; she was far too thin and could wound as easily with that slanted smile as with words. Why on earth had I left Gabrielle for her—

I had *not* left Gabrielle for her. Of that much, I was certain. I halted, coming to the corner of Gilbert Street, and tried to marshal my thoughts. Was I seeing Leonora and Gabrielle at the same time? No, I was seeing Gabrielle, and then I was seeing Leonora, but I had not left Gabrielle, nor had she left me. We merely had not seen each other for some time; that was it, Gabrielle was still there, she was waiting for me.

I began walking rapidly, no longer perturbed by the flitting shadows of the other, nearly invisible pedestrians. Gabrielle was waiting for me on Eclipsion Sunday, even though it had been so long, I could not remember. I paused at the end of Gilbert Street and waited for the semaphore to turn before crossing to Hazard Street. Gabrielle lived at the end of Hazard Street. Behind her building lay warehouses and the dockyards across from the city. All at once the street returned to my memory; there was the beer garden, now shut, where we had toasted each other on innumerable occasions, the marble statue of some forgotten general atop his steam tractor across from a brick meeting house. Soon I would be passing the now-shuttered shops; the one that sold glue and insecticide meant that I was halfway there.

I no longer noticed how cold my feet had become; I seemed to be floating some inches above the marble pavement, envisioning Gabrielle's face as I would fling open the door of her loft. Her black hair would be a nimbus behind her, her laugh soft, purling like low chords on piano. I could remember now one winter night as we walked home in the snow, the flakes in her hair forming miniature galaxies under the streetlamps; and now, Eclipsion Sunday, together—

I stopped, faced with a cracked brick wall, blackened from long-dead flames, its gaping windows screaming silently the purple light beyond. My stomach wrenched, and I felt my throat closing. I climbed the ruins of the front steps and jumped through where a door once hung to land in a field of charred rubble, shapeless blocks of cracked masonry and splintered beams nearly enveloped by sour weeds and tall grasses. The air reeked of cold, damp plaster and burned lumber. Only one other outer wall was standing, at right angles to the one I had faced. From the placement of the windows, I could recognize where Gabrielle's loft had been. As I reached a hand to my forehead, I saw my watch. The hands both pointed straight up; beyond, the sky was the same color as it had always been, as it would ever be.

Gabrielle had *not* been waiting for me. I had seen her to her door, that night before Eclipsion Sunday last year, where I shook her hand and smiled as broadly as I could before walking back to the Elevated station. I had had other plans for ushering in Eclipsion Sunday and had never intended to spend it with her. Our relationship had not yet progressed to that stage; I had carefully mulled over our every conversation after each time we had spent together; it was clear that we still had far to go before our feelings were so congruent as to allow us to have that kind of shared pleasure. Until I had attained absolute conviction of her feelings and thereby been capable of determining my own, our relationship was at a given stage and could not be so advanced.

She had *not* been disappointed, or in any way perturbed. I *knew*, I knew *her*, and besides, I would return the next day. But that day I returned to a smoking ruin, the fire lads still heaving on their pumps, the policemen in their stovepipe hats, gems of office gleaming in the embers, holding back the crowds. There had been no survivors of what had been a gas explosion and subsequent inferno. I learned all this at the Department of Cemeteries office, trying to learn the fate of Gabrielle. Some money changed hands and as I pored over crabbed handwriting in the Register of Deaths I learned that the explosion had started in Gabrielle's apartment; that she had been found in what remained of her bed, apparently peacefully composed.

I had *not* meant that much to her, nor her to me. It was an accident, a leak in the building's ancient pipes, nothing else, nothing that I could have done or said would have changed that. I would have seen it in her eyes, just as I could judge her every word, knowing the meaning behind each spoken nuance, knowing that she was *not* disappointed that I would await the arrival of Eclipsion Sunday elsewhere. I knew that she knew that we had to wait until we were ready, that we would know when the time was right, and it *had not been* right, but it *would have been*—

A sudden roar overhead made me look up and I narrowly avoided colliding with an Elevated pillar as a train rattled and banged above me, disappearing around the curve. I watched it disappear, silhouetted against a sky that glowed with nonlight that was neither dawn nor dusk. Without looking, I knew that the cars on Bullock Street were still rushing by and the pedestrians still scuttled in the shadows of the great brick towers, scarcely seen and unseeing. I thrust my hands in my pockets and resumed walking, puzzling over how I had arrived in this outer borough of the city on such an important occasion, for it was Eclipsion Sunday. I had come down to the city for Eclipsion Sunday, which should be tomorrow. Of that much, I was certain.

Won't You Take Me Dancing?

Esther M. Friesner

Come on, Rachel, it's just a joke!" Lauren rubbed more brown eyeshadow into the faint creases beside her mouth and studied the effect in the mirror. "Yuck. If this is what I'm gonna look like when I get old, I'll kill myself."

"Wait until you use that gray spray-gunk in your hair," Rachel muttered from the bed. She lay there on her stomach in pale peach bra and lace-trimmed panties, staring at an old dress—satin, strapless, a fat tulle gardenia swelling from the waist. She poked at the tiers of stiffly starched net petticoat, but made no move to stand up and wriggle into the garment.

Lauren spun around on her mother's makeup-table stool. "Hey, what's with you? I'm nearly all done, and you're just lying there in your underwear like a lump. You said you wanted to do this. I even gave you first choice about who you got to be."

Rachel stared at the watery shimmer of the sky-blue fabric. The bodice was so heavily boned it seemed to be supported by a pair of phantom breasts. She wondered how many pairs of rolled-up knee socks it would take to bring her own sixteen-year-old measurements up to where the top of the old gown wouldn't flop forward when she moved.

Ghosts weren't supposed to fall out of their dresses.

"I don't know, Lauren. I mean, maybe this whole idea is dumb. What if we really scare someone bad?"

Lauren smeared some more brown eyeshadow under her eyes, then attacked her entire face with loose powder too pink for her true complexion. "Listen, Rachel, I told you: It's only a joke!"

"Yeah, but it's kinda—you know—a sick joke."

Lauren paled down her lips with blemish concealer, then powdered over them too until they looked like withered flower petals. "Those are the best kind." She smiled smugly at her reflection. "First time in my whole life I was ever glad my folks bought this stupid house right across from the graveyard. This is gonna be so cool!" She waited for Rachel's confirming voice, but her friend remained where she was, sprawled on the bed, contemplating the old prom finery the two girls had salvaged from the wooden wardrobe down cellar.

The dress smelled terribly of mothballs. Sequins dripped from a loose thread in the flower-shaped appliqué just over the left bosom. There were slightly darker splotches of fabric where the vanished dancer's sweat had bested the deodorants of the day, and most of the pastel paint had worn off the zipper up the back. Only the dyed-to-match satin pumps looked nearly as good as new. Rachel slipped one over her hand and studied the sole.

"Your mom sure didn't do too much dancing in these."

"Maybe she dumped her steady the week before the prom too," Lauren said, teeth clenched. She glowered at Rachel, defying her to speak up, to contradict her, to say what the whole school knew: that Lauren's boyfriend Mark was the one who'd done the dumping.

If that young man's cool, casual betrayal had come as a shock to Lauren, it came as a worse one to Rachel. Pretty, popular, self-possessed Lauren, left discarded and dateless for the prom? That wasn't the way it was supposed to be. To Rachel's mind, such things only happened to girls like herself. It wasn't an idea she liked, but it was one she'd thought she could depend on. Now she could depend on it no longer. This knowledge frightened her. If even Lauren wasn't safe from the hurts of the world, where did that leave Rachel? She hated Mark for what he'd done, both to Lauren's pride and to her own snug, safe assumptions. Still, if not for him, she would be spending yet another prom night alone.

"Yeah, maybe that's what happened," she said, running the ball of one finger slowly over the barely scuffed sole. "Maybe he was a big jerk too. Maybe—"

An impatient exclamation from Lauren made her drop the shoe. "Are you still dragging it? What's the matter?"

Rachel shrugged. It felt funny doing that without her heavy fall of dark blond hair tumbling down over her bare shoulders. She'd gotten as far in her masquerade as gathering it up into a tight chignon and anchoring it with some white silk roses before the chill realization of what she was doing made her stop.

"Hey, Raych, if you don't want to play the ghost, at least you could've told me before I put on all this old-lady makeup. Shit, now I gotta wash it off and put it on you instead. You really can be a pain in the ass sometimes." Lauren got up and started for the bathroom.

"No!" Rachel surprised herself by how loudly she cried out, how quickly she swung herself off the bed and ran to stop Lauren. "What I mean—I don't want to be the old lady either. I don't think this is a good idea at all."

"Oh, for God's sake." Lauren stalked over to the bed and threw herself down so hard the dress bounced, its heavy skirts rustling with a sound that made Rachel think of mice. "You are so dumb. What's the big deal here? I mean, where were you when we were thinking it up five minutes ago? You were jumping up and down to do it! Remember what you said when we found this old dress downstairs? 'Oh, wow, this is just the kind of dress the girl in that old ghost story would wear,' that's what you said. I had to ask you what story, so then you told me all about how there's this girl out hitchhiking on prom night and this guy picks her up and she asks him to take her home. She says she's cold, so he gives her his jacket and she gets in the backseat, only when he gets to the address she gives him, she's gone and her mom tells him she died fifteen years ago. *Remember?*" She made the last word bite.

Rachel stood in the doorway, feeling colder than any prom-night ghost. The way Lauren told it, the story lost all its delicious tingles, turned itself into a second-rate tabloid item. There was a strange taste in her mouth, even though she hadn't eaten anything since coming to spend the night with Lauren, in the prom-night solidarity of the dateless.

Words clustered on her tongue; that was what left so strange a tang. Words urged themselves to be said, demanded that she speak them and save a tale so special, once so darkly beautiful:

But when he went back to his car, thinking that the old woman was crazy, he found that his jacket was gone as well. Maybe he was the crazy one. The moon still chilled the sky. He drove away, passed several cars on the road, all of them filled with young people coming back from the prom. He could hear their laughter, the music blaring from their car radios through the unseasonably cool June night. Somewhere in his heart he felt the question form: How many of those pretty, laughing young girls were riding away into the night to dance a last measure with death? Had she laughed like that, his lonesome, wistful passenger? Take me home, *she had pleaded.* Oh, please, take me home!

The cemetery gates were locked; he climbed the wall, leaving smears of blood from scraped knuckles on brick and moss and ivy. He knew her name. He had to see, to know for certain, to find her again, even if all he found would be—

The stone was where the old woman had said he would find it (Go and look for yourself if you don't believe me!), *by the south wall, under a black-barked elm. He knelt by the stone, cursing the overhanging foliage that blocked the moonlight and sometimes brushed against his cheek like owl wings. He nearly dropped his cigarette lighter among the weeds* (I'm an old woman, I can't look after her grave the way I'd like.) *and cursed when it would not strike a light until the fifth try.*

Yes. Yes, there was the name the vanished girl had given him, the date of death this very night, fifteen years ago, and there—

"—and he finds his jacket hanging on the gravestone," Lauren finished. She made the climax of the story sound like a hotshot lawyer's slickest, most inescapable concluding argument.

She made it sound like something that happened every day.

Rachel winced. What had gone wrong? Hadn't she told it well enough before, when she recounted the old, old tale to Lauren? The words died unsaid, the story was left as a naked bone of happenings in Lauren's powdery pale mouth.

Kathy had told it better—she must have! Rachel could still feel the short hairs on her forearms rise up every time she recalled Kathy's face when she told the tale, as if the cool, pale lips of the wandering girlish ghost were passing over her skin in a shy, fleeting kiss. Was that summer only a year ago? In the darkness of the camp cabin, in the warmth of their neighboring bunks, she heard Kathy tell the story in savoring whispers from the other side of the shadows, heard her own answering protest:

Don't tell that one again. I'm scared!

Laughter, very soft, so as not to wake the sleeping children. *I want to scare you.*

Why?

Because I can. A whisper, and then Kathy's laughter again, so soft, so cold, trailing through the dark, a graveyard fog. Even when Rachel pulled the covers over her head and lay there, trembling like a child, she could still feel it there, a wraith looming over her bed, mocking her, waiting.

Because I can. Even when Kathy's whisper was no more than a memory, it still twined itself like an iron thread around Rachel's heart and pulled tight, so that there wasn't a breath she drew without knowing Kathy held the other end of the strand.

Summer ended. Rachel slept in her own room, her bed cold and white, lying lone in moonlight. And even so, Kathy was there. Rachel could still hear the whispers in the dark, still feel her skin prickling as Kathy lay down the shimmering filaments of words, one by one, spinning out an icy web that seemed so fragile, but that would cling to Rachel's soul forever.

Rachel never knew quite when it was that she first recognized the spell that Kathy had cast over her. She told herself to be sensible, to throw it off, to be free again. It was an old story, the wistful hitchhiking phantom; it shouldn't have such power. But it did.

That was when Rachel knew that the only way to cast out Kathy's whisper-woven ghost was to raise one of her own. Kathy's power over her was made of fear; she must hold the commanding end of the iron strand if she ever wanted to be free.

She had to usurp the power; she had to make someone else afraid.

"That's not the way I told it to you!" Rachel blurted. She wanted to cry. Lauren was looking at her as if she were crazy. Maybe she was. Crazy to try to conjure something more than friendship with this girl. Crazy to use the old ghost story the way Kathy had used it on her. Crazy to try bringing Lauren—trembling, frightened, open—near enough to—

Nothing. Rachel wasn't Kathy. Rachel didn't have the enchanted words that danced so sweetly, so seductively through the shadows to bring another girl close enough to set the cold hook of fear so deeply, so irrevocably in her heart. In the darkened basement where they found the dress, for a moment it almost seemed as if the words had come to her with all their power of allure. Lauren had trembled (*Hadn't she? Hadn't she?*) and leaned close enough for Rachel to smell the spicy perfume of her burnished auburn hair (*Don't go on. I'm scared!*) and she had gasped and shuddered as Rachel's words crept through all the hidden places slyly, skillfully opening doors (*This is nothing, just a simple story. What, are you crying? Is it making you so afraid? I would rather die than hurt you. I'll stop if you really want me to. But you don't want me to stop, do you Rachel?*).

No. Rachel took a deep breath, and with it she released all her ghosts. "Okay, you're right. I'm being a dork. I'm sorry. Let's do it."

The plan was very simple, really, every detail worked out to provide the "ghost" with a safe and easy time of it.

"The thing to do is make it as quick as you can," Lauren said as they cut through the cemetery, flashlights bobbing like fireflies. "The less time you spend in a stranger's car, the better. Just hang out in the dark around the side of the 7-Eleven next to the Mobil station and you can get a good look at the drivers when they go in to pay at the self-serve pumps. Someone looks like a weirdo, you just stay hidden where you are. But if you spot someone who looks okay—you know, all by himself, clean, maybe a little nerdy, glasses are a pretty good bet—then you go down to the end of the drive and try to flag him down before he gets back on the road."

Rachel shivered, wrapping herself tight in a solitary embrace against the night, against the shuddery brink of the unknown. The white gardenia corsage flopped awkwardly on her wrist, a last-minute touch to match the gown's fake gardenia ornament, a cobble-up job done by Lauren with blossoms snipped from her mother's prized plant, pink ribbons scavenged from the gift-wrap box in the hall closet.

"I'm scared . . ." Rachel's voice faded away into the warm dark, floating above the tombstones like a bat's drifting shadow. "Suppose—"

Lauren stood stock still on the wiry, close-cropped grass. By moonlight her amateurish makeup job stole just enough magic to convince the unknowing witness that she truly was one of the those spry, bristly old ladies. "Look, Raych, you don't want to do this? Fine. I just wish you'd've said something before we got started. You think I like feeling like an idiot, all this glop on my face, in my hair, and all of a sudden calling it quits? Okay. Forget it. Forget the whole thing. Let's go back to my house and you can call your mom to come get you."

"Get—? But I thought I was going to sleep over with—"

"Forget it, I said." Lauren had turned her back on her and was already stomping back the way they'd come. "You are such a wimp. You make me sick. Everything's off, okay? Everything." She stopped and let Rachel catch sight of the calculating curve of her lips as she said, "If I'm half as sick as you make me, you can't possibly sleep over."

Rachel didn't move—couldn't move. She stood there among the gravestones, watching Lauren's briskly retreating shape. "Wait!" she called after her, but Lauren kept on walking. "*Please* wait!" She despised herself for the pathetic, wheedling whine in her voice. She ran over the grass, over the graves, until she caught up with Lauren, tugged at her elbow. "I'm sorry. You're right: I'm a jerk. I said I'd do it, so"—a deep breath of warm, moist air, forced down her throat—"I'll do it."

"You don't have to." Lauren said it so it meant *You have to.* Rachel only shook her head so rapidly that it looked like an attack of palsy and squeezed Lauren's arm. Lauren's teeth flashed white in the moonlight, savoring her victory. *"That's* the way!" she crowed, slipping her arm through Rachel's. "I knew you'd cut this ooh-I'm-so-scared crap. Come on, it's gonna be fun!"

They came up on the 7-Eleven by the back way, where the dumpsters stood waiting and the air smelled like garbage and gasoline. "Okay, you can see good from here," Lauren said, and that was all the parting wish she gave Rachel before scampering back to her house to wait.

Rachel leaned against a dumpster, head tilted back, eyes closed tight against the nausea and the fear that spawned it. A breath, then two, and each one after that drawn in and let out by main effort, gusts of air to make her body shudder. There was a plague of goosebumps all along her arms, as much from fear as from cold. She wondered whether Lauren would believe her if she waited here an hour, then went back to the house and claimed that no one had stopped for gas or coffee, or else that every soul who did stop had been a weirdo.

Lauren wouldn't buy it. Lauren would know a lie. Lauren would send her packing, tell her to go home, hate her forever—no, worse than hate her, scorn her. Hate was a passion sometimes even stronger than love, almost as strong as fear, powerful, long-lived. Scorn only killed casually and walked away.

Rachel opened her eyes and peered around the corner from her hiding place behind the dumpster. The cold white lights of the 7-Eleven illuminated deserted gas pumps, smears of oil soaked into the pale concrete until they looked like shadows left by dead men. Beyond the lighted plaza, cars sped by, pinpoint headlights streaking the night. Rachel knitted her fingers together, praying that no one would stop, then praying that someone would, and soon, so she could get this over with and return to Lauren's house in triumph and relief. ("You were *so* cool, Raych! I mean, I wish you could've seen his face when I told him you'd been dead for fifteen years! Oh, my God, it was so incredible!" And they would go to bed, but not to

sleep. In the darkened room she would have her chance to tell the
stories. The hitchhiker's tale was only one, and old, too well known
to assure its effect on the hearer no matter how well told. So Rachel
would tell Lauren the other stories, all the other tales of terror that
Kathy had used to rob her of everything but chilled bones and dreadful waking nights. She would turn the terror from her master to her
tool, claim Lauren the way Kathy had claimed her and maybe—
maybe if she were very careful—she would at last be free.)

"Miss?"

She jumped, banging her shoulder against the rough edge of the
dumpster where green paint blistered up and peeled away. Her fingertips drove against the metal at her back, as if pure fright could
turn them to talons strong enough to scream through steel.

"Miss, are you all right? Do you need any help?" He was tall and
thin and ordinary-looking. He wore glasses with thick black plastic
frames, a white shirt, a navy-blue bowtie, and a gray suit of herring-
bone tweed. His hair was black, short, neat, and as utterly lacking
in style as the rest of him. All the cold flowed out of Rachel's body;
she basked in the sweet warmth of inrushing relief. He was perfect.

"Please," she said, making her voice tremble just a little bit.
"Please, I need a ride."

He let her get into the backseat of his car without demur. ("You
get carsick if you ride up front? Really? Gosh, I used to have a friend
with the same problem. Small world.") She stood there with one
hand on the open car door, one foot poised to enter, then pulled
back. How stupid: She had almost forgotten the most important
thing.

"Please . . . please, it's so cold, and I've been waiting such a very
long time . . . please, could you lend me—?"

The heavy wool jacket settled itself over her shoulders before she
could finish her request. It smelled of piney aftershave and cigarettes. The driver smiled kindly and adjusted the set of one cuff link.
"That should do you," he said. He didn't for an instant point out that
the night was anything but cold.

The sewn-in tulle petticoat beneath her gown rustled loudly as
she slid into the backseat, across the deeply padded bench. The car

was old, though somehow it still seemed to hold the smell of new leather and fresh oil. She couldn't find her seat belt in the dark. Then she remembered that the joke required her to be able to move fast, when the time came. The plan called for her to wait until they drove up near Lauren's house, then find an excuse to stay behind in the car. ("Tell him you feel sick and you want him to bring your mom out to you," Lauren had said, eyes bright with the excitement of conspiracy. "Yeah, that'll work.") While he went up to the front door, she was to slip quickly from the car, into the graveyard, and hang the jacket on a stone the girls had chosen earlier. Maybe the date of death was wrong, maybe not, but it was a young girl's grave marker and that was all it needed to be.

She stopped searching for the elusive buckle and strap. *This is— this is going to be fun*, she told herself severely, and gave him Lauren's address before she could think otherwise. "Do you know how to get there?" she asked.

"I know," he said.

The car began to move. Rachel settled back in the seat. Outside, the familiar shapes of shops and houses whispered by. She took a deep breath, waiting for the driver to speak to her, to ask questions. The driver in the story asked questions, but the girl never answered a one of them. All she did was insist he take her home, home, she had to get home, her mother would be waiting, would be worrying, she had to get home.

And in the soft silence of the car, Rachel suddenly blinked her eyes over something that had never crossed her mind before, a question of her own about the story: Why home?

Why would a girl, set free of home, ever want to return? Even if death had been the means to let her break away from rules and strictures, family ties like hawsers, shackles, why turn your back on a prize so many kids spent nearly all their waking hours fighting to gain?

Yes, even if it meant dying to win it. Oh, not if you had the choice and chance of living, but still—

I'd sooner die than go back, if it was me, thought Rachel.

Why go back to the four walls of a room too small to hold her, no matter what size that room was? Why go back to parents who stood like walls between their daughter and their daughter's life, their precious, perfect child's true self? She couldn't find fingers enough to number the times she'd tried to tell them about the fear that Kathy's tales had kindled, how it crept up over her in the night-time, how it left her lying there in her bed frozen, in pain. She'd tried.

But she'd never told. She knew what they'd say. First they'd laugh—that would be the hardest thing to bear, to hear—and then after the laughter they'd shake their heads over her, call her a fool. She could hear her father's voice booming, "Afraid of what? Of a story? You're a big girl now, Rachel. Grow up! Before you know it, you'll have *real* worries. We're expecting you to get into a good college, but the way your grades have been—"

And her mother, mouse-voiced: "Why don't you have more friends, darling? Why do you stay home alone so much? Why don't you go to the dances? Why don't you have a boyfriend? Why—?"

The questions would strike at her like needle-sharp hailstones, leaving bruises, drawing blood. Her parents would fix their eyes on her, hungry mouths of eyes, and once again demand to know why she was not as perfect a daughter as they deserved. She didn't dare tell them a thing about her fears. She didn't dare tell anyone.

Maybe it will be different, tonight, she thought. *Afterward, when this joke's done, when I'm back at Lauren's house. After I've had the chance to tell her Kathy's stories, to use the words the way Kathy did. She'll know what I feel, then. She'll understand. I'll be able to talk to her about it. She'll put her arms around me and she'll know. I won't be alone anymore. It will be different. It has to be. If not—if not, I'd be better off—*

"Was it a nice dance?"

"Huh? Oh! I didn't go." Startled from reverie, Rachel forgot her role and answered right out, truthfully, where she should have made some murmured reply and urged the driver to get her home, home, *home.* Too late, she bit her tongue and added, "Please—"

"That's too bad," he said, shifting gears, foot dancing from gas to clutch and back again. "All dressed up and no place to go. Had a fight with your boyfriend?"

Rachel said nothing. The fingers of one hand began to worry the gardenia blossom on her wrist, rolling the silky white petals up tight, one by one, crushing the thick scent free.

"That's too bad," the driver repeated. "It's supposed to be a special time for you—pretty dresses, hair done up just right. Special for the guys too, you know. All the plans, all the dreaming . . . It's a waste to let some silly argument wreck it all, a stupid *waste!*" He smacked the heavy plastic steering wheel.

Rachel clenched her hands, felt the nails sting the soft flesh of her palms. A glance out the window showed only darkness. Where were the streets, the shops, the houses? Where were the other cars? She cranked open the window, thinking the glass was playing tricks on her eyes.

Nothing beyond the window but the dark.

"Take me home!" she cried, leaning forward, hands clutching the back of the driver's seat. "Please, please take me home!"

The driver shook his head slowly. "You don't want to go home, not yet. The night's still young, and you haven't even gone to the dance. He's waiting. He worked so hard to make this night special for you, you can't let him down. You know, if he goes home and says you walked out on him tonight, they're going to laugh at him, his mother, that boyfriend of hers. They'll say how this just proves what they've said all along, how there's no girl who'd give him the time of day. You're a nice girl; even if you don't care for him all that much, you don't want him to suffer that."

He turned around partway in his seat and Rachel saw the flicker of yellow light play over the lenses of his glasses. There were no lights to cast those faint reflections, neither outside the car nor in. She gasped, and the gasp became a sob. The driver laughed.

"Oh, don't worry, Miss," he said, turning to face forward once more. "I'll keep my eyes on the road, I'll get you where you're going. To the dance, right? That's where you're going. When you got in my car I heard you say so. You know, this is a pretty fast heap, if I do say so myself. I bet if we hurry, he'll still be waiting at the gym door, waiting for you to come to your senses, come back to him. After all, it was you who invited him. Unless that was your ideas of a joke. If that's so, it wasn't very funny, not funny at all, but—"

"Take me home! Take me *home!*" Rachel moaned.

"Awwwwww, now stop. You're making too much noise, Miss, you know that?" The driver pressed the gas pedal a little harder and chuckled out loud. "Silly girls, don't even know what they really want. It's your big night, you don't want to go home now. What's at home, anyway? You want to go to the dance. That's what you told me when you got in my car, I heard you. You're sorry for how you treated him and you want to go back. Well, you stick with me; we'll make it right."

Leaning over the front seat, Rachel felt her throat constrict as she watched his foot press the gas pedal all the way to the floorboard. The old car growled, then roared, then screamed like a rising wind as it laid itself flat out to the road, flinging her back, deep into the tuck-and-roll padding of the seat. And over the whine of the engine she heard herself shrieking that no, no, no, she didn't want to go dancing, not tonight, not ever, not with any boy she could name, and that yes, yes, oh please yes, she wanted to go home, her home, Lauren's home, any home, please, please, *please*—!

But the car drove on, raced on, flew on through the night. She scrabbled at the window crank, wrangled it down, stuck her head out into the wind and screamed for help. All that came back to her ears was the echo of her own cries, all that filled her eyes was midnight. She clawed at the door handle, but it was frozen still, cold chrome in her hand. She gave a little mew of terror and sank back against the seat.

Petticoats rustled. Stiff skirts of satin and moiré and tulle bunched and crunched under her, crowded against her sides, rubbed her forearms where the driver's draped tweed jacket didn't cover her skin. She heard the faint, shallow sound of breathing, many breaths, and the car was awash with the tickling aroma of warring perfumes.

The little light on the ceiling went on. The small blond girl wore a pink dress, the dark brunette wore green, the mouse-brown one wore a blue that didn't suit her, almost the same shade as the gown the redhead wore. Four pairs of eyes that were only sockets turned toward Rachel, and all the lingering ghosts of Ambush, Shalimar, Tabu, My Sin, couldn't shield her from that other smell now filling the car with its final reality.

The last thing Rachel felt was someone tearing the gardenia from her wrist. The last thing Rachel saw was the dark.

She opened her eyes to a sky that seemed to have been bled of all color. Dew-heavy grasses hissed and tickled against her ears. She sat up slowly, as if there were a solid weight on her chest. Her throat was sore, every swallow of air an effort, every intake of breath a victory. She stood up and the world spun around her.

What did he do to me? She regretted the question the moment it slipped into her thoughts. She didn't want to know what had happened to her after the darkness came; she was only too glad to be back in the light. Without warning, a fresh wave of dizziness overcame her. She felt as if she were going to topple to the ground again and put out her hands, groping blindly for support.

They fell upon a stone. She pitched her weight against it and bowed her head, eyes tightly shut until the swirling clouds blew away. When her head finally cleared, she saw that she was leaning on a grave marker.

She looked around. There was a stone wall directly behind her with trees beyond. Rows of irregularly spaced headstones staggered away before her, and in the distance the wall ended its solemn circuit at the open gates of the town cemetery. If she strained to see, she could just make out the shape of a lone house across the road.

"Lauren . . ." She started toward the house. Lauren must be worried, Lauren's parents frantic, her own—

She was racing for the gate, running so fast she almost rammed right into the two men who were strolling up the graveyard path in the other direction. The short, wiry one had his nose buried in a newspaper, but the gangly one with the clipboard tucked under one arm was alert and put out his hands to stop Rachel in her headlong rush.

"Hey, where do you think you're going, young lady?" He had a kindly voice, and his hands rested on her bare arms so gently that she could scarcely tell they were there.

"I'm sorry, excuse me, I have to get home," she blurted, trying to sidestep him.

The man frowned, more in concern than disapproval. "What's your rush?"

The one with the paper lowered it, finally aware of Rachel's existence, and gave her a hard stare. "Never mind that crap, Harry, what the hell's she doing in here? The cemetery's not open yet."

"But—but—" In an agony of fear worse than any Kathy's stories had created, she gestured wildly at the open gates. Her chest ached with the wish—too late!—that she'd chosen to go over the wall instead, the way she and Lauren had done last night.

"Yeah, so what? We opened them. We're *supposed* to be in here," the man with the newspaper said. "We've got work to do."

"Jim and me, we're here to check on a gravesite," Harry told her. "I'm afraid"—he sucked a long breath between his teeth and tapped his clipboard—"I'm afraid it might be for someone you know."

She felt the ice begin to form in little beads on her skin, then spread out slowly, seep in deeply. She knew that once the ice soaked its way into her heart, she would be lost.

"*Might* be?" Jim snapped. He was almost completely bald, and his florid face flushed into ugly red patches when his temper kicked in. "Five bucks says it is, a town this size. Stupid kids, always in a rush, always fooling around, sticking yourselves in where you don't belong and then acting like it's all a big joke. Well, make a joke of this, girlie!" He slapped the paper and turned it so that Rachel could see the headline: PROM NIGHT SMASHUP KILLS FOUR. "Some boy named Gilchrist, Mark Gilchrist, that's whose grave we've got to get ready for tomorrow. Real funny, huh? A million laughs."

Rachel wasn't laughing. "I know him," she said, hearing the

words shake and shatter as she spoke them. "He's—he used to be my friend's steady. They broke up the week before the prom and—"

"Lucky friend," Jim said, his lip curling. "You don't look like you were so lucky last night. What happened, you and your boyfriend so drunk that this looked like a nice, romantic spot? Did he forget to take you with him when he was done, is that it?"

"No." It was a whimper. What would her parents say? "Oh, please, no."

"Jim . . ." Harry sounded embarrassed by all this, but Jim held on like a terrier with a rat in its jaws.

"Come on, what're you doing in here? We can have you arrested for trespassing, you know."

"No!" This time it was a moan of despair. She tried to get away, dodging around the men, but the path was too narrow. Jim let his newspaper drop to the grass. His hand shot out to close over her elbow.

"You're coming with us while we check out the Gilchrist site, and then we're going to call the cops." His eyes gave her no more hope of appeal than his words.

"Jim, for the love of God, give the poor kid a break."

"The hell I will!" If words had teeth, Jim's would have bitten Harry's head clean off. "Look at her. Butter wouldn't melt in her mouth. What's she *doing* in here? I've got a real good guess. I say we take her to twelve-J first and find out."

"Where?" Rachel piped. The men ignored her.

Harry made one last stab at reason. "Look, even if it's there, that doesn't mean she's the one who—"

"We'll see."

Jim started off, dragging Rachel along behind him. Harry came after, making impotent objections. Rachel was too scared to speak. She could feel the ice spreading over her limbs, feel fresh terrors welling up with every step. All of Kathy's stories, all their power over her—the same power she'd hoped to claim over Lauren—they were nothing compared to this.

Her feet in the old dancing shoes stumbled over the graveyard path. The farther back into the cemetery Jim dragged her, the rougher and less carefully tended the way became. There were old graves here, old graves for the town's oldest families. Angels wept beside pillars draped with robes carved of stone. Statues of dead children clasped plump hands together and turned their eyes to heaven, imploring a mercy that never came while they still lived.

"Jim, Jim, what's the use of this?" Harry implored. "So the kids pull a prank once a year, what's the big deal?"

"It wouldn't be a big deal for you, Harry," Jim said. He was breathing hard, his teeth set together tight. "You only moved here two years ago; I've lived here all my life. I *knew* those girls. It wasn't a joke to us then."

"You make it sound like I lived on the moon," Harry replied. "I wasn't raised that far from here, I read the papers, I knew the case. Yes, it was horrible, but still, after so long—"

"Why they had to bury him here," Jim snarled, half to himself. "Here, with decent people instead of in the prison graveyard. That's where he belonged. But his mama had money, even if that's all she had, and she *fixed* things."

Abruptly he stopped, froze, went on point like a bird-dog. It was so sudden that Rachel lurched against him from behind. "Jesus. They did it again." He pointed at a stone where the year of death was 1958 and the neighboring markers seemed to stand more than a grave's length away, like dowagers drawing their skirts aside from any fouling thing. A sound of pure disgust tore out of him. "Some people. Idiot kids. Every single prom night since, they've always gotta come in here, drunk as skunks, stupid, no sense of decency, no respect, no—"

Still clutching Rachel's hand, he strode right up to the grave and tore the old tweed jacket from the tombstone. He shoved it in her face and shouted, "Think this is a good joke? All those girls dead, and you damned kids make fun of it? Think this is funny, do you? *Do you?*"

He let her go and threw the jacket in her face. Rachel uttered a little cry that crested to a wail as the scents of aftershave and tobacco, of new leather and fresh oil rose up out of the fabric to smother the breath from her body. She tried to fight it away, but the jacket wrapped itself around her shoulders and set relentless claws into the flesh of her bared shoulders. Moaning, she twisted and spun in desperation to escape.

"Jesus, Jim, what'd you *do* to her?"

"I—I don't know! I just— The jacket, it's— Oh, God!"

Rachel heard their voices only faintly, but it was hard to hear anything at all. That was because of the music. It filled her ears, songs from scratchy old 45s, slow dances to close a prom that ended more than fifty years ago. Her struggles turned into a frenzied dance, a travesty, and her borrowed shoes scraped their smooth soles raw over the graveyard stones.

The jacket shifted from her shoulders, squirmed across her body, wrapped its arms around her. With a last effort, she tore it away and flung it against the tombstone. A flurry of shimmering gardenia petals burst from the sleeve, flew up to veil her bruised body. She heard the men gasp as she felt the ground beneath her feet give way, saw it open to the smells of freshly turned earth and things long buried.

She crumpled to her knees and pitched forward into all the nights to come, nights where cars raced past on a lonesome highway and maybe one in a hundred might stop for a solitary girl in a shining prom dress and offer to take her home. A few white petals fell after her like tears. She wondered if Lauren would remember her.

Visitation

Lucy Taylor

Curtis Mayfield had just settled himself before the fire with a snifter of Courvoisier and a copy of Cervantes, when the knocking started. It wasn't a normal rapping, but a scraping, scrabbling sound, as if whoever was at the door were trying to claw their way up to reach the brass knocker. He glanced at the antique grandmother clock next to the fireplace. It was after nine, and he was not a man in the habit of receiving visitors—expected or otherwise—at this hour, his bedtime being at precisely ten, his few friends of the type who would never think of stopping by without calling first.

The assault on the front door stopped. There was a moment of silence. Then the bell began to chime relentlessly.

"I'm coming, dammit," he grumbled, getting up.

Suffering an unsettling mix of annoyance and apprehension, he went through the elegantly appointed living room, crossed the foyer, and unlatched the front door.

The porch light illuminated a pale cone of saffron white, in the center of which stood a little girl of six or seven. She wore a pastel dress of some summery material, completely inappropriate for early

November. Her dark curly hair fell loose and untamed about her shoulders.

"Let me in!" the child cried. "She's after me!"

"Who's after you?" said Curtis, peering over her head into the dark, wondering what sort of miscreant would menace a small child, especially in this neighborhood of genteel, retired folk and tenured academics.

"Let me in!"

Was this some sort of parent/child squabble? The neighborhood had no children that he was aware of. Had she and her family just moved in? How had he missed seeing her before?

"Please!"

Before he could organize his thoughts sufficiently to question her further, the girl darted past him into the house.

"Here now, wait! Come back!" he shouted, but the child was already pounding up the staircase to the second floor.

"Little girl?" He hurried after her, but there was no sign of the child. He began searching from room to room, expecting at any moment for the girl's irate parents to come to the door, demanding to know why he was harboring their daughter. He wondered if he should call the police, but was loath to involve them—here he was, a middle-age professor, still living in the house where he'd been born, lacking female companionship of a romantic nature now for many years—such were the times that the mere presence of a small child in his house at this hour might be viewed by the authorities as indicative of some sort of prurience or perversion. No, the police weren't a good idea at all.

Having completed his search of his own bedroom and bath, he stepped back into the hall, only to see the girl peek around the corner, spot him, and dash into the room at the end of the hall—Clarice's room. He groaned inwardly. This bedroom, with its Erte bronzes and flocked ivory wallpaper, had belonged to his beloved mother, who had died less than five months ago. So grief-stricken was Curtis still that he had barely set foot in it since Clarice passed on. The room was exactly as she'd left it, a treasure trove of Clarice

Mayfield's beloved antiques, her Lalique glass and Belgian lace, not to mention the curios his wastrel father, photographer Paul Mayfield, had sent back from his travels while he and Curtis's mother were still married: Zambian masks and Alaskan scrimshaw, Hopi kachinas and Balinese prints. Curtis liked to think he would someday donate these items to a museum, but in truth the room had already become his private shrine, one rarely visited, but meticulously preserved.

Of all the rooms for the child to hide in, why this one, he fumed. What if she broke something? Stole something? Desecrated the very site where his mother had breathed her last? Oh, this situation was going from bad to worse.

But the bedroom appeared empty when he flicked on the light. Indigo shadows contrasted with ruby glass in the Tiffany lamps by the canopied bed. Dust motes drifted lazily over the inlaid amber eyes of an African mask, making it appear to blink.

After checking in the bathroom and underneath the bed, he realized the only place the child could be hiding was in the closet, a conclusion that chagrined him even more than her disruption of his evening. It had been years since Curtis had so much as peeked inside it. He'd been planning to go through Clarice's things someday, sort them out, perhaps donate a few of her dresses to charity, but so far, procrastination had always won out over good intentions.

And, although he told himself he avoided going through his mother's things because of the grief that would be stirred, in truth, he associated her closet with excruciating memories of his own.

He took a deep breath, wishing he'd had time to finish his brandy before coming upstairs, and opened the door. The draft of air stirred by this movement caused his mother's clothes to flutter softly, like enormous moths. Several of her dresses had slipped off their padded hangers and lay in a satiny heap upon the floor. Her mink coat, fashionable at a time before fur was deemed a sign of cruelty rather than good taste, had fallen down as well. He bent to get it, at the same time pushing aside the other clothes to look for the girl.

"Come out now. I know you're in here."

But, to his utter befuddlement, she was not.

"Don't play games now."

All he was aware of, though, was the blackness at the back of the closet, a darkness that suddenly seemed much too vast and looming for such a tiny space. As if he stood on the edge of a high balcony with no reassuring railing to clutch.

"Little girl?"

His heart began to pulse and jingle like a tambourine.

He searched the house again, then finished off his brandy and a second, unaccustomary one, and dragged himself to bed. Surely the child was no longer in the house. Maybe she'd hidden behind the curtains in Clarice's room, which he realized now he hadn't checked, and sneaked outside while his back was turned. Maybe she'd crawled out the window and shimmied down the oak tree to the ground, although such a feat of athleticism would seem beyond the ability of so young a child.

Somehow she'd gotten out of the house without his seeing her, he told himself, and he tried to put the incident out of his mind.

A week passed, during which Curtis carried on his usual teaching duties, met with his investment counselor to discuss some stock investments, and squired a colleague, Dr. Emily Estes, to a faculty party for the Humanities Department. The widowed Dr. Estes, whose pearl-wrapped neck approached the length and pallor of a swan's, aroused not a smidgeon of romantic interest in Curtis. On this occasion he found her company unexpectedly grating. She prattled on about her plans to join an archaeological expedition to some obscure village in Peru, growing annoyed when he pointed out sourly that his father used to take pictures in such places and that they were richer in disease and poverty than archaeological treasure.

"Really, Curtis, you have the curiosity of a stump. I think you only leave home to come to campus."

"That isn't true," said Curtis, bristling. "A lady friend and I took a cruise to the West Indies a few years ago—charming little islands . . ."

But Dr. Estes only rolled her eyes as though she thought he'd made it up.

Which, of course, he had. He and his former lover, Miriam, had gone so far as to look over brochures for such a cruise, but Miriam demanded that it be a honeymoon. The problem was that in order to have a honeymoon, there had to be a wedding. Curtis had felt a powerful attraction for Miriam and got a knot in his belly when she talked of moving back to San Francisco to pursue her jewelry-making career, but he couldn't marry her—there was Clarice to consider. She might feel betrayed if he brought another woman into the house, especially one like Miriam, who was as bright and loud and fluttery as some exotic macaw.

"Of course you can't marry me!" Miriam had screamed. "You're already married to your mother!"

A remark that, tainted as it was with equal measures of truth and scorn, had marked the beginning of the end of their affair.

Always one to eschew confrontation, he had ended the relationship with an exquisitely worded, but emotionally empty letter, expressing regrets, but pointing out that they were obviously unsuited for one another. Then, to be on the safe side, he got a new, unlisted phone number.

And yet, during the ensuing years, he had continued to think of Miriam. The texture of her lush, platinum-streaked hair, her proclivity for risqué jokes, her astonishing zest in bed. To dream of her was not uncommon—he'd awake to find his body in a chagrining state of readiness for an act that he could only perform with himself.

Occasionally he'd thought to call her, then put the idea out of his mind. Doubtless she'd gone back to San Francisco by now, selling her jewelry in Ghirardelli Square or wherever one did that sort of thing. Besides, he couldn't have married Miriam or anyone else while Clarice was alive.

But now that she was dead . . .

He forbade himself to even explore the thought. No, he was better off alone than with Miriam Godsey.

Except damn if he still didn't miss her sometimes.

Having deposited Dr. Estes at her door and declined the invitation of a nightcap, Curtis returned home and flicked on a tape of *Moneyline*. He was less than five minutes into it when the bell began to chime with frantic urgency. Curtis went to the door and squinted through the peephole. He could see nothing. Warily he opened the door.

The same unkept child was standing there, wearing the same warm-weather clothes and scuffed tennis shoes, her hair windblown and corkscrewed, mouth puckered in a sob. "Let me in!"

Curtis stared over the child's head into the night. He saw the headlights of a passing car sweep past and the blocky silhouette of the retired deli owner from up the street who stood, stargazing, while his pooch took a crap on the curb. Nothing else.

"Let me in! Please!"

Curtis knelt before the child. "There's no one there." And then, against his better judgment, but because he felt truly at a loss for what to do: "Do you want me to call the police?"

She gave no answer, but slipped past him, swift and fluid as winter fog, her feet pounding up the staircase ahead of him. He galloped in pursuit. At the top of the stairs, he glimpsed her fleeing into his mother's room again. It maddened him—whoever she was, she had no business going in there. That room was sacred.

This time, when Curtis checked the closet, he found the child had moved through it like a whirlwind. More of Clarice's clothes were off the hangers, shoes were flung about, a box of cards and letters had been spilled onto the floor.

"Dammit, what have you done here?"

But scarcely had he spoken than he was almost felled with vertigo and nausea. The closet seemed a vast and undulating void. He had the sensation of depth and fathomless space, the sense that if he leaned too far, he'd be falling out of control, like a man who carelessly blunders over the edge of a precipice and drops like a stone to oblivion.

He clutched his chest and leaned against the door frame. His very spine seemed to be trembling, his ribs quivering like the legs of milk white spiders.

From the far back of the closet, he heard the whisper of fabric, the subtle rustling of a skirt.

"Enough of this nonsense," he said, regaining command of himself. He lunged toward a trio of evening gowns, but his hands closed only on gold lamé and brocade. He lost his equilibrium and tumbled forward. His forehead cracked against the dowel. He sagged to his knees, the skirt of a cocktail gown, weighty with bugle beads, flopping into his eyes. He swept it away. Pain and humiliation made his eyes burn. From his vantage point, here on the floor, it was clear that, unless she'd found some secret passage hidden in the wall, the strange child was no longer there.

The hair stood rigid on the back of his neck. Here in the semidarkness, surrounded by the softest of sounds—the crinkling of taffeta and purring of velvet, the sleek, sensuous whisper of silk—unwelcome memories came seeping back, stopping up the area behind his eyes with unshed tears.

He remembered his sixth birthday, crouching in this very closet, weeping silently and inconsolably. Clarice had lavished him with presents, but there'd been nothing, not even a card or phone call, from his father, Frank, and the pain of that rejection had pulsed inside him like some diseased organ ready to burst and flood his system with poison.

While Clarice had gotten dinner ready, he'd huddled in the cool dark of her closet, ashamed of his tears, which he dared not let her see, but comforted by the bright, soft hems that swished around him. Clutching his arms across his belly, he had rocked himself, and touched himself as well, taking comfort in the subtle fragrances of his mother's clothes, the hint of her gardenia-scented skin. He had felt guilty too, for missing Frank when his mother tried so hard to make it up to him, when her love for him was so unwavering.

Later Clarice had opened the closet door, gently urging him to crawl into her arms and cuddle against her luxuriant breasts.

"There, there, my darling," she had cooed. "Never you mind about Frank Mayfield. He isn't worth one tear from Mommy's little man."

Thus had been born Curtis's fierce loyalty to Clarice. And if Miriam was right, if in some sense he had indeed been wedded, albeit chastely, to his mother, then it was his choice, his gift to her, because she'd earned it—by giving up all other men for him, by sacrificing her life to compensate him for Frank's abandonment.

Curtis dragged himself up off the floor. He knew that he should tidy up, should pick up the fallen clothes and collect the cards and letters, but at the moment he wasn't up to anything more strenuous than pouring himself a drink.

All he knew was that something terrible, something inexplicable was happening to him and that he felt powerless to stop it.

Over the next few days, Curtis's work suffered and he slept scarcely at all. Once, while lecturing a group of graduate students on the works of Lope de Vega, he glanced out the window to see the child's tear-streaked face and terrified eyes peering in at him. Stuttering and stumbling, he blundered over to the window, only to discover that what he'd taken for a human face was merely the arrangement of shadow and light created by the foliage.

So exhausted was he that, by the end of the week, he fell asleep in his study in the middle of the day, his cheek pillowed by a pile of singularly uninspired essays he was trying to grade. A vision of Miriam Godsey, so lifelike he could smell her musk and heather perfume, wrapped itself like luscious tentacles around his mind. His breathing quickened. Miriam floated above him, all glowing gypsy hair and tempting eyes, her skin as smooth and tan as marzipan and looking just as edible.

"In sickness and in health," said Miriam.

In her hands she bounced what Curtis took to be some sort of small stuffed animal—a possum or raccoon perhaps, the fur all gray and matted.

"Till death do us part."

She rotated the frizzy orb and tossed it to him—Clarice's head, which smiled and said, "There, there, Mommy's little man . . ."

Curtis woke up gasping and disoriented. So unsettled was he by the dream that returning to his paperwork was now impossible. Restless and shaky, he found himself wandering upstairs to Clarice's room, where he decided that he'd delayed tidying up her closet long enough. In fact, he reasoned, the nightmare might even have been caused by his guilt at not having already done so.

Opening the closet door, he surveyed with dismay the jumble of fallen clothing, strewn postcards, and helter-skelter shoes.

He leaned forward.

And then, rushing up at him from what seemed to be a headlong plummet into darkness, came a mind-stopping vision. He saw the child he'd chased upstairs go racing toward some unknown street full of speeding cars. She leapt the curb, plowing into the street like a panicked animal, heedless of the vehicles rushing toward her. One car swerved to miss her, but the one behind it had no time and crashed into her head-on. Her body, given gruesome flight, soared high. When it slammed back onto the macadam, Curtis screamed.

At once the vision vanished. Furious at himself for having fallen prey to a hallucination, he was more determined than ever to exorcise his fears by inspecting the closet thoroughly. He did this like a man foraging through a nest of vipers, terrified the vision of the child's ungodly death might thrust itself into his consciousness again.

But what he found was even more distressing.

The letters and the postcards that he gathered up—almost all of them were addressed to him.

From his father, years ago. The dates beginning almost to the day of his parents' divorce.

Does your mother tell you that I call? I've asked if you could come and visit me. She says it is impossible. She says you hate me . . .

Astonished, Curtis read more. Here a letter from Bolivia with a photo of jungly mountains, a postcard from Mexico City (*I think of you all the time*), another card from someplace in Colorado—the picture showed a herd of elk traversing the diamondlike surface of a frozen lake. Jagged peaks against a cobalt sky like a row of vanilla Popsicles with big bites taken out.

And many more, their messages heartbreaking: *Your mother says that you don't want to see or hear from me. Is that true? I'm living in Canada now, on assignment for* National Geographic. *Please stop refusing to take my calls. I want to talk to you.*

But the postcards grew fewer and fewer over the years until finally there was only Frank's obituary, sent to Curtis's mother by the lawyer who had probated his modest estate. Frank Mayfield had reeled out of a bar in Winnipeg one night, passed out in a snowbank, and frozen to death.

Curtis felt as if he'd been frozen too, all these long years and now was thawing out in a rush, to feel a pain he could neither comprehend nor tolerate.

All those years he'd been allowed to think his father had deserted him, left him to be Clarice's "little man," all those years despising the man when, in truth, it was Clarice who had stood between them all along, Clarice who had betrayed him.

Nothing was as he'd thought it was.

He put his head in his hands and wept.

Two days later, having taken a leave of absence from the university, he caught a plane for Denver. Curtis hadn't flown in years. At take-off, the pressure and the dizzying view seemed to be unscrewing the top of his skull, but presently the sensation of flying became more tolerable—he even dared to look out the window and watch the plains of Kansas sweeping by.

Upon landing at Denver's extraordinary airport—the roof designed to mimic the snowcapped mountaintops—he rented a Jeep and set off for the high country. The altitude and sweeping vistas almost undid him. A dozen times he wanted to turn the jeep around and head back, but he pressed on, first following I70 west, then taking less traveled roads that took him to a cluster of cabins at the end of a dirt road in a place with the unlikely name of Rifle, the town from where one of his father's cards had been postmarked.

Was this the place his father might have stayed? Were these vistas ones he'd photographed? Did elk still leave the forest and "wander into town," as Frank had written?

Now, sitting before the fire he'd made, Curtis saw no elk outside his window, but deer passed by at twilight like dusky phantoms and crows that looked to him as big as eagles cleft the sky outside like obsidian boomerangs.

In all his life Curtis had never allowed himself to imagine what might have drawn his father to these godforsaken places. Now he watched the sun sinking like a polished gem into the dark-blue mountaintops and shivered at the beauty and remoteness of it.

He dozed. When he heard the thumping on the door, he gasped, then relaxed when he heard the manager yelling that he'd brought more firewood, should Curtis need any. He heard the sound of heavy boots clomping away. Feeling foolish, he went to the door to bring in the wood.

And yelped with fright.

She looked thinner somehow, scrawnier, but maybe that was because she still wore the pale pink summer frock and outside it was well below freezing. Her hair sparkled with snow, as though festooned with cloudy opals. Ice webbed her lashes.

Curtis stepped aside as she dashed past him into the cabin. Her racing feet took her to the fireplace. Although he realized now that this child was beyond all help, Curtis still cried out a warning. She screamed and flung herself toward the capering flames. He saw the car careening, heard the screech of tires, the dull *thwack* of impact, the spew of blood erupting from her mouth and ears. His vision swam. His knees went liquid. He sank onto the floor.

Curtis returned to Denver the next day and visited a travel agent, where he presented himself as a recently retired teacher, eager to experience the exotic and far-flung. The travel agent grew almost giddy at the prospect of sending Curtis to the ends of the earth.

A day later Curtis flew to Japan to connect with the Greek freighter *Ariadne* in the northern Japanese city of Sapporo. Keep moving, that was his agenda. And there was a curious elation to his flight, as though, having been frightened so thoroughly by the spectral child, the far reaches of the world no longer seemed so dangerous or intimidating.

The *Ariadne* brought Curtis days of welcome calm. A week passed, and the child had not returned. Knocks on the door of his cabin meant only a steward, come to clean the room or bring him toast and coffee. Worlds came and went beyond the porthole—

Hong Kong and Manila and Sumatra. In places that Curtis had scorned as hellholes of pestilence and poverty, he now found peace and respite.

One evening Curtis realized he hadn't thought about his old life or his mother in many days. It was as if they had ceased to exist. Instead, he felt alive in a way he hadn't previously thought possible, awakened to new experiences and possibilities. A mad impulse seized him. What if he called Miriam? Was it possible she might still be free, might even have forgiven him the shoddy way he'd said good-bye to her years before?

Curtis's heart began to trot like a spurred pony. His thoughts flew. If he could find Miriam and if she agreed to it, he'd send her money for a ticket to meet him at the next port where the *Ariadne* docked.

I was wrong, he imagined telling her. *My mother wasn't the person I thought she was. She deceived me all along. I wish I'd married you. I wish it had been different.*

He still remembered Miriam's phone number. When the ship was nearing Singapore, he dialed it. A man with a Spanish accent told him no Miriam lived there. Curtis got information for San Francisco and found that two M. Godseys and one Miriam were listed.

Upon dialing the second of the M. Godseys, a woman who sounded much like Miriam answered the phone.

"Miriam—is that you?"

"*Who* is this?"

He realized this wasn't Miriam.

"Curtis Mayfield." Flustered, he tried to retreat behind formality. "With whom am I speaking, please?"

"This is LeeAnn—Miriam's sister."

"May I speak to Miriam? Is she there?"

"No." To which question, he wondered. Both?

"Well, then . . . ?"

The woman hissed, "How dare you call up now, how dare you!"

"I don't understand. What . . . ?"

"How dare you call my sister after all these years. After you dumped her like spoiled meat, ruined her life, after you got her pregnant . . ."

"*What?*"

His distressed surprise seemed strangely gratifying to Miriam's sister. "You mean she really never told you?"

"No, of course not. I haven't spoken to Miriam in years."

"I used to ask her why she never got in touch with you about the baby, but she said you didn't want her and you wouldn't want her child either. She hated you, Curtis, you can't imagine how much she hated you."

Curtis flinched. Outside the porthole porpoises were leaping, glossy pewter arcs against the sky. "That isn't . . . I would have . . ."

"Miriam couldn't deal with raising a child. Vivian—your daughter—was terrified of her. Last summer she was screaming at Vivian about something. The child ran out into the street. She was hit by a car and killed."

"My God . . . I didn't know, had no idea . . . let me speak to her, I must speak to her."

"You can't," said LeeAnn. "Miriam blew her face off, Curtis, two days ago."

LeeAnn hung up. The porpoises were trying to fly up and singe their sleek hides against the sun.

He put the phone down, stared out at the black-green waves outside the porthole. His stomach fisted with despair.

The sound that he'd been dreading came.

Like a man walking to the scaffold, he went to open the door.

When Vivian rushed toward him, Curtis flung out his arms and attempted to embrace her. It was like trying to catch smoke. He sank to his knees, weeping.

But when he opened his eyes, she was sitting on the edge of the bed, swinging her skinny legs, beating on her thighs with her fists. Her eyes were bright with terror.

The bell outside the cabin door began to ring.

"Mom's found us," she said softly.

Victorians

James S. Dorr

The first thing I remembered of my early childhood was the fog. I must have been only five years old when I left the house that I had been born in—beyond that my mind was still pretty much blank—and I would not have returned even now, more than thirty years later, except that I had finally married. Her name was Amelia and I had met her in Chicago, but now·I traveled home alone. I had determined to open the house first and, only after it had been restored to a livable condition, to send for my bride.

I crested a hill and, just as the road hooked down toward the river and to the town I would find across it, I caught my first glimpse of the house my father had been born in too—the house he had died in and that my mother had fled from just after, never to come back. That, at least, was what they had told me after I had been taken away, to another state, to be raised by a cousin on my mother's side.

The fog, a persistent feature of autumn during those first years of my life, had always been thickest nearest the river. Above it, however, under a pale late-afternoon sun, I could just make out the eight-sided top of the great central tower—the Queen Anne tower that dominated so many Victorian homes of its age—as well as the tips of three of the highest-pinnacled chimneys. Memory came back in driblets and pieces. I knew that when I approached the next day to take possession, I would recognize below them the sharply peaked hip roof, broken at angles by the main gables that clutched the tower within the ell they formed at their crossing. The tower itself, with its latticed, oval, stained glass windows, would soar a full story over even the tallest of these, a clear rise of nearly seventy feet from its base to the scale-shingled dome that crowned it.

Memories continued to come back unbidden. I followed the road down a series of switchbacks until the top of the double-lane iron bridge I knew I would find loomed out from an ever-increasing fog. By now I had lost sight of my parents' home altogether, but in my mind I could hear the voice of a young attorney reading a will.

The will specified that the house would be mine, but only after I had gotten married.

The young attorney, a Stephen Larabie—really no more than a clerk at the time—explained to me what my older cousin protested seemed an unusual provision. "Your father," the lawyer said, "fully expects you not to marry until you've tasted somewhat of the world, just as he did. But at the same time you must eventually take on the obligations of manhood, as well as its pleasures, and settle down. The house, that you will not obtain until you do so, is intended to be a reminder."

My cousin who, in that I was a minor, had been court-appointed to speak for my interests, had laughed at that. "You mean young Joseph"—he gestured toward me—"is being told that he has permission to sow his wild oats when he gets a bit older, but, until he's grown out of such urges, to stay out of town. In other words, not to keep out of trouble, but just out of scandal."

The lawyer cleared his throat. "Something like that, yes. I doubt you knew Joseph's father well—as you do know, he was always reclusive and rarely visited even immediate family members after his own marriage—but he, like his house, was quite Victorian in his nature."

"You mean that he was a hypocrite, don't you?" my cousin asked.

I remember now that the lawyer had glanced in my direction to

see if I had understood anything of what he and my cousin were saying, but I had already begun to play with his pens and inkwell.
"Some people claimed that of him, yes. At least that he might at
times have followed a double standard." He cleared his throat a second time. "In any event," he said as he stood up, having come to the
end of his papers and seemingly anxious to usher us out, "the will
specifies that this firm will keep the house in trust until Joseph is
ready."

And now I was ready, by my father's will. The firm, now owned
by Stephen Larabie, had apparently kept an eye on my own various
comings and goings as well as the house. And so, three days after
Amelia and I had returned from our honeymoon, I received the
telegram that had brought me back to this place, at best still scarcely
half recollected, that yet had so overshadowed my first years.

So ran my thoughts now as I reached the bridge and, turning my
lights on low, carefully picked my way across it. Fortunately, the fog
seemed less thick on the river's town side and, even though it was
starting to get dark, I found the hotel I had made reservations at
with surprisingly little trouble. Since I was tired from a full day's
drive, I checked into my room and showered and changed first, then
decided to have a couple of drinks and something to eat in the small
restaurant I had earlier spotted just off the lobby.

When I sat down, the hostess smiled at me, and somehow I
found that I couldn't help thinking how much the opposite, and yet,
in terms of the abstract of beauty, how much the same she was as
Amelia. Where, for example, my own wife was blonde and her figure slender, the restaurant hostess was every bit as dark and buxom.
Where Amelia was quiet, the hostess appeared, as other customers
came to be seated, almost too vivacious. And afterward, when she
winked at me while I took out my card to pay the bill, I learned that
even her name was much like my wife's, and yet unlike it, as well.

Her name was Anise.

When I returned to my room later on, I placed my wife's picture
on the dresser and went to sleep quickly. The first thing next morning, I looked up Attorney Larabie's office.

As soon as I strode in through the door, I was struck by how quickly my mind recalled the tiniest details of my visit, some thirty years past, down to and including the stain on the wood floor where I had dropped one of the young lawyer's pens. The man who confronted me now, however, must have been fifty-five or sixty.

"Mr. Parrish?" he said, extending his hand. "Mr. Joseph Parrish?"

I nodded and accepted his handshake.

"Are you Stephen Larabie? I got your telegram."

"Yes," he said, before I could add more. Still gripping my hand, he pulled me over to a table and sat me down, then produced a thick sheaf of papers. "Couple of things I'll need you to sign first," he continued. "That'll most likely take up the whole morning so, unless you have some objection, I thought we might have a quick lunch after that and then take a look at the house together."

I nodded, wondering somewhat distractedly if lunch would be at the hotel restaurant and, if so, if the hostess, Anise, would be on duty for that meal as well. I shook the thought away and soon enough became lost in contracts and deeds instead. Lunch, in fact, turned out to be a quick affair at a hamburger place just outside of town, on the way to the bridge. And then, as river fog started to thin, giving some hope of a clear if not wholly sun-filled afternoon, we found ourselves on the steep and winding road up the cliff on the other side.

Larabie turned to me while I was driving. "How much do you remember of your father?" he asked. "Or, for that matter, of your mother?"

"Very little," I had to confess. I searched my memory and nothing came, yet I had the feeling that if I just waited—waited until I was inside the house that they had lived in . . .

"You do know, at least, that your father was murdered?"

Larabie paused, reacting, perhaps, to what I imagined was my blank expression. I had no such memory.

"That's what the police said in any event," he finally continued after some seconds. I *did* remember that when, with my cousin, I had been in his office before, the younger Larabie had struck me as being every bit as taciturn about giving out excessive information.

"Did they catch the man who did it?" I asked. Again, attempt to recall as I might, I had no memory—at least not yet—and hence no real feeling one way or the other. But I was beginning to have a foreboding.

"Figured it was probably a drifter," Larabie answered, his voice sounding thoughtful. "A lot of people were moving from town to town those days—mostly farmers who'd been foreclosed on. Big farms forcing out smaller holdings. And you've got to realize that this was a small town. People generally disliked sharing local troubles with outsiders. So the police just poked around a little outside the house—set up a few roadblocks—but they never did catch him."

"M-my mother wasn't murdered too, was she?" It had suddenly occurred to me what he might have been trying to hint at and, while I didn't really remember her any more than I did my father, the thought of my mother's death by violence somehow *was* shocking.

"Oh, no," he said quickly. "In fact, it was her who phoned the police. Figured she must have been out when it happened and had you with her, but came home just after. Sort of a lucky reversal for her, though, that that's the way it worked out." He hesitated for a moment.

"What do you mean?"

"It was your father who usually went out while she and you were the ones left behind." He hesitated again, then frowned. "I may as well tell you, your father was somewhat of a ladies' man. Good-looking man even in his late thirties, just like you, and everyone knew it—except maybe her. Used to be a whorehouse where the hotel is now, and some said he spent more time in that than he did in his own house."

"Really?" I asked. I was about to ask him more when we reached the crest of the hill we were climbing. The road widened and, just at that moment, a ray of sun burst through the clouds overhead. The house could now be seen suddenly rising, dominating the next ridge over, in all its flamboyant, old-fashioned splendor.

As we approached, it loomed higher and higher, the light glinting off the gingerbread scrollwork that framed the huge front third-story gable. I pulled up into its curving driveway, got out of the car, and let my eyes wander—below the trim of the gable, in shadow, the arch of a balcony pointed yet higher to the great tower, half impaled by the slant to its right, and the cast-iron finialed crest of the main hip roof behind it. And yet above that, thrust to the sky, the three major chimneys—the tallest one crowned with a wired, glass-balled spire that was meant to catch lightning, my new memory prompted—added their own bursting streaks of color. An almost blood-colored patterned-brick red, when the sun struck full on it, that, in the jumbled gray and white of friezes and rails of the building below them, was matched alone by the stained-glass red of the tower's downward spiraling ovals.

I walked, as if in a dream, to the house—apparently long-repressed memories came back of the tower windows lighting a second- and third-story staircase before it curved backward up into the attic. Others of diamond panes in the front parlor. I scarcely noticed Larabie's presence until we stood on the broad front veranda.

"You'll notice we kept the property up for you, Mr. Parrish," the lawyer said. "Painted it most recently only last summer, in fact." He pulled a notebook out of his pocket, along with a large, old-fashioned iron key. "You'll notice we nailed up the lower-floor windows with furring strips—this far from town why take any chances?—but, once we're inside, the smaller fireplaces you'll see sealed off were boarded up in your grandfather's time. After they put in the central gas heating."

I nodded dumbly. Yes. I remembered. One of the lesser, back left chimneys went down to the basement. I watched as he twisted the key in the door, only half noticing that it opened with hardly a squeak. I smelled the fresh oil—they had, apparently, kept up the inside as well as the outside—not just of hinges, but of the darkly polished woodwork that surrounded us as we stepped into the shallow, boxlike reception hall.

"Just a moment now, Mr. Parrish." Larabie spoke in almost a whisper. He handed me the first of the keys, then produced a second. He twisted it in a smaller lock across from the entrance we had just come through, then pushed back the double sliding doors that opened the wall to the huge, oak-paneled, main staircase hall.

"Your mother went with this house, Mr. Parrish," Larabie said as he stood aside to let me look. To try to remember. Second only in size to the large formal dining room, the hall, with its stairs angling up to the right and around the back wall, was the dominant feature of the first floor. "Your mother was frail, white-skinned and slender, with pale blond hair," the attorney continued. "There were times when she would descend, the white of her clothes standing out as well from the dark wood around her, and look the perfect Victorian lady. Times when I'd come here on legal business . . ."

I nodded. I saw. I remembered my mother on that staircase, saw in her now, in retrospect, the thin, almost sickly Romantic ideal that would have held sway not so much in her time here, but generations before when the house had been first constructed. I longed now to climb the stairs—now I remembered how she would pause at the corner landing, letting me dash to her so we could go to the main hall together. But first I had to know something more.

I turned to Larabie.

"You told me just before we came to the top of the cliff that my father was murdered. But not my mother . . ."

"No, Mr. Parrish. She was the one who called the police—I think I may have said that already—but, when they arrived here, they came through the sliding doors, just as we did, and the only person they found in the hall was you. You told them your mother had gone away. That was all you would tell them. But when they asked you about your father, you pointed, silently, to the rear archway that leads to the kitchen."

More memory came back—the memory of blood. Of *wanting* to forget what I . . .

"Under the circumstances," I heard the attorney continue, as if at a distance, "no one blamed your mother. For leaving you that way. She must have been so horribly frightened—and she did keep her wits about her long enough to make sure help came. She had always been such a frail woman . . ."

Incongruously, I thought of my wife then—fragile and pale. The bride I would send for who, people might say, would fit comfortably in with this house as well. Then—stark contrast—of yet another detail I suddenly found I remembered. My father had been murdered in the kitchen, had almost staggered out past the pantry, past the back stairs, and into the service hall when he had fallen.

An ax in his back.

I must have begun to look Victorian-pale myself. I felt the attorney's hand on my shoulder. Now I remembered the men in uniform, blood being cleaned up in the kitchen later by neighbors, my own panic at missing my mother. My wondering when I would see her come down the main staircase again.

"Mr. Parrish?" Larabie's voice was very low. "Mr. Parrish—perhaps you'd like to come out for some fresh air?"

I shook my head slowly. "No," I answered. "Everything does look in order, however, so why don't *you* wait outside if you'd like to. I just want do a little exploring on my own, to get an idea of how much work it'll take before Amelia—before Mrs. Parrish and I can move in."

Larabie nodded. "Upstairs, you'll find we pretty much left everything alone. May be dusty, though. Didn't even put dropcloths down much above the second floor."

"I think you've done an excellent job with what I've seen so far," I assured him. I took a deep breath, then looked at my wristwatch and glanced toward the front door. "I shouldn't be any more than an hour . . ."

I waited, gazing up at the main staircase until I heard the outside door close, then turned to the back hallway and the kitchen. On my left, I passed the downstairs parlor first and then the dining room, noting the bay window in the latter—the first-story bulge that jutted out onto the side veranda, forming the base of the four-story tower. Once in the kitchen, I took a deep breath. I saw, at least in my mind's eye, the stains. I thought for some reason of the ink I had spilled myself on Larabie's floor as I imagined my mother calling me, saw her standing over the sink, the door that led to the yard and the woodshed behind the house still yawning open, her hands red with blood.

My mother's hands. *Why?*

I watched as she washed them, then followed a trail of water stains this time—pale, clear drops diluting a deeper red—back toward my father. It circled, minced, avoided expanding pools of crimson as it reached the telephone in the hallway, then returned to the door by the pantry that led to the back stairs. The stairs my mother would never use because, as she used to say, "It isn't proper."

The stairs that rose toward the outside wall, then curved and spiraled up through the tower until they angled back into the attic.

A child's "secret passage."

I followed the trail.

I heard my mother's voice. "Joseph," she said as we climbed the spiral, "you must forget everything that you've seen. It's only a game, like the games your father played down in the village. Games I might have been told about, but had never believed until he came home, more drunk than usual, early this morning." We reached the top, where the stairs straightened out again for their final climb up to the attic, and the sun suddenly shone through the windows, filling the tower with spotlights of blood red. "While he was sleeping," my mother continued, "I thought of a game too."

My mother had always used the front staircase. The back stairs were dusty. And one had to stoop to get from the attic into the tunnel beneath the front gable. But this was different—this was a game.

I straightened up, bumped my head, realized I stood in the attic myself now.

I had trouble breathing the stuffy air. I leaned against a rough brick column—the front parlor chimney, my memory told me—and felt the flange where it thrust through the roof brush against my shoulder. I blinked my eyes, hard, to clear my vision and, when I opened them up again, I saw what still looked like a pool of blood.

Again a memory—a recognition. I was already within the front gable. The red that I saw was the light of the sun, spilling out from a second low arch where the gable roof met the tower's final top level. I heard my mother's voice warning me to be sure to brush my pants carefully before, once the game we would play was ended, I went back downstairs. I saw my mother kneeling next to me as we crawled through the final tunnel.

We came to a child's hidden pirate castle. A room of oval stained-glass windows that served as portholes, of worn-out sheets and ropes carefully hung from the open beams of the dome roof above as a ship's sails and banners.

I helped my mother build a tower within the great tower's uppermost room, helped her make a stairlike heap of the boxes and trunks I'd dragged in for years from the main attic proper as pirate treasure.

"Now you must help me with one thing more," she said when we were finished. She climbed to the top and began to pull on the ropes that hung toward her. "Hold my legs. That's right. And now I want you to promise me that everything that has happened today will be our secret. Do you promise, Joseph?"

"Yes, Mother," I said. The memory was clear now.

"I want you to think of this as a game. Like playing pirates. Do you understand?"

"Yes, Mother," I said again.

"Good. Now your mother must walk the plank—just like in a game. As soon as you feel me move my feet, I want you to push me off these boxes and knock them over, just as if you were a real pirate captain pushing me off the plank. I want you to go downstairs after you've done that, without looking back. Some men will come later and all you must tell them is that your mother went away. Do you promise, Joseph?"

I had promised.

I blinked again. I stood alone in the tower now. Raising my eyes to the dome above me, I gazed at my mother, her flesh long since shrunken into a parchment against her body, still hanging in the red light of the windows just as I had left her.

And somehow, for no reason whatsoever, I thought of Amelia who so resembled her, walking down the front, formal staircase. Amelia, my bride, also somewhat reclusive, who I was sure, as soon as the house was cleaned and ready, would come to love it and make it her own.

And then, without willing to, I thought as well of the restaurant hostess. I could not help it.

Of dark, round-curved Anise who lived in town and would be waiting.

About the Editors and Contributors

WENDY WEBB is the author of a number of well-received short stories and the editor or coeditor of the critically acclaimed *Phobias* anthologies. She is also a playwright, an actress (TV's *In the Heat of the Night*), a registered nurse, and a college lecturer on writing. Born in Florida, she currently lives in Georgia.

CHARLES GRANT is the award-winning editor of over twenty-five anthologies, including the *Shadows* series and the *Midnight* series. His novels have sold over 2 million copies worldwide, he has had two international best-sellers, and his latest book is *Symphony* (from Tor), the first in a quartet of novels about the Millennium.

CARRIE RICHERSON has had a number of short stories published in many major, contemporary magazines, and anthologies. And while the settings may vary, most of her stories capture the wonderful flavor of the state of Texas in which she lives.

JESSICA AMANDA SALMONSON, who lives in the Pacific Northwest, has made an enviable name for herself as an editor, novelist, and short story writer. She devotes much of her time resuscitating and preserving the names and fine work of the forerunners of contemporary dark fantasy. The latest collection of her own work is *The Deep Museum*, to be issued early next year.

BRAD STRICKLAND, who lives in Georgia, is the author of over twenty novels for both adults and young adults as well as twice that many pieces of shorter fiction. His collaborations with John Bellairs have been critical and commercial successes, as have his collaborations with his wife, Barbara, the latest of which is *Nova Command*.

STUART PALMER has had a number of stories published at home— the United Kingdom—but this is his first professional appearance in the United States.

THOMAS S. ROCHE is no stranger to short fiction, his work having appeared to much acclaim in many major anthologies. He is also the editor, or coeditor, of *Noirotica* and *Gargoyles*. He lives in San Francisco and claims not to be working on his first novel.

THOMAS SMITH is a professional musician (he's played with Doc Watson and Chet Atkins, among others), a magician, and a Methodist minister. He lives in South Carolina.

RICK HAUTALA'S novels have sold well over 2 million copies in the United States alone, and he is getting real tired of being called "that other writer from Maine." His latest book is *Impulse,* and his short stories can be found in most major anthologies.

PAUL COLLINS and RICK KENNET have done just about everything that can be done in the publishing world—editing, novels, short stories, magazine publishing, among others. They live and work in Australia.

BRIAN STABLEFORD is undoubtedly one of England's finest writers of fiction and nonfiction. His novels and short stories are known not only for their content—often a unique combination of science fiction and dark fantasy—but also for their unmistakable style. His latest is *Chimera's Cradle*, the last in an ambitious and superior trilogy begun by *Serpent's Blood* and *Salamander's Fire*.

MATTHEW J. COSTELLO is the author of over twenty novels in the fields of science fiction, dark fantasy, and suspense as well as being the author of the first mega–best-selling CD ROM game, *The 7th Guest*. He teaches, he edits, and in his copious spare time hosts barbeques for starving writers.

KATHRYN PTACEK is the award-winning author of over twenty novels, including *In Silence Sealed* and *The Hunted*. She is also the editor of *Women of Darkness* and *Women of the West*, among others. A New Mexico native, she currently lives in New Jersey, where she edits and publishes *The Gila Queen's Guide to Markets*, a regular market newsletter for anyone working in or trying to break into the publishing field.

NANCY HOLDER, a California writer who has lived in Japan and Germany, is one of the most honored contemporary short story writers and novelists. *Witch-Light* (in collaboration with Melanie Tem) and the award-winning *Dead in the Water* are her latest publications. She has also written computer game manuals and romance novels, and edited a newsletter.

THOMAS E. FULLER is a professional radio actor, manager of a bookstore in Atlanta, and a playwright. In addition to writing short stories, he also adapts stories and novels for dramatic presentation on tape and public radio.

P. D. CACEK has published more than two dozen dark fantasy stories, most of which can be found in the best contemporary anthologies. She is active in local and national writing organizations and lives in Colorado.

ROBERT E. VARDEMAN is an international bestselling author of both science fiction and fantasy, and chances are that any Jake Logan western you pick up is his as well. He lives in Albuquerque, where he is working on a novel about Billy the Kid.

RUSSELL J. HANDELMAN has worked in publishing as an editor and now lives in Connecticut. This is his first story to be published in an anthology.

ESTHER M. FRIESNER is one of the country's finest writers of humorous fantasy (with, one should add, a rather grim bite once in a while). Her short stories have been published in most major magazines and anthologies, and her novels have been published worldwide.

LUCY TAYLOR is one of dark fantasy's newest and best young writers. Her stories generally have a dark erotic edge to them, and her first novel, *The Safety of Unknown Cities*, won the Bram Stoker Award for Superior Achievement.

JAMES S. DORR, who lives in Indiana, has nearly one hundred stories to his credit. His work, which is award-nominated at a regular rate, ranges from mystery (*Alfred Hitchcock Mystery Magazine*) to dark fantasy (*Borderlands*), and generally appears on most Best-of-the-Year lists.